An
Uncommon Market

An Uncommon Market

by

Brian and Marta Bagot

The truth is rarely pure, and never simple

(Oscar Wilde 1895)

author**HOUSE**®

AuthorHouse™ UK Ltd.
1663 Liberty Drive
Bloomington, IN 47403   USA
www.authorhouse.co.uk
Phone: 0800.197.4150

Published by AuthorHouse   12/17/2013

ISBN: 978-1-4918-8711-0 (sc)
ISBN: 978-1-4918-8710-3 (hc)
ISBN: 978-1-4918-8712-7 (e)

Dedication

This book is dedicated to the memory of Marta's father, who served with the Polish Brigade in Edinburgh during World War II.

Prologue

Edinburgh—March 1942

Sadie could see a glistening of tears in the man's sad eyes as she placed another pint in front of him. She saw that he'd been gazing at a crumpled photograph that now lay on the bar. He'd been lost in his private thoughts as he drained the first pint, but now he met her eyes with a nod of his head and the twitch of a smile on soft, generous lips, even if the sadness never really left his eyes. Briefly she wondered who was on the photograph, but knew better than to ask as it was none of her business.

Turning to place the coppers into the till she continued to muse about this man who'd first appeared at the Crawford Lounge just a few days ago. Although wearing a uniform bearing shoulder flashes that informed anyone interested that he was a Polish soldier from the Garrison just outside Edinburgh, he remained an inconspicuous figure. That he was handsome, there was no doubt, but he was not as rugged as she thought so many of his race seemed to be. His grey eyes radiated kindness and a sensuous mouth that would readily smile, in stark contrast to the usual mean-lipped and insensitive clientele that she was so used to serving.

Swinging back round from the till she threw him a bright smile and their eyes met for a second before he shyly dropped his gaze. Slowly he folded the photograph and pushed it back into his breast pocket, and then he looked up again and returned her smile. This single act changed his face completely from the sad and introverted demeanour she had grown used to, turning him suddenly into a younger man with a happy and warm personality. He spoke hesitantly, feeling for the unfamiliar words.

"Dziękuję . . . thanks . . . thank you," he said, his words so heavily accented that they fell from his lips almost unintelligibly.

Sadie Macmillan stared for a moment, her mind replaying his words until she was certain of what he'd said.

"Och, ye'r welcome, laddie," she replied.

The next moment a slap on the bar summoned her to the small group of men at the other end of the room. She knew well that they'd be legless and without a farthing between then in a couple of hours time.

. . .

Ladyslav Dochewski sipped at the unpalatable beer with scant enthusiasm. One week in this country had been sufficient for him to discover that many of the pleasures of his homeland were unobtainable here. The beer was rough, the cheese insipid, and what they called sausages . . . well . . . he could find no words to describe them. Vaguely a local epithet 'shite' touched a familiar nerve. The only things this drinking house offered were a modicum of warmth from the open fire that crackled in one corner, and the pleasant smile of the good-looking blonde lady behind the bar who had served him. It was a far cry from the camaraderie and companionship of the group of students he'd associated with less than two years ago at the university of Krakow, some way north of his hometown of Przemyśl in southeast Poland.

The start of the war had rapidly seen the western half of his country annexed by the Germans and the young and able-bodied students, of which he had been one, began to make their way south towards Istanbul where they had heard there may be a Polish Army forming. With bitterness he recalled how he and his fellow students had suffered several months of privation and hardship as they walked and cadged lifts where possible on their trek to join up and fight. Once they arrived in Istanbul they were accommodated in what was essentially a refugee camp hosted by the Turkish military.

He smiled to himself at some of his memories, and tried not to look sad at others, as he drank from the pint glass. Pulling out a pack of British Army issue cigarettes he was about to light up when a rough hand suddenly landed on his shoulder.

"Can I have a light, Jimmy?"

The owner of the broad Scots voice was some years older than Ladyslav, well into his forties, unshaven with straggling mouse-coloured hair and shifty pale blue eyes. The man's nose had been broken at least once in the past and his hands were gnarled and blackened by whatever work he carried out.

Ladyslav nodded and handed across his box of matches.

"You in fra' Dreghorn then?"

This was too much for Ladyslav, the words more than he could cope with as they were slurred under the thick accent to such an extent that they seemed to make no sense. He gave an apologetic smile and shook his head. "I no understand," he murmured hesitantly as he retrieved his matches and lit his own cigarette.

The man's brows drew together into a scowl, gazing at Ladyslav with obvious distaste. "Ye tryin' tae be funny wi' me?"

Ladyslav shrugged and turned back to his beer, not in any mood to argue with this coarse man in a language he could barely understand. Suddenly his spine chilled as he caught the unmistakable click of a switchblade opening.

Before he could make any attempt at defending himself Sadie stepped between them. He'd not seen her move round the bar moments ago as she unerringly anticipated trouble.

"Put that stupid thing awa' or I'll call the poliss," she shouted in a voice that cut the atmosphere of the bar. "Ye'll not cause a rumble in ma hoose Andy McVey, or ye'll be back in jail."

McVey had no chance and he quickly recalled that Sadie was well known to the locals as being able to take care of herself and any fractious customers. He folded away the blade and slunk back to his comrades who were grinning behind their hands. "Ah'll see tae ye, hen," he mumbled as he retreated.

. . .

Some time later Ladyslav drained his third pint and began to prepare to leave. Sadie approached and leaned across the bar providing him with a glimpse of her superb décolletage. "I wouldna leave now if I were you," she said in a low voice. "McVey will be waiting for ye outside so hang on fe' a half hour an' I'll walk wi' ye ter the bus stop. He'll nae cause trouble while ye'r wi' me."

After a few moments sorting out her words he gave her a grateful smile. He'd expected the man might try to waylay him outside and had been steeling himself for such an encounter. Ladyslav was not a scrapper but he'd been trained in unarmed combat and felt he might be able to deal with the man, but her offer was not one to be ignored. He laid a pound note on the bar. "You have drink with me, please?"

"Aye, ah wull," murmured Sadie looking down the bar. The sole remaining customer was old Jock Miller and he was almost done. "Ah'll have a wee dram, an' so wull ye." She slid the money back towards him. "It's on the hoose."

"Dziękuję," replied Ladyslav in his own language without thinking, then realising what he'd said when she stared at him, "Thank you. I speak English . . . little," he explained.

She smiled, the expression softening her face and making her hazel eyes sparkle. "We'll soon see aboot that," she exclaimed as she poured measures of Vat 69 into two small glasses.

. . .

After locking the bar doors Sadie linked arms with Ladyslav and they strolled along Princes Street towards the bus terminus where the camp transport stopped. The night was clear and starry, cold but not freezing as they walked past bright shop windows. Ladyslav noticed McVey lurking in a deep doorway near the terminus and watched as he turned and pretended to be lighting a cigarette as they passed by.

"That McVey's a sad piece of shite," exclaimed Sadie loudly as they passed. "I'll dob him in if he tries anything on you." It was obvious that she'd spotted the man and wanted him to hear her words.

Ladyslav squeezed her arm and said quietly, "I deal with him my way next time." He was aware that a few packs of cigarettes and possibly a bottle of spirits from the NAAFI would swiftly make him invaluable to the lads, after which it would all be profit.

Sadie glanced thoughtfully at him for a moment, then gave a slight shrug. "Okay, you do it then, but no fighting inside the bar or you'll both be in trouble."

Ladyslav grinned at her concern and shook his head. He liked this pretty lady who was also tough and uncompromising when it became necessary. They stood beside the bus for a moment and she pulled his face down to hers.

"I'll see you next time you're in town, eh?" she murmured as she brushed his lips with hers.

Then she was gone leaving Ladyslav standing in the bus shelter. Several others in uniform were approaching and he knew she'd done her job efficiently.

He relaxed with a smile as his hand strayed to his breast pocket to feel the crumpled photograph inside.

. . .

Ladyslav's idea paid off. Next time he visited the Crawford Lounge he was prepared with three packs of Players Navy Cut and a bottle of Teachers Whisky he'd picked up cheaply on the camp black market. In the temporary Polish camp there were many things available and one never asked where they came from. Within half an hour of his arrival McVey and his cronies swaggered into the bar wilting only slightly under Sadie's glare.

"Ye're not here tae cause trouble, are ye?" were her first words as they walked through the door. She stood behind her bar with hands on her hips, a formidable lady when her temper was aroused.

The three men mumbled their protestations and converged at the far end of the bar with hardly a glance at Ladyslav. For his turn Ladyslav never looked at them either, he could watch their actions in a mirror that was on a shelf behind the bar. He waited patiently until they'd downed their first pint and had been served their second round before he climbed to his feet, shouldered his pack and approached them.

"Well, look who's coming," said McVey thickly. There was a malicious glint in his eye and his hand wasn't far from his jacket pocket where he carried the switchblade. "It's our friend fra' last week. I think we've unfinished business."

Ladyslav smiled at McVey, relaxed and sure of himself. "Business, yes. Maybe we come to agreement." He was at last beginning to feel a little more at ease with the language. He placed the three packs of cigarettes on the bar between them. "I have samples. If you like, we do business."

The eyes of all three lit up. Cigarettes were strictly rationed and one pack represented almost half the week's legal supply for each of them. McVey's expression turned from that of bafflement to one of greed as he eyed the contraband. One of the other men had a pack open and was lighting up already.

The Teachers whisky was next as Ladyslav placed it on a stool under the bar counter and out of Sadie's sight. "We do business?" he asked again as he stared straight into McVey's eyes. He could read the conflict within the man so he reached out his other hand and clapped him lightly on the shoulder in a 'let bygones be bygones' gesture.

The bottle disappeared no sooner than he'd let go of it. A swift discussion in low tones followed and a financial agreement was swiftly reached that was amicable to both parties.

At the finish even McVey shook his hand.

. . .

Sadie was impressed with Ladyslav's handling of the men, knowing what an uncouth bunch they were. His way was certainly not her way but nonetheless she noted how he turned from being the potential victim to the person in control within a few minutes, raising neither his fist nor his voice. The triumph of brains over brawn was, to her, more than impressive, and when she closed up she invited Ladyslav to come with her for a drink before he caught the bus to camp.

It was only a few minutes walk to her apartment, a two bedroomed unit on the second floor of a large tenement block set back from the bustle of Princes Street. Communal stairways lit by dim electric light bulbs led them up towards her floor. The musty smell of sweat, urine and decaying food hung heavily in the still air despite some tenants' efforts to clean and disinfect their immediate surrounds.

"Here we are, safe and secure," she said as she closed and bolted the front door on the smelly corridor. She ushered him into a spacious lounge where a brown settee and two chairs dominated the open fireplace. "D'you want the fire lit?" she asked as she hung his greatcoat on a hook behind the door.

Ladyslav smiled at her and shook his head. The day had been warmer than usual and the flat wasn't cold inside. He liked the way she'd arranged the room, not unlike his old family home in Przemyśl.

"A wee dram then? Or would you prefer coffee?"

He settled for a coffee laced with the wee dram of whisky and she bustled away into a small kitchen with a twinkle in her eye.

. . .

Next morning Ladyslav was still at Sadie's apartment. He'd agreed to her invitation to stay, expecting to be accommodated in the spare bedroom, but she'd soon made it clear that she wanted more than just his company. Thus he was still tired as she prepared toast and tea for him before sending him off back to camp.

"Do you want guest for the other bedroom?" he asked as they finished breakfast.

Sadie frowned back at him with incomprehension. "Whut d'ye mean?"

Ladyslav produced a sheet of typewritten paper from the breast pocket of his battledress, unfolded it carefully and pushed it across to her. She found the first part of the document unintelligible as it was drafted in Polish, then she noticed that it continued in English underneath. It said that as more troops were due to arrive shortly the soldiers were urged to seek accommodation in the city on a bed, breakfast and evening meal basis. A scale of payments was listed at the end of the note and, although not over generous, Sadie could see a small profit element that would most likely be left at the end of each week.

"Well?" she asked gently. "Would ye like to move in with me for the time being, then?" Her eyes met his with frankness. "Mind, I have a temper when I'm roused and I like m'own way, but I like you and I think we could get along fine." She grinned shyly. "Especially after last night."

Ladyslav had no hesitation in agreeing. She'd been a willing and energetic partner in bed; he liked her protective nature and knew he could easily fall in love with this astonishing woman. He promised to make the arrangements and insisted she write down her name and address on the paper for him. He told her he could probably be moving in by the end of the week.

"In that case ye'll might as well start right now," she said with a chuckle. "Ye can have the first week free. Ah'll have dinner for ye tonight at six, okay?"

Ladyslav returned to camp a happy man.

. . .

They stayed together for nearly two years apart from brief periods when Ladyslav was sent away on various exercises after the battalion was formed into a cohesive unit under the command of General Montgomery. The exercises usually lasted for a week to ten days and were not so frequent as to disrupt their lives.

They even discussed marriage during the long summer of 1943 but reached the conclusion that such a step might not be wise until the war was over. Their feelings were mutual on this as Sadie was concerned that she could become a widow within months of their tying the knot, and Ladyslav didn't wish to return from the fight crippled and quickly become a burden on her for the rest of his life.

"No, it is better that we wait until it is over," he agreed in his improving but still hesitant English. "This does not mean that I do not love you, I just want you to have good life."

Their love had never been one of high passion, more a deep and growing friendship that bound them closely. They were both comfortable with one another so the matter of wedlock assumed merely a minor importance within their combined lives. Anyway they both knew that soon the war would be finished and marriage would follow in due course.

It was during the May of 1944 that his Battalion was put on stand-by for yet another exercise, the location of which was not disclosed. For some inexplicable reason the stand-by lasted for several weeks, kit packed and alert to move at two hours notice. The call came during the last week of the month and they parted in a hurry one sunny morning, Ladyslav promising to return as soon as the exercise was over.

It was that morning that Sadie was to visit her doctor as she was suspicious that she might be pregnant, a fact she withheld from him as she didn't want his hopes raised until it was confirmed. Three days later her doctor confirmed her as a new mother-to-be. She was delighted with the news but knew she'd need to wait until his return.

A week later the news of the D-Day invasion was splashed over all the headlines and she realised that she may not see him for some time, if ever again. Her premonition proved correct as there was no letter or other communication from him during the months leading up to her confinement. She gave birth to a girl of seven and a half pounds on 18th December. She christened her daughter Veronica.

Chapter One

Märsta—Stockholm: June 2010

The envelope that was to change Anna Petersson's life lay unopened on the top of the oval, glass-topped coffee table in her living room. At half past eight in the morning the only movement within the apartment was that of the sleek body of Mendelssohn, her Norwegian Forest cat, as he patrolled the kitchen, bathroom and living areas impatiently—breakfast was late this Sunday morning!

In the bedroom Anna opened one eye carefully; her head was throbbing gently as she surfaced from a deep alcohol-induced sleep. She considered herself for a moment; apart from the headache (*Oh shit, let's call it a hangover, she thought,*) she felt warm and contented, her bodily needs well satisfied after last night. A sudden thought snapped open her eyes quickly—the boy? Well, actually a young man of about thirty something, she recalled. She pushed her feet behind her to explore the rest of the big bed, quickly encountering somebody else's legs.

Oh, God, he's still here! And he'll no doubt expect an action replay when he awakes, she thought in horror, her body stiffening and less than comfortable. She wondered why she hadn't kicked him out last night once he'd satisfied her needs.

She could recall the man now, almost fifteen years her junior but keen for all their age difference. She had been able to feel his interest as they danced, parts of his body hard against hers as he caressed her neck. Oh, yes, it had been a good night with plenty of wine and a few vodkas. Later she had allowed him a quick fumble in the back of the taxi to keep his interest alive. She frowned, what was his name? She could not recall.

Once they had arrived at her apartment she couldn't wait to get his clothes off, nor he hers. She almost shuddered at the thought as she spotted male underclothing on the floor beside the bed, socks and boxer shorts. She hoped they hadn't woken up Maria and Jorgen in the flat below with their exuberance during the early hours of the morning.

She groaned, now she had to get rid of him. I must have fallen asleep, she mused, before I got round to sending him packing. This was the first man who'd ever stayed overnight with her since her divorce some six years ago.

Gently she slid from between the crumpled sheets and padded in the direction of the bathroom as she pulled on her dressing gown. She put her head round the lounge door to see Mendelssohn seated at the window with a disapproving look in his green eyes. Something caught her gaze and she raised her eyes to see her newest, expensive brassiere suspended from the light fitting in the centre of the ceiling. With a groan she covered her eyes with her hand. What an idiot she'd been; too much alcohol leading to too much sex, and insufficient forethought to getting rid of Stig or Rune, or whatever his silly name was, before dawn.

Suddenly two hairy arms circled her waist from behind and a stubbly chin buried itself in the cleft of her neck. Mendelssohn turned away indignantly as lips began to fasten themselves onto the skin just below her ear, one of those places she was self-conscious about and hated to be kissed on.

Anna shook herself and disengaged swiftly. "Get off me! You're the last thing I feel like this morning!" She turned and looked at his naked body. Not such a bad choice, she thought as her eyes dropped to his most endearing characteristic, you did yourself proud, Anna. "Get your clothes on, if you can find them after throwing them all over the bedroom floor. I've got things to do today."

His face took on a hurt look. "What, no breakfast? When can I see you again?"

Her mouth tightened. Nice lay he may be, but there are plenty more where he came from. She had some personal rules and no serious boy friend was one of them. She wasn't about to break the rule just for a big dick and a few muscles, nice as they were in the darkness of last night.

"You don't. Put your clothes on, go down and turn right when you hit the street. There's a taxi rank at the end of the block." She managed a thin smile. "Thanks, it was fun, but I'm not looking for any relationships."

The man turned and scrabbled across the floor for his underclothes, snatching them up with a juvenile show of petulance. Anna liked his dark, curly hair and those piercing blue eyes, and she felt just a tiny pang of remorse as he pulled up his jeans and tightened the belt around his narrow waist. With an inward sigh she closed the bathroom door behind her.

. . .

The apartment was empty when she emerged from the bathroom washed and refreshed, even her headache had receded. Mendelssohn strutted across towards the kitchen, brushing himself against her legs with more than a hint of hunger. He stopped in front of his food bowl and stared at it. The doorbell buzzed.

Anna opened the door to find Rune or Stig standing outside looking irritated. "The bloody lift isn't working," he said as if it was her fault.

She lowered her gaze towards his legs for a moment. "What's that in your jeans? And I don't mean your dick. Two of them! Well use the damn things and don't come snivelling back here to me." She turned and slammed the door.

Returning to the kitchen she opened a tin and spooned out Mendelssohn's meal while she kept an eye out on the pavement four storeys below. A feeling of remorse arose in her, perhaps breakfast wouldn't have been too much for her to provide, she mused, in two minds whether or not to rush out and call him back. A couple of months later she caught sight of his dark, curly head emerging from the main door of the building and strutting indignantly away towards the taxi rank. She placed the food down with a sigh of relief. This was the only faithful male she'd ever met, and even then she wasn't sure that he wouldn't desert her one of these days, especially if she forgot to feed him. Her track record with the opposite sex was not a good one, even in her own eyes.

Lars Petersson had seemed like the perfect catch nearly twenty five years ago, tall and blond with attractive dark eyes and a smile that soon charmed her away from her friends. They quickly became an item and were married six months later, Anna Dochewski, as she was born, suddenly becoming Anna Petersson. At the time she was proud to take his name.

Twenty two years, two children and several indiscretions on his part later, she kicked him out of the house to go and live with his latest spindly blond with breasts the size of water melons and a face so perfect beneath the multiple layers of make-up. The tart was welcome to Lars with his expanding girth, daily flatulence problems and chronic indigestion possibly caused by over-indulgence in cheap Vodka.

With her half-share from their house and bank account she'd purchased her apartment on the fourth floor of this quiet block in Märsta, on the outskirts of Stockholm. Her own four walls in which she was the undisputed ruler, apart from Mendelssohn, that is; after all who could rule any feline? Mendel, as she usually called him, had followed within the first months of her new, liberated existence and they bonded immediately. They had an unwritten pact between them, she'd feed him and empty his dirt box while he would stand guard against the ingress of crawling insects and rodents. Theirs was a good life, if a touch smelly at times.

She watched as Mendelssohn sniffed cautiously at his dish before starting to eat delicately. With a smile she pulled her dressing gown tighter round her waist and went into the lounge where the beige envelope was still laying in the middle of the coffee table. She eyed it with suspicion. A motorcycle courier had delivered it yesterday evening, just before she left for the centre of Stockholm to meet her friends. She knew roughly what it would contain.

She was paid a small stipend, a retainer if one wished to be more specific, by the Stockholm Police Headquarters as an adviser on criminal behaviour. For this pittance she was expected to review a selection of their more difficult, and all too often gory, cases and advise whether any of the suspects listed might have committed the killings. Her speciality was murder, serial murders preferably, and she had written several books on this theme, the most recent being a text published last month that had stirred up debate in many academic circles. Her retainer and the royalties from her books enhanced her modest income for lecturing on Criminal Psychology at *Upsalla* University. Altogether it brought in sufficient money to live comfortably in her flat and run her trusty old Nissan Micra.

With a sniff she turned back to the kitchen to make herself coffee. The envelope could wait until she was good and ready to breach its contents.

. . .

An hour later, after some toast and a boiled egg, she pulled on jeans and a tee shirt, moving her bra from its living room perch to the bedroom cupboard. Anna set her mug of coffee down on the table in the lounge and inserted a CD into the new system she had bought a few months ago. The music of *Zbigniew Preisner* had always interested her and this CD was the soundtrack from the *Krzysztof Kieslowski* film, *Trois Couleurs-Bleu*, composed by *Preisner*. As the haunting music filled the room she pulled the envelope towards her and opened one end, emptying its contents onto the coffee table.

The main document was a standard police file concerning the death in suspicious circumstances of a young woman whose body had been found floating in the channel adjacent to the *Klarastrandsleden* road by the *Barnhusbron* bridge. The cause of death had been recorded as 'drowning', but the post mortem report also mentioned the fact that the corpse contained a lethal dose of Heroin, so no final decision had been made as to whether or not this was a murder, accident or just a suicide. The covering letter asked her to help them by going through the victim's documents and personal belongings and offering advice as to whether a full investigation was necessary.

The girl was shown to be Latvian, which was one reason that they might not be so keen on conducting any unnecessary and expensive investigations. Her first inclination was to send the papers back and tell them it was probably an accident and not to be so cavalier in their treatment of foreigners.

The police had already visited an address in the girl's pocket book and her body had been identified as that of Katja Bokov, who was said to have worked as a waitress in some bar in the centre of Stockholm. The report hinted that the girl was actually engaged in prostitution and the post mortem examination indicated that this could be a strong possibility, and the fact that her arms indicated she was using hard drugs tended to reinforce this supposition.

Anna threw down the papers in disgust and sipped at her coffee again. Why do they think I can be of help to them in such matters? So far this is out of my purview and I think I'll send the bundle back with a curt note not to waste my time, she thought as she pushed the police file back into the envelope. A second, smaller envelope caught her eye, open at one end. Inside was a passport and a bundle of photographs held together by an elastic band.

She tipped out the contents and picked up a leaflet folded neatly into the passport. On the front of the leaflet was a picture of an Orthodox Russian Cross and it turned out to be a flyer originating from a church at Västerås, a town not very far from Stockholm. It appeared to be concerning proposed plans to organise evening classes on Icon-painting. She took a deep breath and sipped at her coffee as the first track of *Van Den Budehmayer's* funeral music drew to an end. So, she mused, we have a possibly innocent girl from Latvia, maybe working the streets of the city, apparently taking drugs, but nonetheless still true to her religion, or why else did she keep this leaflet? To her this didn't seem to add up. It looks more like some horrible tragedy, paradoxical in its nature. Could she have been forced to take the drugs against her will? Been held down and injected? The idea didn't bear thinking about, but it might explain the suicide; or even her murder? She sat back and rubbed her eyes, not wishing to acknowledge the beginnings of tears.

With a sniff she turned her attention to the passport. Issued in Latvia, it was merely a standard tourist passport, no visas or work permits. The photograph showed the face of a typically shy student, self-conscious in front of the camera. She was not beautiful but, with some make-up and attention, she would certainly turn heads. The only other information it provided was her birth date, 26 June 1986, which meant that she died just before her eighteenth birthday, which had been yesterday.

This was beginning to depress Anna, she could feel the heaviness beginning to infiltrate her mind and knew she must turn her thoughts away from this case soon or she'd be unfit even to go to Stockholm tomorrow on the train. She suffered from fits of depression at times which could keep her from work for several days at a time. She closed the passport and began to push it back into the envelope when something else between the pages began to make itself known. She pulled out a small identification card that had been issued by the

University of Latvia in Riga, attesting to the fact that Katja was a member of the Faculty of Foreign Languages. The same passport photo, but cut tighter, was inserted into the card.

Anna sighed and leaned back, surrendering herself to Preisner's music for a few minutes. Not exactly the ideal medium to help cheer her up, but it did aid her to relax and let her thoughts wander. What on Earth, she wondered, would an intelligent girl like this be doing walking the streets of Stockholm? Okay, so one must expect that she needed money for her tuition fees, they didn't come cheap these days and she recalled that her daughter had mentioned something about two or three thousand US Dollars per year when she'd met students from mid-Europe at the University in Upsalla. But was that worth selling one's body to attain? She didn't feel so. In which case another party may have forced the girl into prostitution. A sobering thought on a Sunday morning after a night on the binge!

As the tracks changed on the CD player she put the card down and picked up the bundle of photographs, removing the elastic band. This was the moment she looked forward to least, peeping into somebody's private life and sometimes seeing their soul bared. It could often feel as if she was watching them walk around naked. She knew it was essential to help her get a feeling for the victim, but at what cost to her? Money could never replace the horror she could go through at times in this job.

She looked round the lounge and the half-empty bottle of Vodka on the sideboard caught her eye. There was a sudden temptation but she resisted it, the idea of strong drink in the mid-morning was not a good sign in anybody's language.

The pictures were mainly harmless, snaps of anonymous students enjoying themselves, mainly girls but a few boys now and then. Only one picture showed Katja as far as she could tell, her features relaxed and happy, unlike her passport photograph. She looked prettier in the photograph as she sat at a table outside a bar, smiling up at the photographer with a glass of beer in her hand. This was certainly not a shot of any lady of easy virtue, Katja was just not the type to do such a thing, she could read it in her face.

Don't prejudge the issues, she counselled herself, you cannot deny the facts even if all you see is modesty, innocence and inexperience. How many girls have given the impression that butter would never melt in their mouths before turning out to be potential killers? She lectured on just this subject and had always berated her students about forming preliminary judgements based on visual evidence alone, and here she was doing just that herself.

It was the final photograph that brought Anna's day to a halt, making her reach out for the vodka bottle.

It was a man, not young like Katja, but good looking in a mature way. She wondered fleetingly if this was Katja's father before turning the print over to see a message written on the reverse. *'To my little love, can't wait to see you again,'* the inscription said in English. It was signed *'Bob'*.

The face of the man was somehow familiar to her, but from where? Covering up parts of his face narrowed down the familiar areas to the man's eyes and mouth. She wondered why this picture left her short of breath; it must resemble somebody close to her, she thought.

She poured a tot of spirit into the small glass she'd used the night before and sipped it slowly, then stood up and walked over to the framed prints she had standing on her sideboard. Her first impression had been that the man looked a bit like Lars, but when she eventually found a picture of him she knew she was mistaken. Who then?

She walked into her study and to the old oak desk she's so lovingly brought across from Poland. It was a genuine antique with rich hand-made woodcarvings on the front of the two doors. It had been her one special reminder of her childhood, one that she needed to keep with her. Momentarily she recalled the look of utter disdain on Lars' face when he'd seen it, and her feeling at the time that he couldn't even appreciate a beautiful piece of Gdansk furniture.

Rummaging into the top drawer she unearthed an old photo album from her youth and began checking the pictures from the back towards the front, working backwards in time. She knew this person must be somebody she was close to at some time in her life so she concentrated on her old friends from her early days in Sweden but to no avail.

The first three or four pages contained old photos from her youth in Poland and she was just about to close the book when she came across a print of her parents, blurry but recognisable. She looked closely at the picture of her father and there was a likeness there.

With a grunt she turned to the first page where she knew she'd inserted a studio portrait of him at one time. Her father's face jumped out of the page at her, mouth, eyes, just like the picture in Katja's collection. Her heart beat faster as she gazed at that photograph of her long-dead parent, it couldn't be! Surely this was some bizarre coincidence!

She gulped down the vodka and peered closely at her father's picture. She pulled it from the album and took it into the living room where she laid the two prints side by side. Finding a magnifying glass in her bureau drawer she compared the features carefully, they were sufficiently alike for her to catch her breath.

She needed to know who this Bob might be, his background and parents. She sat down heavily and reached for the bottle again as she realised she'd never rest until she'd sorted this out one way or another.

Chapter Two

"This is becoming too much like a habit," muttered Anna to herself on Monday morning as she washed down two Ibuprofen Tablets with her coffee.

This time her headache wasn't so bad, she hadn't mixed her drinks like she had on the previous night, but it was still intrusive and a sore reminder that she'd overdone the Vodka last night. I've only myself to blame, she thought as she stumbled towards the bathroom and turned on the shower.

Standing under the warming spray was a pleasure, easing away many of her aches and pains within minutes. She soaked her hair and lathered it with Garnier Fructis to remove the grease from the previous day. As she worked the soft lather deeply into her head she could still see the face of 'Bob' from the girl's photograph superimposed upon her father's face, and it niggled continually at her mind. Surely, she thought as she rinsed her hair, there must be some connection here, there were too many points of likeness to be coincidence. Deeper within her the voice of reason cautioned that there was probably no relationship whatsoever between this 'Bob' and her father.

Clambering from the shower she towelled herself down before gazing at her reflection in the full-length mirror. Not so damn bad, she thought with a smile. Fifty-one years old without a grey hair, I still have a waist, only a little excess fat, and my breasts are still firm with hardly any sign of heading south. She turned sideways and continued to admire herself, liking what she saw. She knew that her body would look good even on someone twenty years her junior.

Her gaze dropped and she considered the stretch marks that extended down her lower abdomen to disappear into her dark pubic hair. She was pleased that they were hardly noticeable as she ran her fingers over them before pulling on a fresh pair of briefs.

"Not half bad, my old dear," she said to herself as she wandered back to the bedroom and began to dress for the day ahead. She selected a dark blue 'power suit' with pencil skirt and a white blouse that wasn't transparent for her meeting with Superintendent Vickström, the Stockholm Controller of Police.

Quickly she fed Mendelssohn and gulped down another cup of coffee before dropping the pack of Ibuprofen into her fashionable handbag. No sense in denying herself relief if she needed it, she thought as she opened the front door.

. . .

The train was crowded when it arrived and she felt lucky to get a seat amongst the morning commuters. Gazing out at the countryside as the train passed through *Upplands Våsby* and *Rotebro* she was reminded of her childhood in Poland. The main difference was the graffiti daubed along the rail-side buildings and walls, much of it exceptionally artistic if somewhat gaudy and out of place. From all those years ago she couldn't recall anything ever written or painted along the tracks.

Forty-five minutes later they pulled into Stockholm Central, crowded and bustling as ever. Anna walked the half-mile to Police headquarters over the *Klarabergsviadukten* Bridge to *Kungsholmen* Island in the warmth of the June sun. The temperature was not as high as it had been this time last year, she recalled as a cooling breeze made her walk pleasant rather than uncomfortable. Last week had seen rain and unseasonable cold but today was promising a spell of settled weather.

She knocked on the door of Superintendent Vickström's Office ten minutes early for her appointment. "He'll see you straight away," the Desk Sergeant had said when she arrived. "He's only sitting in his office picking his nose." She doubted that very much, but she waited for his call rather than walking in, she didn't wish to catch him in an unguarded moment.

He called her in almost immediately, offering her coffee and a comfortable seat in his well appointed office. Vickstrom was probably about six or seven years her senior, tall and lean with a hawk-like nose under a high forehead that denoted intelligence. He waited until she was settled before asking her if she'd had time to consider the case. "What d'you think?" he finished.

Anna shook her head slowly with a grimace. "Depressing. It doesn't feel right that an eighteen year old girl, a student of languages at a University, should commit suicide in such a manner." She fixed Vickström with her gaze to ensure he was listening to her. "The heroin makes little or no sense either. This has to be deliberate, most likely she was murdered."

Vickström nodded slowly, saying nothing. He knew she hadn't finished talking yet.

"The photograph from someone called 'Bob' is also a loose cannon in this scenario, very much out of place from the rest of her stuff. For a start it appears to have been developed and printed in England, there's a company name and address on the back of the photographic paper. All the others were obviously from Sweden or Latvia, different paper and the Swedish ones are all showing locations in and around Stockholm."

She stopped and drew breath for a moment. "The message on the back of the photo might have been to any girl, not necessarily Katja. Is it possible that this got into her collection by mistake?"

Vickström shook his head as he replied. "I shouldn't think so. The girl who shared the flat with Katja helped us remove all of her belongings. She'd have known if anything we took was hers and not Katja's."

"In that case I would suggest that you try to find this man, Bob. You might need to speak to the English Police, they might know the man." She thought for a second. "Er . . . Bob is short for Robert, I think."

"Maybe." Vickström lit up a cigarette. There were 'no smoking' signs scattered around the building, but he obviously ignored such trivialities. Leaning across he pulled open a window to let out the smoke. "We'll see. Shall I get the personal effects sent up here, or would you prefer not to see any more?"

"Why not," Anna replied nodding, "Having got this far there might be something of significance amongst them."

Ten minutes later a large cardboard box had been delivered to Vickström's spare table at the back of his office. He opened the top and started to lay out an assortment of items, toiletries, make-up and brushes, underclothing and a heap of personal jewellery as well as a bundle of clothing and shoes. Outdoor items he left in the box as being of little interest.

"These have all been fingerprinted so you can handle them without worry," murmured Victstrom as he sat back and watched her.

Anna examined each item carefully, trying to connect every object to the dead girl. Most of them were just cheap pieces that Katja had brought over from Latvia, with the exception of a single item that stood out from the rest. This was a gold crucifix on a chain, not the standard cross one sees so often, but a large Russian Orthodox cross, extremely detailed within a design that is rarely seen.

She laid it carefully onto a sheet of paper and turned to Vickström. "Look at this. This is a Russian Orthodox Cross, see the small horizontal bar above the main one and the extra lower sloping bar below? This isn't just a simple crucifix, but a bearer of other religious elements as well."

Pointing out the base of the cross where what appeared to be a skull had been engraved she explained, "This shows the skull of Adam, our original forefather who lost Paradise. Here it is shown hidden under the earth." She edged the tip of her little fingernail up the crucifix to a further engraving just below the sloping cross bar. "See here there are what appear to be four letters engraved, they look like M A F and E. These are Slavic and stand for 'The place of the skull becomes paradise.' It all means that Christ is the new Adam who brings us salvation and paradise through the tree of the cross."

Lecture over she placed the paper and cross into Vickström's hands.

"Hmmm, very interesting," he mumbled, obviously not impressed by her knowledge of the Russian take on Christianity.

"Yes, it is very interesting, especially because you can't buy these just anywhere. This has been specially made and, even though it's probably only gold plated, it's likely to be well beyond the means of any young University student."

He took the pendant from her carefully, holding the paper by its edges, and gazed closely at it through a magnifying glass. "This looks almost new," he murmured, then peered closer for a moment. "There are prints on this so we probably have these on our records" he concluded dropping it into a plastic bag and writing on the label.

"It might be useful if we could find out who made it, or at least distributed it. A list of dealers might reveal something."

He nodded slowly then met her gaze. "How's your Russian?" he asked quietly, his face thoughtful.

Anna laughed. "I think I'd better explain my life's paradox to you." She sat back in an armchair beside the open window. "I'll borrow one of your cigarettes if I may."

"Never knew you smoked," said Vickström in surprise. He pushed the pack of Prince and his lighter towards her.

"Only now and again when the mood takes me," she said as she extracted a cigarette from the pack and lit up. "Thanks. This case is probably getting to me." She blew smoke towards the window. "Russian? You have to remember that I was raised in a Communist country where Russian was taught compulsorily from the fourth year onwards, we had no choice but to learn the language. So I can say that I have a working knowledge of Russian."

She leaned back in her chair and took a further long drag, enjoying the feel of the cool smoke penetrating her lungs before she exhaled towards the window. "The paradox is that when I was a child I attended a private nursery where English was the main language spoken. I still remember 'Humpty Dumpty sat on a wall,' from a time when I was four years old." She grinned at Vickström across his desk. "So you see, I am fluent in Polish and Swedish and nearly as good in Russian and English."

He reflected her smile as he stubbed out his cigarette. "That serves me right for asking, doesn't it? The summer holiday season begins in a couple of weeks, how do you fancy travelling for a short time?"

Anna extinguished her cigarette thoughtfully then looked at the Superintendent with raised eyebrows as she smiled encouragingly, waiting for him to elaborate.

"Truth of the matter is that we're very short of Police Officers at the moment. My staff are up to their eyes with investigating the recent murder of a prominent politician, keeping close tabs on members of our Royalty and too many of them are on secondment to SÄPO while there is such a rise in terrorist activity. Basically this means that we are unable to spare a lot of time and effort into investigating this particular case." He reached across and pulled another cigarette from the pack, lit it and pushed the pack towards her. "It would make a big difference if we could send somebody, say like yourself, to England to liaise with their Special Branch and do some simple research there."

After a brief pause he met her gaze directly. "So? Would you be willing to help out?"

Anna tried not to let her face give away the fact that this was more than she had hoped for, she was being offered the chance to possibly trace her father's movements in the UK during the war. She frowned for a few seconds to give the impression that she was reluctant, then suddenly appeared to change her mind. "I guess I could spend some time on it," she replied in her most off-hand manner.

You're lucky I didn't bite off your hand, she thought to herself as she took another cigarette, lighting it from Vickström's lighter with a feeling of satisfaction.

Chapter Three

The shop door closed behind the last customer of the day. Duncan Macmillan sprung the lock and turned the sign hanging in the window to read 'closed'. He'd had a good day, the customers had been more than generous in their purchases and he appreciated their delight as they discovered many of the more specialised items he stocked.

He grinned to himself as he turned back towards the glass display counter within which the most expensive of his items were housed. He looked at the array with pleasure, noting the welcome gaps where he'd not had time to replenish the stock. These were items made of gold or silver, often set with expensive stones as they were laid out for all to see; crucifixes of all types, clan pins and many rings of special local significance, formed the bulk of the display together with other jewellery that helped to fill the case.

Opening the till he made a quick estimate of the contents, bundling all the notes and credit card slips into a bag and tipping the small change out onto the counter. He proceeded to count out £100 in small piles of change to be replaced in the till tray that he took through to the rear stockroom where he slid it into the safe which was set against the back wall. The remainder of the change was swept into the bag and finally he dropped a paying-in book in with the cash before tying it off.

Duncan spent a further ten minutes inserting gold rings into the gaps in the display and straightening the mats on the counter top. Rolling down the metal shutters before setting the alarm and finally locking the door from outside, he strolled along to the multi-storey car park on Cambridge Street off Sauchiehall Street to collect his car.

He waved at the other shopkeepers who were engaged in their closing operations as he walked.

"Good day to you, Mrs McGlone," he said to the red-haired elderly lady who was struggling with the enormous padlock that held the shutters of her dress shop secure overnight. "Did you have a busy day?" He'd noticed that she'd been blessed with a few more visitors than usual during times when he was idle.

"Aye, y'could say that," murmured the woman with a grin. "Ah'll no grumble tonight, and have maybe a dram or two before ma bed."

Duncan laughed and strolled onwards to the car park. His red Vauxhall Astra awaited him on the first floor, gleaming in the evening sun.

As he drove north out of the city his mind wandered over the recent years of his life since his mother had died. He had started the business with the money he'd been left, his share of her estate that was divided between him and his twin brother, Robert. The house was supposed to be sold and the proceeds split equally between them, but they'd decided to keep it on together until one or the other of them wished to move away or get married. His business had flourished as much as the relationship between them had swiftly deteriorated. Robert appeared at Glen Cottage for short spells about three or four times each year, the rest of his time being spent on some nefarious project or other abroad. Duncan was aware that his twin brother's projects were usually somewhat less than legal, and he knew never to ask exactly what he did when he was away.

He recalled the last time his brother had been there for a few days, it had been sometime in June, about six weeks ago. Robert had insisted on taking a few of his more expensive items of stock, without expecting to pay for them.

"These are imported from Eastern Europe, very special and rare pieces, and they cost me more money than I like to afford," he'd said naming a figure that was less than fifteen percent below the retail price. "I only make a low profit on these and can't afford to give them away, even at cost price."

Robert had looked down his nose at him, mumbling something that sounded like "fucking skinflint". That hadn't been the end of the conversation, however, as two days later he'd discovered that two of the items were suddenly unaccounted for, they had disappeared from his stock without trace. Instantly he knew that his twin brother had lifted them, but how could he prove it? Robert gave a well rehearsed impression of surprise when the theft was mentioned.

They'd argued again and Robert had left early the next morning. Now he was due to return and, like as not, would probably want more of those items. He smiled as he drove along the country road as he'd specially locked those particular items securely in his safe. That would teach the thieving beggar, he mused, he won't have things all his own way from now on.

The sun was dipping behind Glen Cottage when he pulled into the gates. As he cut the motor he noticed another car tucked away close to the south side of the cottage, a black Mercedes with a new brand new '04' registration. For a moment he wondered who must own the car, then he realised that if nobody was waiting outside, the owner must be his brother, for he was the only other person with a key to the cottage.

'But he isn't due until next week,' he thought to himself. 'Why the early return? Most unlike him to arrive beforehand, he's usually a few days late if anything.' He closed and locked the car and walked up to the entrance porch, opening the front door and placing his black bag with the cash and paying in book into the hall cupboard out of sight. He turned and saw Robert step into the hall from the living room.

"Hello, early bird," he said with what he hoped looked like a welcoming smile. "Didn't expect you for a week or two yet."

His brother nodded his greeting, a man of few words, and then he shrugged. "Happens," he muttered offhandedly, as if this explained everything from immaculate conception to the increasing price of haggis.

Duncan's mouth tightened; there was hardly a greeting or word of welcome from his brother. 'We might as well be total strangers,' he thought with a mental shrug. Earlier he had resolved not to argue with the man if possible, but now he felt the stirrings of anger welling up inside him. He took a grip on himself. "Hungry?" he asked.

"Had a pork pie at the service station a couple of hours ago, but I could use a tea and maybe a sandwich."

'Welcome home,' murmured Duncan sotto voce as he made his way towards the kitchen. He was well aware that Robert's 'sandwich' could easily stretch to a three-course meal if that was on offer. Opening the freezer he pulled out a tray of chicken breasts and a pack of frozen oven chips.

. . .

Anna stretched her legs out under the seat in front of her and laid back against the head rest. What a pleasure it is to fly in luxury with Scandinavian Airlines, she thought with a wry smile. On previous occasions she'd travelled Tourist Class, with the accompanying constraints of space and comfort, but in contrast this journey was an unexpected pleasure. The MacDonnell Douglas MD90 was only about two thirds full and there were barely half a dozen passengers in the front Business Class seats, giving room for them all to stretch out.

Her flight, SK 0531, had taken to the sky from Arlanda Airport in Stockholm at a quarter past eleven, a sensible time in the morning. Drinks had been served about twenty minutes after take-off and she'd enjoyed the luxury of a miniature of Famous Grouse whiskey before the lunch was served. The steward turned out to be a personable young man in his late twenties and she'd surveyed him closely with her experienced eye as he dispensed drinks from the trolley. 'Nice bum' she mused as her eyes travelled down from his light brown hair (a trifle too long), strong muscular shoulders (but not overdeveloped) to his slim waist (yum!) and finally settled just below that region with amused interest.

When their eyes met she had suddenly realised why he wasn't displaying any similar interest in her. "*Tak så mycket*" she murmured with a resigned shrug as he turned away with more enthusiasm to administer to a younger male passenger. 'Can't win them all,' she thought as she broke the seal on the scotch and poured it over the ice in her glass.

The cigar shaped MD90 touched down at Heathrow after the 90 minute flight and she passed straight through the formalities, collected her luggage and walked through the green Customs gate onto a crowded concourse. She stopped and gazed around her spotting a woman holding a card with 'Petersson' printed on it in black felt pen.

"You will be met at London Airport," Superintendent Vickström had told her, "and escorted to your hotel. Anything you might need, just ask the escort and he or she will try to help."

She'd forgotten his words until this moment as she smiled across at the young lady and gave her a wave. Her escort was in her early thirties, dressed in a charcoal suit with a crisp white blouse beneath, her dark hair cut short and brushed back from her fresh, tanned face. There was an air of hidden strength about the woman, like an athlete at the peak of her training, thought Anna as she approached.

"Miss Petersson?" she asked as Anna put down her case. Anna nodded with her smile still in place. "I'm Justine Baker, yours for the time being if you need me. I work for the Home Office."

. . .

Justine turned out to be surprisingly open and talkative, much to Anna's delight. Her previous contacts with people from Government departments had all been intense and non-communicative, but Justine was a breath of fresh air, young and obviously enjoying her life as she chatted about various places in the city that Anna might wish to visit. She obviously didn't know that Anna had been to London several times during the late eighties and had seen most of the usual sights.

The black limousine drew up silently in the forecourt of the Royal Standard Hotel in South Kensington, just off the Brompton Road where the main shopping area was located. Justine got out and escorted Anna to the Reception desk where she laid a card in front of her.

"This is my telephone number, both office and my flat, so if you need anything, or get lost, or just want to talk, just ring me and I'll be there for you." She put a hand gently on Anna's arm. "If you want to have a day or two taking in the sights or doing any special shopping, and you would like company, just call me. I'm at your disposal for the duration of your stay here."

Anna raised her eyebrows in mute question. This was an unexpected service and she was wondering why she'd been selected for this special treatment. She asked the question quietly.

"Your chief, Superintendent Vickström, has met our head of section, Brigadier Kelso, in the past. I get the distinct feeling that they're actually closer than the casual acquaintances my boss will admit to." She grinned and winked at Anna. "I understand that our Brigadier was on active operations in your country not so long ago."

Anna raised her eyebrows but didn't comment on the information she'd received. She thanked Justine for her help. "I'll be in touch if I need anything, thanks" she said as the receptionist approached them with a welcoming smile.

. . .

Her room was a dream, more a suite than a room, she felt. A lounge fitted with plasma television, luxury seating for four or five people and a small bar at one end. To one side was the bedroom, a double, with an en suite bathroom, and . . . 'Oh boy! Look at this!' She thought. 'A Jacuzzi, even!'

"Wow," she exclaimed out loud as she gazed around the charcoal grey and cream tiled enclosure. Her first thought was to run a hot bath and just lay in it to let the bubbles work their magic for half an hour or so. Then she began to realise that she was hungry.

Turning back into the lounge a clock on the wall informed her that the time here in England was one forty-five, so she adjusted her watch back an hour and decided that her first priority must be to find some food. She stepped round her bags that lay on the floor where the porter had placed them, locked her door and hurried across to the lift.

Walking down Old Brompton Road in the direction of South Kensington Underground Station she stumbled upon a small but attractive Italian Restaurant a few yards past the turning into Queens Gate. The sign over the door indicated it was called the Bella Italia and she could see that it was still serving customers. Walking over to the menu she concentrated on the lunchtime sea-food options, one of these being her favourite dish that was not usually available in Sweden, mussels with pasta and garlic sauce. She stepped into the restaurant without any further hesitation.

The manager, or proprietor, was effusive and insisted on placing her at a 'very special' table right in front of the window, no doubt to reinforce the fact that they were still open for business. He continued to fuss around her for a few more minutes, taking her order for the mussels and her preference for a drink, a glass of white wine, before retiring to deal with other customers.

The food was excellent and the wine just sufficient to leave her feeling relaxed for the first time in several years. She lit up a cigarette to go with her coffee and considered how lucky she was to be here. She need not continue playing the part she'd allotted herself in life; the tough, self sufficient predatory female persona could be consigned to the back seat for now and she could revert to the 'old Anna', a person she hardly knew these days.

As she gazed out of the window she could see that London didn't appear to have changed very much since her last visit, she felt it was still a home for a wide variety of cultures, all rubbing shoulders with one another in a more or less amicable fashion. The word 'polyglot' popped into her mind from some long forgotten text she'd read during her Psychology studies; how aptly that word could describe the population of this city, she thought with an inward smile.

As she sipped the coffee she considered her plans for the rest of the day. Explore the hotel, take that long and sensuous bath she'd promised herself, catch up on some sleep and eat in the hotel dining room before a few drinks and an early night. The fleeting thought that there might be some personable young man available in the bar was dismissed almost immediately. Let go of the old life in Stockholm, she told herself, you can become a 'new and improved Anna' while you're here! Perhaps it might actually be the 'real' Anna, the 'old Anna', after throwing off the mask of toughness she had got used to since her divorce? Whatever it might be, she thought, it felt good.

She stretched her legs with a sigh of contentment. Working can wait for a day or two.

Chapter Four

"Hello Justine, this is Anna from the Royal Standard Hotel. How do you fancy showing me around a bit today? I'm dying to see Betty Boop's latest collection of handbags, and a nice English pub with some life to watch, if you know what I mean?"

Anna had slept well and was looking forward to an afternoon out before settling down to the mundane business of checking on the suppliers that Vickström had come up with.

"I think the Kings Arms by the river at Weybridge might be right up your street," suggested Justine. "It's a lively pub where we can at least get a good meal."

"Okay, we'll meet here at the hotel at, say, eleven? I'll buy the lunch today so don't worry about the cost. And we can have some fun, I feel the need for it." Anna was hoping for a complete change in scenery and somewhere where she could just be herself, without any pressure or hassles.

Their meeting arranged she decided to take a walk along the Old Brompton Road. The sun was hot and the sky cloudless, ideal for a trip later, but for now all she was interested in was a spot of casual window-shopping.

Strolling down the road turned out not to be as pleasant as she'd hoped, heavy traffic making the air heady with diesel fumes and smoke while the noise was incessant as vehicles raced between sets of traffic lights. She soon decided to try to escape the noise so she turned off onto a side road and walked along beside a row of stunted and dusty trees. About fifty yards along she came upon a parade of small shops; a newsagents, convenience store, dress shop, then she halted at the next window, intrigued by what she was seeing there. The display was mainly various items of Scottish traditional dress and ornamentation like clan pins, dirks and tartan items, but amongst these was a tray of crucifixes. The centrepiece of the tray jumped out at her immediately, a decorative Russian orthodox cross, similar to, but not exactly the same as the one she was searching for.

She stood there and stared closely at it for about one minute, then stepped back and checked the name of the shop, 'Macmillan' was all it said. On impulse she pushed at the door and entered the premises, noting immediately that she was their only customer.

"Good morning, can I help you?" The lady behind the counter was elderly but had a welcoming smile and a friendly face. Her hair was tight to her head and she wore a severe black jumper over a green and black patterned skirt that Anna recognised as a Scottish tartan.

"That cross in the window, the Orthodox Russian Church," she said indicating the left hand window. "Is that the only one you stock?"

The lady walked to the window and extracted the display tray with the centrepiece that Anna had been looking at. "You mean this?" she asked, pointing to the crucifix.

"That's it. It's unusual and not easy to find in this country," said Anna. "But I'm looking for one a little larger than that."

The woman's lips tightened slightly in thought. "We don't get asked for this very often, maybe once a year if that. This is the only one we hold, but I can ask the owner, Mister Macmillan, if he has any others if you like."

"How long would that take?"

The lady shrugged slightly and shook her head. "I couldn't say, perhaps a couple of weeks?"

Anna grimaced and smiled. "I'll probably be out of the country by then. Does the owner have any other branches?"

A nod and a smile indicated that there was at least one other branch. "Our head office is in Glasgow, Sauchiehall Street, number 242 I think, or something like that. That's a long way away I'm afraid."

Anna agreed with a grin. "I think I'll give it a miss then," she said as she turned towards the door with a vague feeling of disappointment.

. . .

Justine was in the foyer when Anna walked in through the main door. She put her book into her handbag and rose from the armchair when Anna approached. She was wearing a casual tee shirt that accentuated her pert figure and jeans, perfect for the excursion.

"We have transport outside, so there's no worry about travelling. It's on my expense account," grinned Justine as she flicked her dark hair back from her eyes.

"I hope you won't get into trouble for all this will you?"

She shook her head immediately. "Our expense accounts in the Department are massive. They cover foreign travel, meals and accommodation as well as entertaining, like this. Nobody queries them so long as they don't exceed the limit, and there isn't too much alcohol on the bills," she said with a grin. "Even if they do go over the top a little the Brigadier countersigns them and there's never any hassle. Finance has more sense than to argue with him!"

Anna nodded briefly, relieved by her words. "You're lucky. I was fortunate to have my flight paid for and a basic living allowance that wouldn't cover the costs for a toilet in this hotel." She pushed open the swing doors. "Your boss is more than generous."

Justine chuckled, a gentle tinkle in the air. "I believe he might have reason to be generous in your case. It's rumoured that if he hadn't gone to Sweden he'd never have met his wife. Her name is Ann, like yours, and she was a stewardess on the Scandinavian Airlines flight he went out on."

Anna grinned as they piled into the rear of the black Daimler that was waiting outside, and the car pulled smoothly away from the forecourt.

. . .

Anna was enthralled with the journey towards the pub at Weybridge; the country road was narrow and she was surprised that the car was able to find solid ground under its wheels. A sharp turn to the left and they were on an equally narrow roadway running alongside a riverbank.

The sun shone down on canoes and other pleasure craft as they drifted gently up and down the water. Houses were set back along either bank and their gardens were all beautifully kept, adding to the peacefulness of the scene. All too soon they pulled into the car park belonging to a Public House overlooking the river Thames, and there was a large patio with sun shades where people were seated looking out over the tranquil water as they ate and sipped their drinks.

"You find a table while I get the drinks," suggested Justine as they approached the doors.

"What about our driver?" asked Anna, concerned that he'd stayed with the Daimler. "He looks so nice it seems a shame to leave him here."

"He doesn't drink. Anyway his remit is to stay with the car and make sure nobody tries to steal or damage it. He carries his lunch with him," added Justine casually. "Is it a Vodka and tonic you'd like?"

The day was just perfect, motorboats chugging up and down as the ducks and geese fed voraciously on the leftovers cast onto the river by children. They ate grilled salmon steaks followed by crème caramel as they relaxed in the sun. It was about half past two when Justine rose and suggested they go into Weybridge and walk round the shops.

"I'd like that," said Anna as she picked up her bag and walked back towards the car with Justine. She noticed the driver climbing out of the front seat and opening the rear door for them. "Things aren't like this in Sweden, only perhaps for the King and the very important national guests. The rest of us have to open our own doors."

Justine grinned as she helped Anna into the back seat. "It's just ole English courtesy. Men never open the door for me these days," she laughed. "Not that I want them to, I'm far too independent."

Weybridge turned out to be merely a couple of miles away and they spent well over an hour touring the shops, buying little apart from a few trinkets Anna wished to take back. They finally sat outside at a street-side café with cups of coffee. Eventually Anna glanced at her watch and saw the time was almost five.

"I think we ought to be getting back, don't you?"

Justine nodded agreement and they rose. She pointed to a back street across the road from them. "If we go down there we'll cut across to the car park. It'll be quicker than walking back round the main streets," she suggested.

Anna nodded, content to follow her guide who obviously knew exactly where she was going. They strolled past a terrace of older houses and Anna could see the car park some hundred yards ahead of them, across a small grassy square. The place was deserted, not a sign of anybody on the street or in the gardens of the adjacent houses.

As soon as they had entered the car park a voice intruded from behind them. "Excuse me, but have you got the time?"

The voice startled Anna for a moment. She stopped and turned to be confronted by a half-caste youth with long black hair and bushy eyebrows beneath which his staring eyes were almost devoid of emotion. She noticed that his pupils were dilated far too much for the bright day and her first thought was that this character must be high on drugs. Whatever his problem, she didn't like the look of him, but had no intention of being impolite.

Glancing at her watch she answered, "Just after five," as the man stepped closer, too close. She edged backwards away from him.

"I'll have the watch, and your purse," he growled threateningly. In his hand there was suddenly a knife, a vicious looking weapon with a skeleton metal handle and a blade that had a serrated edge along the top.

Justine appeared at her side looking angry. "You've got a cheek," she said through clenched teeth. "Just piss off and we'll say no more about it."

"Fucking slag, I'll have your purse as well," he threatened as he jerked the knife in her direction.

Justine's foot came up from nowhere, connecting on the side of his face with a sharp sound like a slap. He staggered back for a moment as she grasped his wrist in one smooth movement, twisting his hand backwards as she turned away slightly. Suddenly there was an audible crack and a scream as their attacker appeared to turn a somersault in mid air to land with a sickening crunch on his side, knocking the wind from him with a woosh.

Anna stood and watched, speechless in her surprise, as her friend delicately stepped across his body and twisted his arm like an iron rod against his shoulder. She gave it a quick jerk, applying pressure on the back of his hand with her fingers and thumb, his grip opened and the knife clattered harmlessly to the ground.

"You fucking cu . . ." His words choked off into a scream as she levered his arm high and across his back. Suddenly it seemed to flop uselessly in her grasp and every time she moved it the man cried out in agony.

"Just lie still and it won't hurt so much," hissed Justine with contempt. "Turn your head the other way to ease the pain." He slowly rolled his head away so he wasn't looking at them. "Now isn't that better?" Silence from the figure on the ground. She glanced round at

Anna. "Pick up that blade carefully, use your handkerchief and wrap it up, then put it into my handbag."

Anna stared silently at the knife, hesitating to touch it.

"Come on, we have to do this properly. Make sure you don't leave any prints on the thing."

Using a tissue, Anna lifted the weapon and swiftly folded it into the soft cloth. It was heavier than she expected. Picking up Justine's handbag she opened the zipper. The first sight that met her eyes was the ugly butt of an automatic pistol. She almost dropped the bag in surprise.

"Don't fumble with it, put the knife inside and get my mobile phone out." Their eyes met and Anna could now see steel in her gaze. "There's nothing else inside that bag of interest to us at the moment," said Justine quietly.

Anna suddenly realised that her friend didn't want the man to know that she'd been armed. Carefully she pulled the Nokia cell phone out from the bag and zipped it up, hefting it onto her shoulder.

"Okay, now hand me the phone." Justine's eyes were on her captive. "Just slip it into my hand."

Anna did as she was bid, watching as Justine used her left hand to operate the buttons. She brought the phone up to her ear.

"Hi, this is Justine. Will you call the Met Police and tell them that I've immobilised an armed mugger in Park Square, Weybridge. We'll probably need an ambulance as well." She paused for a moment. "No, nothing like that. It's just that I managed to dislocate the scum-bag's shoulder in the process of disarming him. We'll need a doctor, or somebody qualified, to establish the extent of his injuries in case he tries to sue us for unnecessary force."

She grinned across at Anna with a wink. "Yes, she's okay. A bit shaken but hardly stirred."

She handed the phone back to Anna. "Thanks, they'll be here in about five minutes. You are all right, aren't you?"

Anna was beginning to tremble. She nodded. "Yes, but I think I'd better sit down for a moment. I'm beginning to feel a little dizzy."

Chapter Five

Anna was ushered in to see Brigadier Kelso precisely at ten the next morning. Justine had telephoned shortly after breakfast to advise her that her boss wanted to have a chat, and would ten be okay? Now here she was, a little nervous and unsure of herself, after all if Justine could handle herself like that, what sort of monster could her boss be?

As the door closed behind her she gazed at the figure seated at the desk who dominated the room, a lean dark-haired man, greying at the sides, who had an engaging, almost boyish, smile on his lips. He was very attractive in a masculine way and this was definitely not what she'd expected. The Brigadier rose to his feet, proving himself to be a six-footer dressed in a grey pin-stripe suit, white shirt and a regimental tie of some description.

"*Hur mår du*? Come in and have a seat," he welcomed partly in Swedish. He walked round the desk and shook Anna's hand. His grip was firm but gentle; giving her the impression he could crush her fragile bones with ease. He pulled across a comfortable armchair for her and, instead of merely retiring back behind his desk, he pulled over another chair for himself. "Don't get too excited, that's about the most I can say in Swedish, but it was good to see your look of surprise just then. Can I get you a drink of some sort? Or coffee perhaps?"

Anna was tempted to settle for Vodka, but decided on coffee as being more appropriate at this time in the morning.

"I asked you here for two reasons," started the Brigadier somewhat hesitantly. He seemed to be a little embarrassed, or ill at ease, for some unaccountable reason. "I need to brief you on our role, and explain what you should or should not mention in your statement about yesterday's incident when you make it later. Secondly, I wanted to meet you personally and welcome you to our 'patch'. I met Gunnar Vickström about three years ago when I was in your lovely country."

The door opened behind her and coffee appeared on a small side table. The young lady pushed her trolley back out of the door and closed it gently leaving them in silence as Kelso dispensed milk and sugar. It seemed somehow demeaning for him to play 'mother', but he completed the formalities with efficiency and sat back in his chair.

"I'm afraid I have no idea of how your department fits into the scheme of things here, nor what you actually do for the Government," said Anna, more at ease with the situation now she had met the Brigadier and had a cup of coffee in her hand. "I presume you must be some sort of counterpart of our SÄPO, a type of Special Intelligence Service that takes on cases with a national or international significance?"

Kelso nodded slowly. "That seems to be a reasonable approximation of our remit. The most important difference is that we're not identifiable in the way that SÄPO is. The 'man in the street' has never heard of us; neither have our Local Authorities, or the ordinary Police. That's why we need to speak before you're interviewed later on today."

Anna grinned as she placed her coffee cup onto the side table. "Just tell me what I must avoid saying. If they ask any embarrassing questions, I'll refer them to you if you wish."

"That's fine by me. The various Chief Constables are aware of our presence and they tend to keep a lid on anything if we ask them." He rose and picked up a folder from the desk. "Let's go through your statement first, and then we'll try to deal with any possible questions you might be asked."

. . .

"Okay, so you're sure you feel happy with everything we've discussed?"

Anna sat back in her seat and grinned. "Absolutely. Now I'll accept that drink if you're still offering?"

The Brigadier nodded and strolled across to a small mahogany drinks cabinet to one side of the desk. "Don't get the wrong idea here, this is just the courtesy suite for special guests. I don't keep drinks in my office which is several floors down from here. I expect you'll visit it sometime. Now, what's your poison? I'll be having a straight Scotch myself."

"Vodka and tonic would be good," suggested Anna with a smile. They had been talking for over an hour, going through the whole incident until she knew what she needed to tell the police almost by heart.

The Brigadier held up a bottle of Krupnik. "Half and half?" he asked with raised eyebrows.

"That will be just fine, Brigadier. Thank you. Nice to see you have a good Polish Vodka in this country"

He put down the bottle and regarded Anna with a serious face. "I think, now the formalities are over and we're about to have a drink, you ought to call me Danny. Everybody else who's not in the Department does, so why make an exception in your case?" He laughed as he passed her the drink. "My wife, Ann by the way, thinks I'm stuck-up by insisting the staff call me 'sir', but you must have some formality in this type of organisation. My predecessor insisted on it, and I'm not intending to change anything."

"Quite right . . . . Danny . . . . thanks," she said as she held the half full tumbler aloft, waiting until he was seated again. "*Na zdrowie*, er . . . cheers," she said as she toasted him.

"*Skal*," he replied, "I still remember that at least." His expression altered subtly as he changed the subject. "So how are you getting along with our Justine? Is she taking good care of you?"

"Very much so, I'm obviously in extremely good hands. What she did to that mugger was awesome. Did you train her yourself?"

Kelso laughed and shook his head. "No, we've got a lot better qualified trainers than me. She's one of our best Martial Arts practitioners and holds black belts in Karate, Aikido and Judo, which more or less covers the spectrum. She's also a crack shot with the pistol and most other small arms," he grinned again, "and she's kind to old ladies and dogs."

Anna smiled at his obvious sense of humour. "What more could you wish for? Which of those categories might I fall into?"

Kelso smiled in his turn and shook his head. "Woof, woof," he said with a cheeky expression, then he changed the subject. "I gather you've got some shops to check out like the one you visited yesterday morning. I'll get Justine to go with you from now on, just in case."

She caught his eye as she suddenly understood just how much silent authority this enigmatic man wielded. She was more than impressed that he knew where she had been yesterday. Opening her handbag she pulled out a sheet of paper, unfolding it on her lap.

"I have three addresses here, the one in Kensington that I've already stumbled upon by accident, one in Southgate in North London and one in Wimbledon. I also have another address, but that one's in Glasgow. When I've done here I want to go up there and stay a couple of days as I understand that the city is something of a cultural centre for Scotland."

"It's a long way away," he cautioned gently.

She nodded. "I know where the place is. I'll get an overnight sleeper or a morning flight, book into a hotel and take in the sights the next day." She finished her drink and placed the glass on a small table near her chair.

Danny got up, a move to indicate the end of their meeting. "Right, I'll get Justine to take you out for lunch, then up to Southgate to check one of those addresses. Tomorrow morning you're due to go to the police station and make your formal statement, after that she'll take you to Wimbledon. I'll be pleased to help you arrange the trip to Glasgow afterwards."

They shook hands formally again as Justine arrived to escort Anna away to the car.

. . .

"All sorted with the Boss?" asked Justine as they settled into the back seat of the car provided by the service. This time it was an impressive Rover 75, black and shining as it drew up in front of the building in Old Holborn. "I gather we're bound for Southgate?"

Anna nodded, still deep in thought from her meeting with Brigadier Kelso. She was trying to fathom out why she's detected just the slightest edge to the man's voice when they were discussing Justine. It seemed almost as if he was unsure of her.

Mentally she shrugged and made an effort to concentrate on the matter in hand. "Yes, I have the address here," she murmured, opening her handbag and pulling out the sheet of paper. "It's a shop on Chase Side, quite near to the Tube Station I understand."

Justine copied the address onto her notepad, tore the page out and passed it to the driver, and then they both sank back into the soft seats to enjoy the journey.

"What did you think of our Brigadier?"

"He's a charming man, and quite young for the position, I think," answered Anna as she recalled the past two hours with warmth.

"He was in the chair when I joined, but I understand the previous Brigadier was quite a bit older and a grumpy old sod at the best of times. Brigadier Kelso has always been helpful and polite to me, but I wouldn't like to get on the wrong side of him. I understand he's a hard man when he's crossed."

"That's not the initial impression I got, but I understand what you mean. He seems to have a subtle authority about him."

"Well, I think there are some who would disagree with you. He's recently fired two or three of the agents for not pulling their weight and other minor offences." Justine sat back and laughed, a snort of mirth that seemed out of character for her. "One of them was actually snorting cocaine during his lunch break, would you believe. The story goes that Kelso caught him red handed, took him by the scruff of the neck and threw him down a flight of stairs. Next day he was suspended and we never ever saw him again."

Anna shook her head slowly. "Somehow I don't find that difficult to believe. That's probably one of the most dangerous things you could do in your profession, and if I was the Brigadier I'd have probably done the same thing."

Justine touched her hand for a moment and then squeezed it gently. "So would I," she agreed with a twinkle in her eye.

. . .

They stopped for lunch at the Cherry Tree Inn, about half a mile from the main centre of Southgate. Anna settled for a traditional meal of fish and chips with a small glass of French lager, while Justine went for a more exotic dish of Chicken Curry Thai Style that she washed down with a glass of sparkling mineral water.

"I don't like to drink alcohol during the day, especially when I'm on duty," she explained when Anna commented on her choice of drink. "Even though we're relaxing and I'm not engaged in my normal activities, I'm still expected to be vigilant and look after you if anything nasty happens." She grinned at Anna. "Just like yesterday. If I'd been drinking I'd probably not have reacted as quickly."

Anna nodded agreement as she placed her empty glass on the table. "I thought you were awesome yesterday. I guess you must be one of the best in the Department?"

Justine's face lit up with pleasure for a moment. "I try to be the best, but when the Brigadier decides to visit our training sessions he shows us all up so easily. He's the best I've ever seen."

"That's no surprise to me," said Anna, "It's the way he moves, more like a tiger than a man." She grinned at her friend. "At least not like any man I've ever known. Do you have a husband or a partner?"

"No, I haven't time for men. They're all after one thing when the chips are down. Our job attracts a certain kind of man, like the James Bond stereotype; a collector of trophies. See who can shag the most females each year to gain the trophy." She shook her head, black hair bouncing against her ears. "They're not for me."

"Yeah, I guess you're quite right," agreed Anna as they rose. Though I don't think Danny would fall into that description, she thought with an inward smile.

. . .

"Oh, you mean those big crucifixes!" said the little man behind the counter, his stomach wobbling as he spoke. His eyes appeared to dart around the shop, refusing to look directly at Anna or Justine. He shook his head sadly. "No, we haven't had any of those for over a year now, there's just no call for them in this area." He assumed a thoughtful look for a moment. "We ordered a couple of them after a specific request from a customer who never returned. We sent them back in the end."

"So you never sold any of them?" asked Justine casually.

He shook his head again, jowls jiggling from side to side. "Not a single one. Too expensive by far if you ask my opinion. We get customers for Russian Orthodox Crucifixes occasionally, maybe one or two each year, but they all want the cheaper, inexpensive type." He scratched his nose. "Those others were over three times as much as the ones we sell."

They retreated from the shop gratefully. Once out they turned to their right and started walking towards the Underground Station where the car was parked illegally between some taxis. Their driver had just flashed his Authority when the taxi official had approached, and told him they'd be out of the place within a few minutes. The man had checked his badge and walked away quietly.

"I didn't like that chap at all," murmured Justine as she pulled a face. "He looked as if he's had a nasty accident in his trousers."

Anna laughed, the thought of the obese little man crapping himself tickling her sense of humour. "He couldn't look us in the eye, I noticed. How on earth could somebody like that be employed in a shop where he deals with people every day?"

Justine shook her head slowly. "The idiot probably owns the business himself. I'd guess he doesn't do a whole lot of trade."

They reached the car and climbed into the rear seats. The driver set off towards Wimbledon. There was time to make the final call in London before Anna flew north.

"Once we've finished at Wimbledon, what're your plans for tonight?" asked Justine as the car slid round Brookwood Park towards Palmers Green and the main road into Central London.

Anna shrugged. "Nothing in particular. Eat dinner and maybe a couple of drinks at the bar." She glanced at her companion. "Why d'you ask? Have you something in mind?"

"How d'you fancy eating out, then going to a club in the West End? A few drinks, maybe a dance or two, who knows?"

"Sounds good to me." Anna paused. "But don't you have friends to give your time to? I mean, it can't be much fun baby-sitting me all the time. You don't have to take me out in the evening as well."

Justine laughed, this time a melodic tinkle. "No, I have very few friends, I'm afraid. London's not the place to make proper friends, at least not lasting friendships. You're not exactly old enough to be my mum and I'm sure you'd appreciate a good time. I'd love to show you some of the sights."

"Okay then," said Anna, warming even more to her companion. "You're on, what time and where?"

They arranged to meet in the hotel foyer at seven, have a meal locally then take the tube to Trafalgar Square for some fun. Justine said she was a member at a club where they could drink and dance all night if they wished.

When the car slid to a halt near Wimbledon Central Station, Anna was feeling pleased with her day so far. It had been unusual and she was looking forward to the forthcoming evening, the meal, the drinks and Justine's company.

Chapter Six

Anna eventually settled for a long charcoal skirt under a pale cream blouse. A black bolero top with a red and cream design made the outfit suitably formal to pass for most occasions. She decided on tights rather than stockings and suspenders as those might spoil the drape of her skirt. Her ensemble complete she regarded herself in the bedroom mirror, turning from side to side to assess the possible impact on the male population. She especially liked the way the bolero top partly hid the line of her breasts, providing her with a slight air of mystery even though it did nothing to lessen the jut of her best assets.

"You'll do nicely," she told the reflection in the mirror, and then sat down to apply some make-up to her eyes and lips. She never overdid the cosmetics on her face, preferring a more natural look. A touch of eye shadow and lipstick was usually all she wore apart from a quick splash of Chanel No 5. She eventually opened the door to the suite with the hope that tonight would prove to be more enjoyable than their unsuccessful trips to Southgate and Wimbledon earlier.

With her evening coat over her arm she took the lift down to the foyer where she immediately spotted Justine seated opposite the reception desk. Her friend's eyebrows rose when she saw Anna approach, and she got to her feet with a wide smile.

"Wow, you look great. I love the top," murmured Justine as Anna brushed her cheek with a kiss. "And that fragrancy . . ." Her eyes shone as they parted.

"You look good too," replied Anna, pleased that her friend wasn't the typical standoff English type and accepted her traditional kiss of greeting that reminded her of her past days in Poland. "I'm glad you decided on a long skirt too. I'd have felt a bit uncomfortable if you'd turned up in a miniskirt, patterned stockings and bits of metal stuck in all parts of your face," she laughed.

"There's a nice restaurant just up the road if you appreciate Italian, the Bella Italia. I just happen to know the proprietor. Would that be okay?"

Anna laughed again. "I went there just the other day. That would be fine, they do a good meal."

They walked through the hotel doors arm in arm.

. . .

Anna used the meal as a chance to find out more about Justine. Her newfound friend came from a good family, and she told her about her father who was a Barrister, and her mother, who owned an exclusive West End Travel Agency before Justine was born. Her parents, she said, now lived in Harrow while she owned her own flat in Bayswater. She explained how she had been educated at Milford School in Somerset and later gone on to Oxford to take her degree in Politics.

"The subject soon bored the pants off me, to be frank," Justine admitted over dessert. "Once my studies were over the last thing I wanted was to exercise the scant knowledge I'd retained." She pushed her plate away with a sigh, "That was heaven in my mouth."

She grinned across the table in an intimate way. "Actually I enjoyed my stay at Oxford, the social side more than made up for the grind; it's just that the studying got in the way most times. My sex life was tremendous during that time, we all took as many different partners as we wished, and there was no shortage of opportunities." Her expression reflected her words as she sipped her wine.

"I know what you mean. My University days were second only to the nights. It was a hectic time, especially during the early seventies when Sweden was far more liberal than it is now."

Her friend nodded thoughtfully. "I gather the pendulum has swung quite severely back the other way recently."

Anna grimaced. "We all enjoyed ourselves then but that doesn't happen quite so openly now. I'm considered to be something of a rebel because I don't want to form any permanent attachments."

"Okay, so what did you read?"

Anna looked puzzled. "Sorry?"

"Study. At Uni?"

"Oh, Psychology. Now I lecture courses in Criminal Psychology at Upsala University, near Stockholm."

"Ah, so you're a doctor? Or a professor?"

Anna nodded with as off-hand a manner as she could muster. "What did you do before you got into this line of work?" she asked in an effort to change the subject.

"Oh, not much really. When I got my degree I decided that the Army might be a good thing to try." Justine laughed as the memories began to flood back. "Problem is that I'm too independent. I managed the basic training all right but once I was posted away to a unit I found I couldn't cope with some of the stupid rules and regulations."

She produced a pack of cigarettes and handed one to Anna. "Even worse, I hated being told what to do or say by people with the brains and charisma of an ard vaark. I could out-run, out-shoot and out-drink most of the male contingent and the rest of the women were only good for one thing. The men took their pick," she gazed across at Anna. "And so did I." Her tone implied something that nudged Anna's imagination.

Anna lit their cigarettes and raised her eyebrows. She'd wondered about her companion at times, not that her sexual orientation made the slightest difference to their friendship as far as she was concerned.

"Needless to say," Justine continued, "I found myself on a series of disciplinary interviews within the first few months. Eventually they sent me to the office in Holburn where the Brigadier interviewed me. Suddenly I discovered it was a pleasure to meet another rebel like myself, so here I am, more or less on permanent secondment to the Department in the rank of Lieutenant, and with little prospect of quick promotion." She grinned. "But at least the work's fun!"

Justine flicked her ash into the glass ashtray provided. "So now you know my life story, while I know very little of yours."

Anna averted her eyes. "I hate talking about myself. I'm sorry, perhaps I'm a very private person, but I couldn't summarise my life as you've just done." She glanced up and met Justine's eyes with defiance. "It's very difficult for me to talk about it . . . complicated . . . but perhaps another day?"

"Okay, a nod is as good as a wink. We ought to get on our way, eh?"

They rose and moved towards the restaurant door, paying at the counter and leaving a generous tip before picking up their coats.

. . .

Together they strolled along the road past Knightsbridge Station and onwards towards Piccadilly, turning off opposite Green Park into a quieter area of residential properties. At the end of a short terrace of tall houses a basement had been converted into a small night-club that went under the name of 'Sappho Club'. The doors were heavily bolted and guarded by a body-builder type who smiled welcomingly as soon as he recognised Justine, opening the door for them.

Justine noticed Anna's grin as they entered and murmured, "One of the boys at the office doing a spot of moonlighting. We'll be safe as houses while he's at the door."

"The Sappho Club?" asked Anna pointedly. "Wasn't she one of the original Lesbian poets from ancient Greek times?"

Her friend nodded. "It used to be the best gay club for 'ladies who need to be discreet', but now any Tom, Dick and Mary uses the place. You'll find more straight than gay inside, which is why I brought you."

"I'm not looking to get laid," murmured Anna.

"Here you work to your own agenda, there's no pressure. We can just have a drink and leave if you like."

"Well, let's test the water, shall we?" Anna said as she finished freshening up. She turned to see that her companion had applied fresh lipstick and heavier eye shadow.

"Can't let my image slip," laughed Justine as they exited the cloakroom.

The lights were dim and romantic music played softly through slim speakers placed around a central dancing area. The interior reminded Anna of some of the clubs she frequented from time to time in Stockholm, small tables for two or four scattered round the outside area. Only about half the tables were occupied while a handful of couples undulated slowly on the dance floor.

They selected a table in one corner that was quiet and discreetly away from the dancers. Justine ordered drinks from a waitress who gave her a bright smile of welcome and a knowing look.

"Oh," said Anna when the waitress had left. "I get the feeling I've just been labelled by our waitress." She found it amusing that because she was with a younger woman she was automatically categorised as an 'Old Dyke'. "I don't mind really, perhaps it could be seen as a mild compliment in this place?"

"Depends on your point of view," suggested Justine. "Maria, the waitress, knows me very well and no doubt thinks any female company I come in with is like-minded." She lowered her voice slightly. "I'd be stupid to try anything with guests of the Department. I'd lose my job over it."

Anna nodded slowly and replied, "If you did I'd never tell. I'm 'straight', as you call it, and I'd only be very disappointed with you, even if it was a compliment. Do your work colleagues know about this?"

"I think Brigadier Kelso is aware of my position, he's just never mentioned anything about it to me. I'm surprised that none of the male staff have ever 'come on' to me, so they probably know as well."

The drinks arrived and they sipped as they watched the couples dance. Anna drank in the club's atmosphere and found she liked it more than most she'd been into, perhaps because she wasn't being pressurised to dance all the time. After some time and another round of drinks, she suggested that they get up and take a stroll round the floor.

"Let's give our waitress something to talk about, shall we?"

Justine smiled and readily accepted.

Anna found that her companion was good to dance with, her body lithe and responsive to her every move. After a couple of sessions on the floor they returned to their seats and she noticed Justine stifling a yawn behind her hand.

She glanced at her watch. "Shall we finish up our drinks and walk back? Time's just after eleven thirty already and I want to be up early to catch the morning flight to Glasgow."

Some minutes later they were walking back, arm in arm, past Hyde Park Corner Station, enjoying the unusually warm, dry night. Anna felt comfortable with the company and the groups of people strolling past them in both directions. She could hear music playing from several shop fronts and noticed that everybody looked as if they were enjoying themselves. She turned to her friend with a smile.

"You probably don't realise just how much this all impresses me. In Sweden everybody is at home or in bed by about ten in the evening.

Here we are walking out at almost midnight, it's warm and there are people everywhere." She gazed around as she spoke. "This is a wonderful city, you're very lucky."

Justine's eyebrows rose for a moment. "It's good that you have this impression of London. Most foreign visitors are afraid to walk out at night with all the stories they've heard."

They were approaching Anna's hotel when Justine stopped to light up a cigarette. "Look, I'll leave you here. It's only about a hundred yards to go and you'll be quite safe. You've got a plane to catch and transport's arranged in the morning. I'll book you into a hotel and text you the address for when you land." She raised her hand to stop a passing taxi. "See you when you get back."

They embraced swiftly and Anna gave her more of a hug than she intended. She pulled away and strolled towards the hotel feeling a little embarrassed with the thought that she might have given Justine the wrong impression.

Chapter Seven

Duncan Macmillan left his shop earlier than usual complaining that he was suffering from a headache. He entrusted the rest of the day to his assistant, Mary McCartney, knowing that she was well capable of locking up after trading was finished.

'Oh Lord,' he thought as he walked slowly away, 'don't say I'm coming down with the 'flu!' He unlocked his Astra and sank into the front seat with a sigh, leaning his head on the backrest and closing his eyes to shut out light from the dying sun. Thoughts of his brother Rob erupted in his mind, lazing at home with his feet up for the last couple of days. He'd hardly stirred from the house since he'd arrived.

"Why the hell do I put up with him," he mused out aloud. "He does nothing around the house, expecting me to clean and cook for him, and all he does is complain about everything!" He noticed that his teeth were grinding together as these thoughts passed through his mind, his fists clenching involuntarily with the deep seated anger he suddenly felt.

He knew he was no match physically against Robert. His brother was street-wise and possessed a vicious streak when it came to fighting. He recalled the only time he'd found himself in trouble as a boy, three youths threatening him and demanding his money. His brother had intervened and seriously hurt the three lads, getting away with it only because it was one against three and their pride prevented them from going to the police. He'd never been sure whether Rob had done it to help him out of trouble or just because he'd spotted an opportunity to hurt somebody else with his fighting skills.

He shook his head slowly, realising with a flash of rationality that he only put up with Rob because he was frightened of what his brother might do. 'He may be my twin brother,' he thought, 'but he's not really of the same blood as me. Something dark's lurking in his head. There's something not quite right with him.'

He stirred and sat up, aware that several people who passed by were looking round at him anxiously. With a sigh he fumbled in his pocket and pushed the key into the ignition. He started the car and began to drive slowly round the car park towards the exit.

. . .

Robert's black Mercedes was parked on the road outside his cottage when he reached home. It had been cleaned and polished sometime recently and Duncan wondered whether Rob had actually done this himself or got one of the neighbours' children to do it for a pound or two. As he turned into the gateway, his brother was coming out of the front door with two suitcases in his hands.

"I'm away now," said Rob as Duncan shut off the motor and stepped from his car. "I'll see you sometime in the next few months."

"Cleaned your room after packing, have you?" asked Duncan, then instantly regretted his words as he saw Rob's face darken.

His brother dropped his suitcases and grabbed Duncan by the shirt front, his face red and twisted with sudden rage. "Ye'll no speak tae me wi' that tone," he snarled as he brought his face close to Duncan's. His accent thickened as it always did when he lost his temper. "Ah'll clean if and when I feel it needs tae be done!" His breath reeked of garlic and Duncan was hard put to remain facing Rob under the caustic blast of his stale odour.

Duncan had the sense to relax in his brother's grasp, well aware that he was helpless against him. "Sorry," he gasped. "I expect the room is tidy anyway." In the back of his mind he knew that he'd need to open the window, wash the bed linen and vacuum the carpet to freshen up the room. His brother always seemed to leave a bad smell behind him whenever he stayed, in more ways than one.

Robert thrust his brother away towards the front door, picked up his two cases and walked out of the gate to his Mercedes. He opened the boot and placed the cases neatly inside.

Duncan stood silently and watched as he got into the car and started the motor, pulling away with a quiet purr. He didn't bother to wave as he made sure his brother drove away. He stood there for a few minutes, dreading the possibility that Robert might turn round and come back. As he turned to go indoors he suddenly became aware that his 'headache' had miraculously eased.

. . .

Anna's flight from Heathrow on a British Midland Airbus arrived at Glasgow on time, and some twenty minutes later she was in a taxi and on her way to the hotel. Her booking details had been waiting for her as a text message once she'd switched on her mobile when she exited the airport building. The Kelvin Ambassador Hotel turned out to be a delight and she found her room was almost as comfortable as her hotel in London. She was pleased that Justine had made such a good choice.

After slowly unpacking she locked the door and took the lift down to the bar where she was served with a light lunch accompanied by a small lager. The restaurant was not too crowded and she managed to get a small table to herself with views out of the window to the beautiful gardens at the rear as she ate. Her meal finished she stretched and felt she was ready to pay a visit to the Macmillan Head Office or Shop in Sochihull Street, wherever that was.

She consulted the receptionist and he advised her that a taxi might be the most appropriate mode of transport. He agreed to order a cab for her and at two o'clock a sleek dark blue Mondeo arrived outside the main entrance, awaiting her presence.

"Where're ye gang?" enquired the driver in his strange, thick accent.

Anna had never met any Scottish people before and she found the man's speech extremely difficult to understand. After a moment's thought she guessed he was asking her where she'd like to go. "Er, Macmillan's the Jeweller, in the town centre," she said hopefully.

"Aye lassie, nae problem."

That sounded like a positive reply so she climbed into her seat and relaxed, leaving the navigation to him. She closed her eyes for a moment.

"Ye'r fust time in oor city?" The driver was turning round and obviously intent on making sure she didn't drop off to sleep.

"Er, yes, this is the first time I've been to Scotland," she said in the hope this was the appropriate answer. "I have great difficulty in understanding the accent here," she added in the hope he would take this as an excuse if she made the wrong answer to any of his questions.

"Ah, lassie, stick wi' me and ye'll come tae nae harm. Ah ken the city inside oot and the local boys won't mess wi' me an ma pals."

Anna considered his words for a few moments. They seemed to indicate a certain fatherly concern, so she smiled and thanked him.

"Ye'r noo from England then?"

She explained that she was Swedish, just over here on a short break.

"Ah, ye ken we have a lot of travellers from your country through the city," he said, slowing his speech for her as he stopped the car outside a double windowed shop that bore the sign 'Macmillan The Jeweller' over the front door. "D'ye want me tae wait?"

"Yes please. I'll let you know if I change my mind."

He got out and opened the door for her with a kindly smile.

. . .

The shop front looked like any other jewellers, plated glass windows with drop down metal cage shutters, items displayed on velvet trays carefully lit by spots to show their contents in the best possible light and side displays of watches and other sundry items. She spotted three trays devoted to crucifixes, both silver and gold, but none of the kind she was searching for.

Anna's heart sank as she began to wonder if she hadn't come here on some wild goose chase, and she even considered jumping back into the taxi and returning to the hotel. Her conscience dictated, however, that she at least go into the shop and ask, that way she would never feel she'd backed away from the issue. With a sigh she pushed open the heavy shop door, a gentle ringing sounded as the door jogged the spring bell mount above. A woman of approximately her own age appeared as if by magic behind the counter to her left.

"How can I help you, madam?" Her voice didn't have the broad, coarse accent she expected to hear as she greeted Anna with a welcoming smile. "You aren't a regular customer with us; are you on holiday, perhaps?"

Anna was startled for a brief moment. How did the lady guess that she wasn't a local? She smiled back. "Good guess," she said quietly, raising her eyebrows in mute question as she assessed the shop assistant thoughtfully. She didn't want her to be reading her mind too closely.

The assistant grinned for a moment. "Ah, I can see from your clothes, your earrings and the rings on your hands that you come from somewhere quite a distance from here. Now I've heard you speak I'd guess you must be from the Continent, perhaps Denmark or Germany?"

Anna smiled broadly. "Not a bad guess, I'm actually from Sweden." She allowed her eyes to gaze round the displays inside the shop for a moment. "I'm looking for something very special and I've been told this is the place to come. I want a crucifix to wear on a neck chain. A Russian Orthodox cross in gold, similar to this one." She opened her bag and passed the photograph of the cross that had recently been around Katja's neck to the assistant.

"Ah, you have very good taste. We don't sell many of these, but they're lovely aren't they. Let me take a quick look in our safe, that's where we keep them. We don't usually put them out on display." The lady disappeared into the back of the shop while Anna perused the rest of their displays. Some minutes later she reappeared with a tray in her hands and a sad look in her eyes. "I'm afraid we've sold the last one. I didn't realise they'd gone, but we only keep about three at any one time."

Anna didn't really mind that they'd sold out but knew she must play along with her story. "When will you be expecting some more then?" she asked.

The assistant shook her head slowly. "I don't know, but I'll speak to Mr Duncan Macmillan, he's the owner of the business, he should know when replacements are due in." Lifting the telephone she keyed in a number.

"Hello, Duncan, this is Mary at the shop. I've a customer asking for one of those Russian Crosses, you know, the special ones? We're out of stock and she wants to know when more will be arriving."

Silence for a few moments.

"Oh, okay, just a moment." She looked up and smiled at Anna. "He thinks he might have one in his safe at home. He's just gone to have a look." She turned back to the receiver. "Yes, I see. Just a minute, I'll ask her."

Anna raised her eyebrows.

"He says he's got one there, but he can't get here tomorrow. Are you here for long?"

Anna shook her head doubtfully. "I'm not sure; I might have to go to Edinburgh later tomorrow or the day after."

Mary murmured into the telephone, then turned back and asked, "Where are you staying? He says he could drop round and show it to you at your hotel."

Anna told her the details and her name.

"He says he'll be there at about six thirty in reception. Would that be all right?"

Anna agreed and moments later she got back into the taxi with a feeling of satisfaction.

. . .

The call from reception came at six twenty, just as Anna was about to go down to wait at the bar. She thanked them, locked her room behind her and walked to the lift. The doors opened onto the reception area, arranged like a huge lounge, and she walked across towards the main desk in the centre of the hall.

"Excuse me, are you Mrs Peterssen by any chance?" enquired a gentle voice from just behind her.

She swung round to be confronted by a slim man in his mid-thirties with startling blue eyes, sandy hair and a smile that immediately reminded her of her father. Catching her breath for a moment she recalled the face in the photograph in Katja's possessions, but this was not the same man.

Mentally she shook herself. "Oh, yes, of course. You'd be Mister Macmillan?"

"Aye," he said as he held out his hand.

His grip was firm and cool, and his manner polite, just the qualities she always appreciated in a man. There was still something about him that reminded her of someone, apart from his smile, but she couldn't put her finger on exactly who or what it was.

"Shall we go into the bar? I'm sure you'd appreciate a drink," she offered quietly. "We can talk there away from the crowd."

Duncan nodded and followed this beautiful and enigmatic lady into the sparsely populated bar. At half past six few of the regular drinkers were installed and they found a quiet table away from the early customers. Anna went to the bar and ordered a tot of Macallan malt for Duncan, taking the same herself with a dash of water.

"So, how many years have you been in the jewellery business?" she asked as she sat down and pushed his glass towards him.

"All my adult life," he replied as he inhaled the fumes from the scotch. "I got into it soon after I left school, working for a large jewellery firm in Princes Street in Edinburgh." He glanced around for a moment to check that nobody was listening to them. "I'm a canny Scot; I saved up my money and when this place came onto the market I jumped in without hesitation." He raised his glass. "Cheers, er . . . skal?."

Anna was impressed with Duncan's basic honesty, no dressing up his decisions or showing off to impress her. "So you'd saved sufficient to buy the business outright?" she asked.

He smiled at her naivety. "Oh no, not by a long way. I had a good deposit and the bank gave me a business loan for the rest. That was all paid off a few years ago and the entire business is now mine."

She nodded. "I admire anybody who knows exactly what they want and goes all out to get it. Well done." She sipped carefully at her scotch, it was smooth and very much to her taste. "Now, you have a Russian Orthodox crucifix for me to see, I believe?"

"Ah, yes indeed. These are some of our speciality items. I import them directly from Russia." He reached into his pocket and pulled out a small packet which he placed on the table in front of her. "Open it, it'll not bite you."

Anna opened the packet and pulled open an elegant box. Lifting the lid she saw the crucifix nestling under a pad of polystyrene foam and on top of a dark blue velvet backing, it looked beautiful in its setting. The carving was intricate and the whole thing was indeed a work of art. Gently she plucked the cross from the box, it was heavy and exactly the same as the one she'd seen at the police station in Stockholm.

Rummaging in her handbag she produced a small magnifying glass, using it to check the hallmark on the reverse. She murmured to herself as she did this in a language that Duncan did not recognise. Turning it back she examined the front with a smile of delight.

"Are you familiar with the meanings of all these extra carvings on the cross?" she asked as she pointed to the Skull of Adam. Duncan shook his head so she went on to explain the full meaning of each of the parts of the crucifix to him. When she finished and put her magnifying glass away he looked nonplussed.

"I find it hard to believe there is so much detail in such a small item," he said in an awed voice. "I'm impressed. It's very symbolic, rather like a Masonic Scroll. I'm not allowed to tell you any of the details, but that's the same sort of thing."

Anna was herself impressed by his interest, the way he never interrupted her when she explained the intricacies of the decorations. Most men, she knew well enough, would have lost attention after the first couple of minutes, but here was a man, an attractive one at that, who obviously enjoyed the finer things in life.

"And how much is this going to cost me?" she asked. She knew she was going to buy it, unless it was prohibitively expensive, but needed to ask the price as a matter of course.

Duncan named a figure well within her means, but certainly not cheap.

"I presume you'll want cash?" she said. "I can drop that in to the shop tomorrow morning."

"Cash is fine," he assured her. His tone of voice told her that he'd expected her to try to barter with him. "Would you like dinner?" he enquired gently. "My treat since you are such a good customer."

Anna thought for a moment. She felt attracted to this man, the first since arriving in England, but she wanted to take this slowly. She knew instinctively that he was no 'two dances and a quick bang on the back seat' kind of man. Obviously he was more a 'meaningful relationship' person, one who only entered into a liaison with genuine intentions.

Did she want this? More to the point, was she ready for this type of contact? One part of her mind yelled, 'Yes, yes, go for it!' while another was whispering, 'back off, it's not worth it'. How should she answer?

"Tell you what," she replied with a smile. "If you really want to buy me dinner, let's do it tomorrow evening. Pick a nice restaurant and escort me so we can dress up and make the most of it. How's that?" She saw a look of disappointment cross his face for a moment, then brighten as she went on. "As for this evening, why don't we eat here in the hotel and go shares on the costs while you explain how on earth you manage to sell these Russian crucifixes here in Scotland."

It was Duncan's turn to consider her offer. He fancied her like crazy, even if she was a touch older, but he was inexperienced at the dating game. Her suggestion sounded too good to be true.

He grinned across the table at her. "Okay, with one stipulation. If either of us end up by not wishing to see the other tomorrow—so be it. No recriminations, no hard feelings. Okay?"

Anna nodded. That suited her just fine.

Chapter Eight

When Anna awoke next morning she was looking forward to her evening meeting with the boss of the Macmillan Empire, such as it was. Last night Duncan had been the perfect gentleman and her recollection of him escorting her on his arm into the dining room, pulling out her chair and generally being attentive gave her a warm and comfortable feeling. He'd seemed to be everything she'd always dreamed of in a man, courteous, kind and respectful, without any obvious signs of a hidden agenda.

She rolled slowly from her bed feeling cosy and sensual, possibly the anticipation of another perfect evening with this attractive man. A hot bath and breakfast set her up for the lazy day ahead. She went out onto the main street and walked down to a bank where she drew out sufficient cash from her *Handelsbanken* Visa Card to pay for the crucifix.

Once back at the hotel she made arrangements for the taxi again and when it arrived they set out for the shop. When she got there Mary was behind the counter arranging one of the display trays, her smile warming as Anna walked in.

"Good morning, Mrs Petersson, it's nice to see you again," said Mary as she pushed aside the tray. "I hear you enjoyed a pleasant meal last night."

"Oh, how did you know?" Anna was startled at this greeting and she wasn't used to people speaking about her business openly. In Sweden people were generally much more reserved and would wait until she brought the subject up herself.

"Duncan . . . er . . . Mr Macmillan, telephoned me earlier and told me to expect you." She reached across the counter and laid a well-manicured hand on Anna's arm. "And I hear he's taking you out again for a special dinner tonight. He's a lovely man and you're a very lucky lady."

Anna raised her eyebrows in surprise. She wasn't used to such intimate talk with somebody she didn't really know.

"He doesn't date many women," explained Mary quietly. "He's quite shy by nature, but he's obviously taken with you."

"That's very kind of you and I am looking forward to tonight." Anna opened her purse and pulled out a wad of notes. "Now, to business. I have the full amount here, just check it please."

Once Mary had counted out the money and produced a receipt, Anna went back to the taxi, quite glad to be away from the shop. She found Mary's directness difficult to deal with even though she'd volunteered to go and pay at the shop last night. Duncan had given her the crucifix after dinner, saying he knew he could trust her to bring the cash next morning.

"Where would you like to go now, lassie?" asked the driver as he held open the door for her.

"I'd like to see the main city centre. Some large department stores, all that sort of thing. I'll have lunch there and you could pick me up later, say at four this afternoon? How's that?"

Their arrangement made he drove her towards the main centre of Glasgow.

. . .

During dinner the previous evening Anna had tried to learn as much as she could about Duncan, meeting with only marginal success. He was obviously a very private person and hesitated to speak openly about himself, always changing the subject to more impersonal matters at the first opportunity. She'd managed to discover that he lived in a cottage some way out of the city, drove a late model Vauxhall and had a brother who he couldn't get on with. He also gave her the information that he'd been born in Edinburgh and only moved to Glasgow in his mid twenties when he purchased the business, his mother moving with him to the cottage that she bought and then left to him and his brother after she passed away.

She found that getting this much information hadn't been easy, and she mulled over it as she changed before meeting Duncan for their first official date. He was due to pick her up at seven so she'd had a long, hot bath, done her hair and put on something suitable for the occasion. She was now putting the final touches to her make-up as she mused on the possible outcome of their forthcoming evening.

Did she want him to make love to her? Yes, there was little doubt about that, but perhaps not tonight, that would make her seem too easy. This man was something special and she felt she ought to savour their courtship for a time before taking the plunge between the sheets. The others before had been overtly obvious and just with her to satisfy their needs; but Duncan seemed just that more special and at least deserved to be treated with the respect he was showing her.

The biggest question in her mind was whether or not he might try to seduce her at some point this evening. Somehow she didn't think that very likely from what she knew of him thus far—but if he did, how should she react? Outright rejection was out of the question; perhaps some carefully intimate moments stopping well before the point of no return would be most appropriate.

She rose from the dressing table with a final glance at herself. If he tries too hard, she thought, then I've made a mistake and he isn't the man I feel he might be, she mused. With a smile she checked herself in the full length mirror. Now she had a little time to reflect and await his arrival, and she could see that the three-quarter length black cocktail dress would look in place almost anywhere. She was pleased with the result. She'd decided to wear the cross tonight, not from any religious reasons but because she liked it and it did look good with the dress.

The telephone rang to announce that her escort was waiting for her in the reception foyer.

. . .

Duncan paced nervously in one corner of the reception area, unable to be still for more than a few seconds. Last evening had been comfortable and relaxed, but this arranged meeting was, he soon discovered, far more stressful. He sat down on the edge of a seat and tried to analyse his feelings. There was something about Anna that just seemed right, he'd immediately felt comfortable in her company, as if he was talking to an old friend, and for him that was both unusual and surprising as he was rarely at ease on a one-to-one basis with any attractive woman.

He hoped she had similar feelings from last night and this was to be an intimate and enjoyable evening. He hadn't dated in almost 12 months, and his previous liaison with the younger blond woman in her twenties, Bonnie, had petered out within the space of a couple of weeks. He'd soon got the feeling that Bonnie was after him for what he might buy her, and he'd felt less than enthusiastic once he realised this. At that time he recalled that he'd sworn this would never happen again, he hated being the victim of a half-hearted attraction, and here he was now pacing about like some love-struck teenager.

When Anna stepped from the elevator he saw that she was wearing a slinky black dress that accentuated her figure, his breath catching momentarily as he stared at her. My God, but she's beautiful, he thought as she spotted him and smiled across the foyer, and she's wearing the cross. It looks wonderful with that outfit, he mused as he fought to turn on his most charming smile.

Duncan gave Anna a chaste kiss on the cheek. "You look like a cover girl," he said with awe in his voice. "Absolutely terrific." Holding her at arm's length he gazed into her eyes. "I don't deserve to be seen with anybody as gorgeous as you."

Anna laughed and squeezed his hand to thank him for the compliment. "You look pretty good yourself," she said as she appraised him openly. "I was afraid you would be wearing a Scottish kilt and all the regalia, but I'm glad you're not." She caught his arm as they walked through the swing doors to where his car was waiting.

Duncan had selected his best pale grey wool/mohair DAKS suit that he knew tended to complement his build and make him look mature. He wasn't a person for flashy clothes and this suit was the first expensive one he'd ever bought. It only came out maybe once or twice each year.

He grinned at Anna's remark. "I do own a set of Highland Dress, but you don't want to see me in it, it doesn't really suit me."

He opened the passenger door and helped Anna inside.

. . .

He'd booked a table at the restaurant in the Glasgow Central Hotel, widely reputed to serve the best meal in town, and they were escorted to a dark corner that offered some privacy. He wanted to learn more about Anna and last night he'd got very little information other than she was Swedish and taught part time at a university.

Aperitifs served and their orders taken he launched into his objective with questions about her job at the university.

Anna smiled and told him, "I run a course in Psychology for students at the University at Upsalla, that's a bit north of Stockholm. Even though it's only a part time appointment it helps with the bills," she murmured. "Living in Sweden is quite a bit more expensive than here in the United Kingdom, the tax system takes more of your earnings than over here, and the pay scales are much lower than they are in UK."

Duncan pulled a face and shook his head slowly. "And I thought our country's system was designed to milk us dry!" He grinned suddenly. "It's comforting to know that other people are worse off than we are."

Anna began to tell him about the local Swedish rates and taxes, stressing the fact that the level of hidden taxation in the UK probably made up for the extra Income Tax they paid in Sweden. "And of course we don't have the awful housing problems that you have here. There are many more houses and flats than there are people and everyone can get accommodation—what you call council housing—if they need it. Our state system will pay you, keep you healthy and even train you for a job as well. Add to that the fact that housing is much cheaper than in Britain. So it's not all bad."

Their meal arrived and they ate in relative silence for some time.

. . .

"Would you like to dance?"

A trio had begun to play at the far end of the dining room where there was a small dance floor and two couples were sliding gently around to their music. Their meal was now finished and they were enjoying coffee and brandy to complete the evening.

"Why not," said Anna nodding her assent. The idea of a few turns round the dance floor appealed to her and the mood of the evening was far more comfortable than the frenetic club atmosphere she was used to in Stockholm.

Once on the dance floor she found Duncan to be smooth and easy to follow, their bodies moulding neatly as if they'd been dancing together for years. After a moment she laid her head on his shoulder and allowed herself to relax, drifting round the floor as if walking on clouds. Suddenly she became aware that she'd inadvertently turned him on; he now had a rather obvious erection. Startled, she drew back for a moment, then relaxed again, turned her face up and kissed him.

"Perhaps we ought to go and sit down before you have an embarrassing accident," she whispered with a laugh, pressing herself against him. He's certainly a big lad, she thought to herself with an inner smile, perhaps he might invite me back to his cottage tonight. If he does I'm not sure that I could resist.

They walked slowly back to their table and as they sat down Anna's mobile telephone began to ring in the bottom of her handbag. She frowned and fished for it, who would want to call her at after ten at night, she wondered. "Sorry, but I must answer this," she apologised. "Yes?" she murmured into the telephone.

"Hi, this is Justine. Sorry to break into your evening but the shit's hit the fan! You have to come back right away, or at least first thing tomorrow. We've booked you on the first flight at 7.30 in the morning, and your tickets will be waiting for you at the British Midland Airways desk. Don't miss it for God's sake."

Chapter Nine

"Sorry, but I need to go," apologised Anna as she shut her mobile. "There's urgent business of some description that I must be in London for, like yesterday, then I need to return to Stockholm once that's done."

Duncan's face showed his disappointment as he nodded. "I understand, we'll go right now. Will you be back? I'd hate to think this will be the last time I ever see you."

Anna smiled across the table as she zipped up her bag. She hated to leave now as they were just getting acquainted. "I won't let you go that easily. I'll be back soon. I have personal business to see to in Edinburgh, family research; so perhaps we could meet there? What d'you say?"

"Of course." He dug into his wallet and pushed a card across to her. "My home telephone, mobile number and the shop number are on this. Ring me whenever you like. Let me know when you are coming across and I'll try to arrange a few days' leave. I could meet you in Edinburgh; how about if I book hotel accommodation for us both if you like? Separate rooms of course."

"*Toppen*, er . . . perfect, I mean. I'll let you know how I'm getting on and we'll arrange the Edinburgh trip as soon as possible." She shouldered her bag and they walked to the cloakroom where she plucked her coat from the rack.

The drive back to her hotel was conducted in silence as she mulled over her thoughts, wondering what could have happened in London while Duncan pondered upon which hotel he could use that might provide them with adjoining rooms.

Once at the hotel she suggested that he escort her to her room. "I can't offer you a drink as I need to pack and get some sleep, but at least we can have a few moments together."

Her suite was elegant and comfortable, well furnished with mahogany units and a carpet that must have cost a fortune. No sooner than he closed the door behind them she grabbed him, their lips meeting in a kiss that made him dizzy. Her tongue passed silent messages as he pulled her to him and he quickly realised that she wanted him as much as he wanted her.

Moments later she pulled back slightly, brushing her fingers slowly down the front of his shirt. "Just keep yourself safe for me and we'll enjoy ourselves later, perhaps separate rooms aren't necessary when we meet again." she whispered as she nibbled his bottom lip. "Drive carefully."

They said their 'goodnights' and he walked slowly along to the lifts as he pulled on his coat.

. . .

"Hello Justine? Okay, I'm alone now. So what's happened?"

"A body's been found in a shallow grave on Wimbledon Common, young girl about sixteen to twenty, and wearing one of those crosses. That's all we know at the moment. The place is under canvas now and the forensic guys are going over the area with a fine tooth comb."

"*Jävla skit*! Sorry, er, that would translate to 'bloody shit' I think! This is rapidly becoming a case for Interpol, isn't it. I'll be on the flight in the morning. I've ditched my date and am packing right at the moment." Anna caught sight of herself in the mirror wearing only her panties. She laughed. "I look like an advert for one of your strip clubs at the moment."

"Wish I was there," murmured Justine wistfully.

"Don't you start! I've just said goodnight to a sexy man, and due to your call I never even got my hands on him. Count yourself lucky I didn't throw this mobile into the river Clyde when it rang."

"I'll meet you at the airport when you land," said Justine with a laugh.

. . .

Her friend was at Heathrow Airport at nine next morning as Anna walked out from the Arrival Lounge. Justine was wearing a full length black plastic mackintosh and boots, despite the fact that it was barely raining outside.

"Hey," said Anna with a laugh, "You're dressed for an Atlantic Crossing in an open boat? Or is this the latest city fashion for the gay lady?"

Her friend gave her a peck on the cheek. "Neither, I'm afraid. We're going straight from your hotel to Wimbledon Common. You'll have five minutes to change into something similar because it's wet and muddy on the common." She lifted Anna's bag and swung it easily as they walked. "The car's just outside, illegally parked, but we can get away with anything while we're on duty."

They piled into the back of a large Daimler and the driver took off from the terminal building like a Formula One rally star.

"So tell me exactly what happened."

Justine's face darkened as she began to speak. "The call was made at about six last night. Some nerd walking his pooch on the common, let go of the lead and it took off after a rabbit. He followed it into the trees at the edge of the golf course and discovered Fido scratching and yelping at what looked like a finger covered with bracken."

Justine smiled and pulled a face. "Then he began to check exactly what it was and discovered that the finger wasn't alone, there were three more just like it, and a thumb. About then he began to panic, pulled out his trusty mobile phone and screamed at the Emergency Services Operator. She said she needed ear plugs!"

Anna tried to repress a smile at Justine's description.

"Two hours later our Department was alerted. We'd flagged up the Russian Cross as being something of special interest to us, and once they found that, one of their office staff logged a call to our Headquarters. Kelso received the call at home, right in the middle of his dinner, so he called me out. He was not a very happy bunny! I gather he had dinner guests at the time." She leaned back on the leather seat. "So here we are, off to see the body; that is if they haven't moved it yet. Forensics reckoned it wouldn't be away until lunch time today."

Anna nodded. Peering at dead bodies wasn't exactly something she wanted or expected to do, but as she was here representing the Scandinavian authorities she couldn't very well refuse.

"Does it smell horribly?" she asked with a note of trepidation.

Justine pulled a face. "Let's say that the girl has seen better days in the past. I'll give you a mask to wear when we get there. It doesn't get rid of the entire pong but you can stuff a tissue laced with Chanel No 5 inside the mask before putting it on, that helps." She sat up and looked round at their surroundings. "Here we are, the hotel is just a few moments away."

. . .

By the time they arrived at Wimbledon Common the rain was falling harder than ever and rivulets of water were cascading down the sides of the road. Armed with umbrellas and boots, Justine had given Anna a spare pair of Wellingtons she had in the back of the car, they splashed their way through the police cordon and onto the common where a canvas tarpaulin had been stretched over the site on tent poles to keep the body as dry as possible while the police worked on it. Four men wearing full waterproofs were gathered round the corpse, scooping semi-liquid earth and grass roots away to expose the grey/green flesh to daylight. One of them looked up as Justine approached.

"We're almost ready to move the body," he said in a low voice, one eye speculatively on Anna who had hung back a little. "We've managed to get it just over halfway into the bag and will be pulling the rest of the bag under the top half in a few moments. We only need to lift the top of her trunk and all will be finished."

Anna could see that they had wriggled strips of canvas under the corpse's shoulders and back so they could support its weight as the bag was pulled up. Once this had been done the bag would be sealed and transported to the morgue for a post mortem to take place. The body was virtually unrecognisable as regards age, sex or any facial features, just a grey, muddy, half clothed lump of rotting flesh. How anybody could do such a thing to a young girl was a complete mystery to her despite her professional qualifications and familiarity with death in all its forms.

"Any idea how she died?" she asked as she moved forwards to join Justine.

Her friend shook her head. "She wasn't shot, stabbed or bludgeoned to death. Other than that we have no idea at this moment."

The man who'd first spoken looked up again. "The doctor said she'd probably have been here for about a week, and that the post mortem would soon establish the exact cause of death. From what we've seen it is possible that she might have overdosed on some drug or another. There seem to be some track marks on her left arm, but only a proper post mortem will confirm that." He turned back to the task in hand.

"I've something to show you over here," murmured Justine as she led Anna across to a small folding table at the other end of the area. It held several personal effects taken from the dead girl, and she pointed to a sealed plastic bag in which Anna could see a crucifix caked in mud.

She picked the plastic pack up and looked closely at the contents, a cheap gold chain, most likely plated, and what appeared to be a similar crucifix to the one she'd purchased the day before yesterday. A cold shiver ran down her back as she gazed at the mud-encrusted chain and pendant. She half turned towards her friend.

"Yes, it looks the same," she began hesitantly. "I've seen this . . ." she was lost for words for a moment . . . "back in Stockholm," she whispered. Then half to herself she murmured, "It is the same as Katja had, and now I too . . ." She drew a long breath as a fear began to cloud her thoughts.

Her friend glanced at her in surprise, suddenly aware that she was emotionally involved in some way. She decided to try to defuse the moment with a question on a different subject. "How did your search go in Glasgow?" she asked quietly, then added, "Besides meeting sexy, well-endowed men and night-clubbing every evening."

Anna turned to Justine and tried to shake off the feelings she had by thinking of a witty reply. "You should try a few before you dismiss well-endowed men as some stereotype female fantasy," she replied with a grin.

I guess I asked for that, thought Justine. "I did when I was in my teens," she retorted. "Tried three or four and didn't enjoy any of them. All testosterone and self satisfaction. All taking and no giving. All 'how was it for you?' I prefer the real thing." She looked at Anna with a frown. "You should try it a few times before you knock it."

"I didn't mean teenage boys, I meant real men. You mustn't judge all books from a few cheap paperbacks bought at a market stall."

Justine turned away so Anna couldn't see her face. Her eyes had suddenly filled with tears as memories of the only man who'd ever got close to her sprung into her head. He'd left her for some younger bimbo after a few months and she'd never taken another man since.

"If you say so, professor." Her voice was frosty. "I guess you have the knowledge and experience that I haven't as yet." She strode away towards the waiting Daimler.

Anna regarded at her receding figure with an empty feeling. She realised that she'd unintentionally upset her friend. She hoped Justine was big enough not to permit a few badly-chosen words to ruin what could be a good friendship.

She started slowly back towards the car.

"I'm sorry," said Anna as she climbed into the back seat of the Daimler beside her friend, "I didn't intend to insult you."

Justine glanced at her and summoned up a tiny smile. "No, you didn't insult me, it's just something that you said brought back a cartload of very painful memories that I'd sooner not have hanging around. I'm fine now."

"Do you want to talk about them? That can sometimes help; and I'm a good listener."

Justine took a deep breath as she considered the possibility of opening her soul to Anna, something she'd never done before. She knew Anna was a psychologist and not based in Britain, so she'd have no worries that her story would reach anybody else that mattered. "Can I come to the hotel tonight? We could have a meal or a drink and I could unburden myself, unload all my troubles onto you?"

Anna reached across and squeezed her hand. "Of course you can. Whatever you tell me will be completely confidential."

They arranged a time so they could eat together and have a couple of hours alone. When the car drew up in front of the hotel Anna climbed out and ran up the steps to the front doors, turning to wave to Justine as the Daimler pulled smoothly away. Surprisingly she felt she was looking forward to their meal tonight.

As she reached the reception desk she was given a message that had been waiting for her, it asked that she ring Brigadier Kelso at his office as soon as she arrived, short and to the point. She went up to her suite and removed her wet clothes, then sat on the bed and lifted the telephone. She was put straight through to the Brigadier himself.

"Ah, Anna! Good! We need to have a chat face to face before you go. Can you make it at three this afternoon?" Kelso was brief but friendly. "This time we'll actually be in my office."

She agreed to present herself there at three.

"I'll arrange for a car to pick you up at twenty minutes to three precisely. Be there waiting in reception, okay?"

She agreed and the line went dead. She smiled and shook her head slowly as she replaced the receiver. Moments later she picked it up again and asked for an outside line, dialling Duncan's number as she continued to relax on the bed with her new crucifix in her hand. There was a smile on her face for the first time today.

. . .

Anna stepped into Brigadier Kelso's office at precisely three that afternoon. She gazed around the room, compact with a cheap but cheerful carpet on the floor, bland pale green colour-washed walls that could do with a repaint, old grey metal filing cabinets along one side wall and a shabby melamine desk supporting a computer, laser printer, scanner and a fax machine along the opposite wall. There were a few faded framed prints of soldiers on the walls and cream curtains hung listlessly from the window. The Brigadier was seated behind a new mahogany desk with a black leather insert on which to write. In-trays were piled with papers and there was a large ash tray half full of cigarette butts in front of him.

She was surprised that an officer of his rank and stature should be forced to occupy what in Sweden would be little more than a store room.

"Please take a seat Anna," he said rising to shake her hand. "You must excuse the ancient and modern décor and furnishings but I only took over a year ago and it's taken me all my time to achieve just this desk. Getting new office fittings here is like trying to extract hen's teeth."

She sat down as she wondered where hen's teeth fitted into the picture, did hens have teeth? She didn't think so. She gazed across at the Brigadier with interest. In contrast to his surroundings he was handsome in a weather-beaten way and his eyes seemed to miss nothing. 'Wow' she thought, 'now that's what I call a man!'

She looked enquiringly at him. "Hen's teeth?"

"Ah, yes, sorry, it's an English expression like 'getting blood from a stone'! Means that something is virtually impossible to do or to get. I'll try not to confuse you again," he said with a wry smile.

Anna nodded, grateful for the explanation.

"So, how did your investigations go? I gather you went up to Glasgow?"

Anna explained how the outlets in London didn't have or currently stock the crucifix. "The only business that appears to stock these is Macmillan the Jewellers, with a branch in London and main office in Glasgow," she said as she passed one of Duncan's business cards across to Kelso. "You'll need to check their sales records against imports," she suggested as a fresh thought crossed her mind. "Oh, and you'll find my name on his books as probably the latest purchaser, so bear that in mind."

The Brigadier opened a drawer and pulled out a plastic packet containing the Russian Cross, now cleaned and polished. "It does look magnificent, doesn't it?" he said as he gazed closely at its intricacies. "I'm sure these engravings all have some significance," he murmured pointing to the skull.

Anna took the crucifix from his fingers and laid it on the desk. Then she went into a careful explanation of each of the carvings on the cross, their meaning and purpose.

Ten minutes later Kelso lit up a cigarette, offering one to Anna who accepted with pleasure. "I'm impressed," he said with awe, "you certainly know your stuff. Surely that isn't in the remit for a lecturer in Criminal Psychology, is it?"

"You could call it a pastime, a hobby of mine perhaps. I have a special interest in carvings within churches around the world. The Russian Orthodox church is one of the most prolific for this kind of thing." She smiled apologetically for a brief moment. "I was brought up as a Catholic myself and our embellishments are not up to the level of those of the Russian Orthodox."

Kelso nodded as he removed the crucifix and returned it to his drawer. "I shall be sorry to see you leave, but I understand that you're due to return to Stockholm tomorrow?"

Anna nodded with a measure of sadness. "I'll come back soon as I have some family history research to conduct in Edinburgh." She rose slowly. "Would you do me a favour and not mention my name during your investigation of the Macmillan Jewellers? Duncan Macmillan and I have been out together, and I would like to continue this friendship in the future."

He raised his eyebrows for a moment, then obviously decided this was none of his business. "Oh, okay. Not a problem. We never reveal any of our sources anyway, but I'll brief the officer who goes there." He grinned momentarily. "As it'll probably be Justine, you could mention the request to her yourself."

They shook hands formally and Anna left the room, closing the door silently behind her.

Chapter Ten

Anna relaxed into her window seat as the jet lifted off from Heathrow Airport, content to be leaving the frenetic atmosphere of London behind. Her stay had been eventful, she'd made a few new friends and been shown kindness far beyond her expectations. Now she was relieved to be returning to her comfortable flat and familiar surroundings. With some surprise she realised that she was actually missing Mendelssohn, despite his attitudes. Whatever plans she might have for the future could wait for a while.

She knew her first stop had to be Superintendent Vickström's office to report back what she had seen and done. Her final talk with Brigadier Kelso had pointed his investigation in the right direction, and now she needed to alert Vickström to maintain a liaison with Kelso.

Her dinner and chat with Justine had helped to cement their friendship. She'd been interested to discover that her friend had only turned to her own sex after being badly treated by a man she'd loved and trusted, a time when she was at her most vulnerable. She could empathise with Justine's situation in many ways, especially as the man ran off with another girl shortly after they'd declared their mutual love and begun to plan their future together. Her own enlightenment had only come after many years of what she'd felt was basically a happy marriage. She was always amazed at the lengths men would go in order to achieve the target of his current desires, and it mattered not from which country they originated.

Her friend had been put off all men and found comfort from the far more tender couplings of other women, while Anna had gone in the opposite direction and begun to use men to satisfy her own personal needs. She knew that her's was a similar reaction following rejection, but now she felt that she'd possibly met somebody who she could trust once again.

Her conversations with Duncan had swiftly convinced her that he was sincere and as trustworthy as any man could be. The Scotsman's gentle ways tended to remind her of her Polish boyfriends. She smiled as she recalled how sweetly he had kissed her hand at one point, so different from the average Swedish men she'd known, including her ex husband even during the first years of their marriage.

Slowly she drifted off to sleep as the MD80 sped across the North Sea towards Stockholm.

. . .

"Mrs Anna Peterson to see you," said Vickström's secretary into the intercom. A moment later she looked up with a smile. "Please go right in," she said as she turned back to her work.

The Superintendent's office was so different from Kelso's that it startled Anna, even though she knew what to expect. Bright and modern as opposed to dim and ancient, furnished with new filing cabinets and tables in cherry wood veneer, comfortable and stylish armchairs and a settee sitting over a thick pile red carpet that covered the majority of the parquet floor. There was a matching drinks cabinet and a workstation with an ultra-modern computer, television set and all the usual accessories. Vickström himself was lounging in one of the armchairs. He indicated for Anna to occupy the other.

"Welcome back," he said with a smile. "Tell me all about your visit to England and what you've managed to find out. Coffee will be here in a few minutes."

Anna sat back and outlined all that she'd done during her stay, leaving out the more personal aspects and Justine's treatment of the mugger in Walton on Thames. Coffee arrived in the middle of her story and they sipped it as she continued.

"You will need to liaise with Brigadier Kelso for the time being," she finished. "I understand that his Department will be controlling the investigation in the UK. He said he'll send somebody up to Glasgow to get the customer list from Macmillan's and they'll check on each one separately."

Vickström has sat up with interest in his eyes at her mention of Kelso. "Do you mean Danny Kelso?"

Anna nodded. "Yes, he's in charge of the Department in their Ministry of something or other. I don't know the details but he did mention that he knew some areas of Sweden." She looked at him and noted that his eyes were shining. "Why? Do you know him?"

"Indeed I do," said Vickström. "I was the Superintendent at Örebro a couple of years ago before I was promoted to this position and Kelso was there with some officers from SÄPO. They eradicated a nest of Al Quaida terrorists who were training recruits just outside the town." He smiled as he recalled the incident. "Kelso was extremely good, but unfortunately our ministry didn't quite see things his way and they ordered him to leave the country immediately."

Anna raised her eyebrows and shook her head.

He looked sad for a moment. "It appears that our government originally invited him to come here to help as a token gesture. I don't think they expected the success he managed to have and it caused a few red faces within political circles." He suddenly broke into a smile again. "There is a happy ending to the story, however. I understand that he was later awarded the Medal of Honour and an official apology was issued over that decision by the King himself."

"Good," Anna nodded with satisfaction. She liked the man and hated the fact that he was treated so badly by their government. "Now you and the Brigadier can pursue the two cases together while I go and resume my quiet life." She grinned at him. "That is until you need to call on me again."

She caught his eye as she rose. "But don't call me in the middle of the night, will you." She gave him a cheeky wink as she walked to the door.

He nodded and she shut the door quietly behind her.

. . .

"*Hej* Mendelssohn," she called as she opened the front door to her flat. No answering meow came, no hurried patter of soft pads coming to greet her, no cat. "Mendelssohn? Where are you?" she called again as she put her case down beside the shoe rack.

She headed for the kitchen as she checked the small pile of post that had been stacked neatly on the hall table. There seemed to be nothing obviously urgent amongst the envelopes. A fresh dish of cat food in its usual place greeted her as she stepped into the kitchen, noting that the place was clean and tidy thanks to her downstairs neighbour. A tiny feeling of panic suddenly took hold of her and she whirled round and strode into the living room.

"Mendelssohn?" No answering call. No cat.

She moved on to the bedroom but there was no cat to be seen. His favourite place on the window ledge was unoccupied, and by this time she was at the edge of tears, where was he? Had something horrible happened? She gazed carefully round the room.

Suddenly a slight movement between the pillows of her king sized bed caught her eye. Pulling away the duvet she discovered Mendelssohn curled up in a ball fast asleep. Gently she reached out to touch him, still afraid that he might be cold and stiff.

The cat let out an angry mewl, jumped to his feet and stalked away towards the kitchen, ignoring her entirely, his head held high. Moments later she could hear the unmistakeable sounds of Mendelssohn eating.

Anna felt a deep sense of relief as she padded after him, consigning her shoes to the rack as she passed it. She knew he'd thrown tantrums like this before when she'd been away for a few days, but they never lasted for very long. Now she could hear him purring loudly as he gulped down his food as if he hadn't had a proper meal for a week.

With a smile she took her case into the bedroom and laid out its contents, tossing aside the used underwear for the washing bin and putting the unused clothes carefully back into her wardrobe. Anna was a meticulous packer and everything had to be ironed carefully and folded precisely each time it was put into her case.

As she finished Mendelssohn jumped up onto the bed and nuzzled her arm, purring constantly now that his temper had abated. She picked him up and gave him a hug, walking with him in her arms to the bathroom where she turned on the taps to fill the bath.

"You can join me if you like," she murmured to the cat, who scrambled away to relative safety on top of the washing machine. "It's a long time since I had any male creature in the bath with me."

Mendelssohn walked quickly out of the bathroom as she stripped and climbed into the warm water. The post can wait, she thought as she slipped under the surface, beginning to relax already.

. . .

At half past nine she telephoned Duncan. She knew the time would be an hour earlier in UK, about the time he usually finished his evening meal. The telephone was picked up almost immediately.

"Aye?"

"It's me, Anna. How are you?"

"I'm good. How was your flight?"

They exchanged small talk for a few minutes, relaxed with one another as if they were man and wife, then Anna broached the subject of her return.

"I'm hoping to come back to Edinburgh in about a fortnight's time. Would you be able to get some time off?"

"Oh, aye. I am the owner after all. If you tell me when you'll be arriving I'll book a hotel for us." He paused for a moment. "Is a double room still on the cards?"

Anna smiled to herself, trust him not to take her for granted. Most men would have booked a double and only told her once she was at the hotel. "No need for the question, a double room will be fine. It will save some costs, but if you snore I'll kick you off to the downstairs lounge!"

She could hear Duncan's pleasure in his words as he agreed.

"I'll phone you once I've booked flights, okay?"

Moments later she replaced the receiver on its cradle; she would call and arrange the bookings tomorrow morning. For the time being she intended to go downstairs to her friends and thank them for looking after Mendelssohn and the flat. She expected that the large bottle of scotch whiskey she'd brought back for them would be sufficient encouragement for them to do it again in a couple of weeks.

. . .

Anna was walking along a river bank holding her father's hand. The sun was shining and she could hear the eager chatter of birds in the nearby trees. She looked up at her father who seemed as if he was ten feet tall as he strode along the path, Anna needing to half run to keep up with him. She tried to slow him down by pulling back on his hand but nothing she did would reduce his speed.

As they walked she could see clouds suddenly begin to darken the sky ahead and the first stirrings of a cold wind began to start her shivering despite the speed that she was moving. Moments later the first drops of rain began to splash down and within minutes became a deluge as her father pulled her along behind him. He began to run along the river bank, leaving her behind so she could trail along at her own pace.

Ahead, a bridge loomed up from out of the misty rain and she could see the outlines of the village, the tiny houses, the school and church in the background. She could also see that the river was rising dangerously and she realised that the bridge would be swamped within a short time, as it always was during a bad storm. She knew they must cross within the next couple of minutes or they would be stuck and unable to get home. She ran after her father as he turned to cross the wooden bridge about twenty meters ahead of her, and as she took her first steps on the planks a sudden clatter announced the collapse of the centre section of the side railings, just adjacent to where her father had stopped and turned.

He held out his hands for her to grasp but before she reached him a sudden gust of wind swept brown muddy water across the planks and her father lost his footing. She could see the panic in his eyes as he fell, his hands grasping at the wooden supports of the bridge. Running forwards she cried out only to see him swept off the bridge and into the rushing water. She looked down at him as he tried to hold onto the wood . . . . only it was not her father she was looking at. His face had altered subtly and she was now gazing into Duncan's frightened eyes as his hands finally lost their grip on the bridge sub-structure, and he disappeared beneath the swirling surface of the river, carried away by the flood as his last words echoed in her head—'meet me at the cemetery!'

Anna stood on the bridge in a couple of inches of fast flowing water, still shouting as the river soaked her shoes and lower legs. She no longer cared whether or not she could walk to safety; Duncan had gone from her life forever. She turned her head and looked towards the village as warm fur enveloped her face, bringing her up from the nightmare and slowly back to the present. Mendelssohn purred in her ear as she opened her eyes and began to breathe normally again.

With a sigh she sat up and glanced at the clock, it was now four in the morning and the sky was still dark and cloudy outside. She switched on the bedside lamp and pulled on her dressing gown.

"Come along, lovely boy, let's have a cup of coffee," she murmured as she rose and padded towards the kitchen. "Meet him at the cemetery? I wonder what that could mean?"

. . .

The idea of a cemetery sent shivers through her as she sipped at her drink. Mendelssohn sat in silence on the table top watching as she drank, possibly in the hope of a titbit of something more acceptable than coffee. Anna met his gaze and grinned as she leaned across to the kitchen drawer to extract a small pack of Purina Lickins. As she took out several of the small sweets designed for cats, Mendelssohn stood up and moved slightly closer. She offered him the sweets in the palm of her hand and he took them delicately, purring as he chewed them with obvious enjoyment.

"What with Vitbe vitamins and these Lickins, you do better than me for treats," she murmured to the cat as he licked his lips and looked up at her in expectation. "Me? All I get is this cup of coffee and horrible dreams about some cemetery or other."

She rose and carried her cup into the study, switching on her computer and watching the boot up screen slowly turn to a scene from the coast looking out towards the islands of *Öland* and *Gotland* that formed her desktop image. She activated her Broadband icon and tapped in '*Polish World War 2*' as a start. Then she refined the search to Scotland, and then to Edinburgh. Surprisingly enough there were several sites listed that were dedicated to the Polish Troops during the last war and there was even a Polish Cemetery listed, but as her father died back home in Poland she felt that was not relevant.

"What the devil am I looking for?" she asked herself out aloud. She sat back and tried to recall what few details her father had told her about his stay in Scotland during the war. Suddenly she remembered that he'd been billeted out from his camp for some time and she wondered if that might throw some light upon his activities. What does a soldier do when he's staying in a foreign town with no family nearby? He goes out for drinks, looks at the local sights and maybe finds himself a woman? Somehow she couldn't see that in her father, but one never knew.

She checked out the sites for over half an hour until she suddenly came across one that purported to have a copy of the official records of soldier's billets during the years 1941 to 1944. She soon discovered that the list was not uploaded onto the site, but it was available to personal callers at their office with positive identification of a relationship to, or a genuine reason for discovering the billet of any particular soldier. There was a short paragraph at the bottom saying that *'although most of the original house owners have now moved on there are still a few who may not appreciate callers without prior notice'*.

She made a note of the office address in Hanover Street, then began to search for flight details to Edinburgh through Scandinavian Airlines. She was pleased to find that there were regular flights between Stockholm and Edinburgh at reasonable prices. After some more searching she settled on an outward flight during the morning from Arlanda Airport that eventually arrived in Edinburgh at 12.30 local time. She booked a return a few days later leaving from Edinburgh and arriving back at Stockholm at 21.25, via London Heathrow. She wondered if she should call Justine once she'd had her booking confirmed and meet her at the airport for a coffee or something on her way back.

Satisfied with her progress she shut down the computer and made her way back to the bedroom where Mendelssohn was curled up in the middle of her duvet. I'll telephone Duncan tomorrow and tell him my arrangements in the hope that he can book us into a hotel for the three days, she thought as she climbed into her bed with a wistful smile.

She was looking forward to this trip for more than one reason.

Chapter Eleven

Mary McCartney looked up from the tray of rings she was arranging as the shop door pushed open. She'd never before seen the two people who stepped inside. The man was well over six feet tall and tough looking. In his forties, he had an air of authority about him, and similarly the younger lady with him was attractive but also had the same indefinable something that quickly told her these were not ordinary customers.

Reluctantly she plastered a smile onto her face. "How can I help you?"

The man stepped straight up to the counter and introduced himself as he laid his police authority open on the plate-glass top. "I'm Detective Inspector Mc Graw," he said as he turned to the young lady, "and this is Miss Baker. She's with the Home Office in Whitehall and has come all the way from London just to speak with you."

Miss Baker grinned and extended her hand. "Justine Baker, I'm with a special Department attached to the Home Office. I'd be pleased if you'd call me Justine. We're investigating a homicide that possibly has implications abroad and you might be able to help us with some minor details."

Mary's insides seemed to convulse despite the fact that she'd done nothing that could possibly be connected with any murder, it was just a reaction to the situation and she tried to calm herself before answering. She had paled visibly and she stammered her reply. "Yes . . . yes . . . of course. Er . . . how on earth could I be of help?" She instantly hated herself for her obvious show of weakness.

"Don't worry, this is purely an enquiry and nothing to do with you personally," said Justine as she opened her purse and produced a small plastic wallet. She opened it and took out a gold crucifix, one of the Russian Orthodox crosses that they supplied. She laid it on the counter. "This belonged to a young lady, and we think it might have been sold by your firm. I gather that you have a branch in London as well as here?"

Mary nodded slowly as she gazed down at the cross; it was beautiful and intricately formed. "Yes, we sell these," she agreed. "Though we don't supply very many. They're quite expensive so they mainly go to tourists, the local population couldn't afford this sort of jewellery, even if they knew what it was."

"I expect you keep records of all your sales?"

Mary considered her reply carefully for she was fairly certain that Duncan would never be able to account for every one that had been supplied to them. She recalled his brother taking several from their stock over the last two or three years.

"Mister Macmillan does all the record keeping. If I sell any item I make sure there is a copy of the receipt in the till, or in the safe after trading, with all the details of the customer. I give these to him when he comes in, or he takes them later after I've gone home, but I've no idea what he does with them from there on I'm afraid."

"Have you any idea just how many of these crucifixes you could have sold over the last couple of years?"

Mary thought for a few moments, doing a quick calculation in her head. "Well, I think we've probably sold about three so far this year. Funnily enough we sold one only last week, to a very nice lady from Sweden. Last year I would guess we sold about six or seven, mostly to American tourists." She paused and returned a wan smile back to Justine. "That's only my guess, you really need to speak to Duncan Macmillan. He's away today somewhere on business. You might catch him later on at his home."

The Detective Inspector asked for Duncan's address and telephone number, which she supplied. "We'll try to call him later today," he said. "If you see him please tell him we called and to expect us later. This is quite an important matter and we'd appreciate it if you could say nothing to anybody except Mr Macmillan about our visit here."

Mary gave her assurance that she's keep this to herself and watched as they departed, noting that Justine opened the door for herself.

No shrinking violet this one, she mused. She knows exactly where she's headed in life, and the kitchen sink is certainly not her intended destination.

Once they were well away she fished her mobile telephone from her bag and punched in Duncan's number.

"Hello Duncan, Mary here. Look, we've just had the police here asking for records of sales for Russian crucifixes over the past couple of years; you know, the same as we sold to Ms Petersson a few days ago."

She listened for a moment.

"No, I didn't give them any details. I told them to speak to you personally. You'd better expect them to call at your home sometime this evening."

. . .

Duncan slammed his car door and aimed the key fob at it like a missile launcher. He strode to his front door and resisted the temptation to kick it; he was not in a good mood. His business trip to Hamilton had been less of the bargain he'd expected and the call from Mary had started him wondering just how he could manage to account for the crucifixes that had been taken from the business.

He couldn't believe that Robert could be mixed up in any murder, but knew that if he told them about his pilfering ways they'd naturally become suspicious. Pain in the arse or not, Robert was his brother and he wasn't about to cast suspicions on him in front of the law. So how many of the pendants had he taken? About six or seven, he thought. It was his habit to order half a dozen at a time, so if he could conveniently lose the paperwork for one order that would more or less keep the books straight in the eyes of the police.

Once he closed the door after himself he went straight to the desk where he kept the files he used for his business. He opened the main ordering file and selected one order delivery note and its accompanying order duplicate. The note was from about one year ago and he knew it wouldn't unbalance the sales by date order. He did some quick calculations and saw that Robert had taken three at one particular time, so the following order didn't look out of place. He put the paperwork into an envelope and stored it in his safe, leaving the order files and receipts out on the dining table.

Typically, the front door bell rang just as he was preparing his dinner. When he opened the door he recognised DI McGraw from a meeting he'd attended some months ago on crime prevention, but the other lady he'd never seen before. He held out his hand to the policeman.

"Well, well, Inspector McGraw, we meet again," he said as they shook hands and he ushered them inside.

"Oh aye, I recognise you now," said the policeman with a slight smile. "This is Justine Baker from the Home Office in London. Did your assistant speak to you earlier about our visit?"

Duncan nodded as he led them into the dining room. "I have the details ready here," he said with a smile and a shake of Justine's hand, cool and firm, with a grip just like a man's.

"Thanks, we need to check your stocks and clients because I think you're the only supplier of these items in the United Kingdom." She glanced at him searchingly. "That is unless you know different?"

"No, lassie, you're right. Nobody else in the trade that I'm aware of holds these, they're very slow to move and too expensive to leave lying on the shelf." He ushered them to chairs beside the dining table. "To be frank, they're somewhat of a liability to me as well, but they're lovely pieces and there is quite a good mark-up on them, plus the fact that if we stopped holding them we might lose our hard-earned reputation."

"We?" McGraw raised his eyebrows.

Duncan managed a cheeky grin as he shook his head. "Well, no. Me actually. It's just that I usually refer to Macmillans the Jewellers as a generic 'we.'"

McGraw nodded slowly, not looking totally convinced.

"Do you have any other family?" asked Justine.

"Only one twin brother, but he's not connected with the business. He works abroad mostly, somewhere on the continent."

"An identical twin?"

"No, thank God. The world could do without two of him." Duncan saw Justine's eyes flicker at his words and quickly realised he needed to explain himself. "It's just that he's a lazy, scrounging pain in the backside. Seems to think the world owes him a living. He stays here a couple of times each year and after a few days I'm glad to see the back of him when he leaves."

He grinned at the look of surprise on Justine's face. "It's just that we never could get along together. We've always been like chalk and cheese, so to speak."

She dropped the subject and picked up the files of orders and receipts. "Would it be possible to take these away with us and photocopy the ones we're interested in? I'm sure DI McGraw will manage to get one of his officers to drop the files back here tomorrow."

McGraw nodded disinterestedly, he was only here because his Chief Inspector had insisted that the Home Office investigator be accompanied and not permitted to trample across their residents as she felt fit.

Duncan handed over the files with some misgivings. He was now beginning to wish that he hadn't removed one of the orders. He knew he could have refused to part with the file but they would have been straight back with an official warrant and he didn't fancy the idea of them searching his premises.

He showed them out a few minutes later and breathed a sigh of relief as they pulled away in McGraw's battered Sierra.

. . .

The telephone rang just as Duncan had finished eating his meal. With a sense of foreboding he lifted the receiver but was delighted to discover it was Anna on the other end instead of the police that he'd half expected.

"Hello, it's so good to hear your voice—I miss you already," he greeted her warmly.

"Same here, I'd sooner be there with you at the moment. You sound a bit up tight, is something wrong?"

"I've just had the police round to see me. Some young hen from England, the Home Office no less. They were asking questions about those crosses like the one you got."

"Oh," Anna had expected this to happen sooner or later. "Now I really wish I was there. Why were they asking about them?"

He explained that apparently there had been a woman murdered and there'd been one of the crucifixes around her neck. "I'm the only supplier in the country as far as I know, so they were after sales details over the past two years. I wish you were here as well, it would have been much easier with you by my side."

"Was that a problem? I mean the sales details, not me here in Sweden."

"Well, yes and no. I can't account for about six or seven of them. They were pilfered from the shop but I never told the police. That's embarrassing because I know who took them and didn't wish to get him into trouble." He sighed for a moment. "Perhaps I'm too nice at times, but he is a relative and I can't do much more than grin and bear it."

"I see," said Anna slowly, her mind racing. "I really wish I was there to help, it can't be much fun under the circumstances. Could you not explain this to the police if they query it?"

"Even worse, I'm afraid. I've done something stupid and removed one of the orders from the files. It won't be obvious unless they manage to get the records from my supplier in Russia." He smiled thinly. "If only you were here I'd feel so much better."

"Well, you've dug a hole for yourself all right. Try not to make things worse. I'll be with you soon, that's what I rang to tell you. I've booked flights to Edinburgh for a fortnight's time." She gave him the flight numbers and times. "You said you'd book us a hotel for that time. I hope the offer is still on the table and you don't feel too down to want to see me?"

"No way; only the police slinging me in jail could stop me from being there for you. The best news I've had all day. Leave it to me, I'll get back to you when I've found suitable accommodation, a double room with en suite bathroom and room service at any time, how's that?"

"Toppen," she said. "Best news I've had today too."

They said their goodbyes after a few minutes more and Duncan laid down the telephone with an easier feeling than when he picked it up.

. . .

Next morning as Anna was just about to leave her flat to visit the ICA Superstore when the telephone stopped her. She tossed her shoulder bag on the hall table with an upward cast of her eyes and picked up the receiver. She was surprised and pleased that it was Justine. Her friend got to the point pretty quickly after the initial pleasantries.

"I went up to speak to Duncan Macmillan yesterday and got back late last night to Heathrow," she started. "Would he be the guy you were dating when you were in Glasgow by any chance?"

Anna wondered whether or not to deny it, then decided that the truth was her best bet. "Yes, as a matter of fact. What did you think of him?"

"He seems okay, very Scottish. Says little and takes a long time to make his point," she said without enthusiasm. "Not exactly my type, wrong sex for a start and a bit too old for me." Suddenly she laughed down the other end of the telephone. "But go for it, girl, I wish you luck!"

"Thanks, I intend to be 'going for it' as you so delicately put it, the weekend after next. I'm flying to Edinburgh and staying over until Tuesday. I have some family research to do so we'll take advantage of the time. I have to return via Heathrow and I have several hours stopover between connections on Tuesday about midday. Would you be free to meet me for a drink, or lunch, for a chat?"

"Why not? I might have some information for your use in Stockholm."

"Good idea, we could make it sort of official, an exchange of information. But lunch on me, okay?"

"Could you do us a favour when you see Duncan? Would you try to get some information on his twin brother? I think he said his name was Robert, and he seems a bit of a minor villain. I wasn't convinced he was telling us the whole truth about him."

Anna breathed a long sigh, she didn't like the feel of that. It was as if she was being asked to spy on Duncan, and that made her feel uncomfortable. "Sorry, I don't think I could do that. I can't do that to somebody I'm involved with, it wouldn't feel right and I'd be ashamed of myself. What would YOU do in my shoes?"

"Ah, okay. Point taken. I didn't realise that it went any further than a good bonk. In that case just forget I asked."

"Let's put it this way," suggested Anna, "if he volunteers anything significant about his brother, I'll tell you. That way I won't feel that I'm two-timing him. That's the best I can offer." She could almost see Justine's smile.

"What's that word you use? *Toppen*? That might be very useful, thanks."

"*Varsågod.* You're welcome."

"Yes, all right! Don't confuse me. By the way I'll need to speak to your Inspector Vickström later this morning and see if he has any connections to the police authorities in Moscow. We have the address of the guy who makes the crucifixes and need somebody to check his records against Macmillan's documentation."

Anna suddenly got a sinking feeling. Poor old Duncan was going to have to explain himself to the police in the end.

"What's Vickström like? Is he co-operative, helpful, or is he just another pain in the butt?"

Anna summoned up a chuckle. "He's probably one of the best we have in the country. Very conscientious and likes to dot every 'I' and cross every 'T'. I'm sure he'll be only too pleased to help."

"That's good to know. Most of our leads have drawn a blank so far and we seem to be making little or no progress with the case." Justine paused for a moment. "Uh oh, I need to go. Kelso wants my body, in the nicest possible way of course."

Lucky you, thought Anna as a picture of Brigadier Kelso popped into her mind. On second thoughts, she mused as she replaced the receiver, I'd sooner be cuddled up with Duncan.

She picked up her handbag and opened the front door.

Chapter Twelve

Two days before Anna was due to fly to Edinburgh she received a telephone call from Superintendent Vickström. "I understand you are going to England again soon," he said no sooner than she'd picked up the receiver.

"Yes," she said guardedly. "That isn't a problem, is it?" How the hell did he know about my impending trip, she thought.

"Of course not. You're free to do whatever you please with your time," he said in an off-hand manner. "I just wondered whether you might possibly run into Miss Baker during your stay?"

Ah, she thought, they've spoken together, that's how he knew my intended movements. "That could happen. Why d'you ask?" She knew by his tone that he was getting round to asking her to do something.

"I have a small package for Miss Baker, and would be much happier not to entrust it to the postal system. I'm looking for somebody to deliver it by hand, and as you're going that way I wondered if you might help? We'll pay something towards your flight, say a third?"

"I hope it isn't some illegal substance!" she quipped, then noticed his sudden silence. "Sorry, I was joking. Of course I'll help" She resigned herself to the status of messenger for the Stockholm Police. "Okay, as it happens I shall be returning via Heathrow where I have a couple of hours to spare. I'll make sure she gets the parcel from you. Will you send it to me here?"

Vickström agreed without any argument and told her that the package would be with her by late afternoon. His immediate acceptance of her implied terms, delivery rather than her collecting the package, told her that it must be very important.

. . .

Anna's flight to Edinburgh was delayed by half an hour due to weather conditions. Once in the air, however, the Boeing 737 made up several minutes of time before arriving over the airport. From the air, as she gazed through the cabin window, she could see the main terminal was shaped like an ice hockey stick with a shortened handle.

The interior of the relatively new International Arrivals block was fresh and airy, and her progress through Immigration and Baggage Reclaim was efficient. Her case was one of the first few on the belt and she put it onto a wheeled trolley and headed for Customs. The Customs Hall was deserted as she strode through and out onto the Arrivals Hall to see Duncan waiting anxiously near the gate. His face lit up as he spotted her, making her feel warm and wanted.

He swept her up into his arms and gave her a quick but very pleasing kiss. "It's good to see you again," he breathed as he slowly replaced her onto her feet. "I was worried in case you'd changed your mind."

"I'm here, am I not? You've nothing to worry about."

He picked up her case. "The car's just outside, I'll take you straight to the hotel."

Anna wondered what the next couple of hours might hold in store for her.

. . .

Duncan had been feeling extremely nervous as he paced about waiting for the passengers to appear from flight SK 2541. He'd been at the airport for just over one hour, drinking coffee and unable to sit still for more than a few moments. Every time a plane landed his nerves jangled as he checked the arrivals board to see if it was from Stockholm, and now her flight had docked at the terminal safely and the passengers were due any minute.

He had checked into the room at the Ambassador Hotel two hours ago. This was one of the best hotels in the city and he'd made sure that there was a chilled bottle of champagne waiting for them and a bouquet of fresh flowers had been placed on the main table to greet Anna's arrival. He was well aware of the age difference between them, she was some years older than he and he couldn't help wondering if she was just playing with his emotions. Their initial time together had begun to ease that undercurrent in his mind, but their recent separation had not helped. Now she was coming he felt like some love-struck teenager on his first date with a more mature and experienced girl. One part of his brain was laughing at himself for his naive excitement, while another part was worrying that she'd not turn up.

A sudden burst of passengers erupted through the double doors that led from the Customs area, and his heart skipped a beat when he spotted Anna's figure striding purposefully towards him. She looked so calm and cool, thoroughly in control of herself; so unlike the nervous wreck he felt. How on earth this beautiful, mature woman could be remotely interested in somebody like me is unbelievable, he told himself as their eyes met and her face broke into a smile. He could see her gaze appraising him as she walked unhurriedly out of the Terminal suite. She looked just as lovely as he remembered and his heart melted as she dropped her case and they embraced. He lifted her off her feet and kissed her, tentatively at first and then with fervour as her lips responded. He distinctly got the feeling that he was embracing a young girl half his age rather than a mature and self-confident woman approaching middle age.

Their initial embrace over, he carried her case out to where he'd left the car and loaded it into the boot. "I've booked us into the Ambassador Hotel, I'm sure you'll like it," he murmured as he opened the passenger door for her.

"Of course I will," she replied as she buckled up her seat belt. "I know you wouldn't book us into some squalid dump." She grinned and touched his cheek as he shook his head and pulled his door closed. "I've missed you these past few weeks."

Ten minutes later he parked the Astra on the forecourt of the sumptuous hotel, squashed between a gleaming new Mercedes and an equally posh, but older, Daimler. Anna looked at the cars either side of their modest saloon and grinned.

Duncan didn't comment as he climbed from the car and opened the boot to get Anna's suitcase. He escorted her through the heavily engraved entrance doors.

"*Herrgud*," exclaimed Anna as she gazed round the reception area. "I like this, it's magnificent." She looked at him with raised eyebrows. "I can't wait to see the room."

"Good," he replied with a pleased smile. "I've already booked us in so we can go straight up." He looked at her with an air of apology. "I'm afraid I took the liberty of booking us in as Mr and Mrs Macmillan. It was easier that way, I hope you don't mind? Saves you being hassled about your passport and completing forms before we can get the room."

Anna's smile was warming as she accepted his lead. "That's okay, I can cope with being Mrs Macmillan, at least for a few days." She stepped into the lift and Duncan pushed the button for the 4th floor.

"Hope you don't mind heights," he said with concern. "I couldn't get anything lower I'm afraid."

Anna looked at the lift controls and noticed that there were nine floors. She squeezed his arm gently. "That's not a problem for me, I live in a flat on the third floor myself."

They stepped from the elevator and walked across to a door which Duncan opened with a digital card. Anna stepped into the room, stopped and gazed round in wonderment. *"Herrgud,"* she said again. "What luxury. Are you some sort of millionaire?" She turned to Duncan with a twinkle in her eyes. "I know you told me it was a good hotel, but you didn't tell me it was actually a palace!"

He beamed with pleasure. "Glad you like it, but don't expect this every time you visit. This is, after all, a very special occasion." He stepped across to the table where the bottle of Moet & Chandon nestled in its bed of ice beside the flowers. "A tiny welcome present." He grinned, still feeling like a young boy. "We ought to drink the flowers and display the champagne before they get too warm."

Anna put her arms round him and kissed him long and hard. "Thank you for this, I don't deserve it."

Pulling away breathlessly, he said: "Oh yes we do." He picked up the champagne bottle and pair of glasses. "Shall we have this before . . . or after?"

"How about with?" she grinned, then she looked around the suite. "That is if we can find the bed!"

Chapter Thirteen

"Do you know where Hanover Street is?" Anna asked next morning as they sat at the breakfast table.

Duncan smiled across at her and nodded. "Aye, it's not too far from here." He sipped his coffee for a moment. "Why d'you ask?"

"There's an office there which holds records of the Polish soldiers stationed here during the war." She selected a slice of toast from the rack and buttered it. "Don't forget that I'm here to research my father's movements from 1942, as well as to get to know you better." She grinned across the table and raised an eyebrow. "And I certainly did that a few times last night!"

Duncan's eyes sparkled. "Aye, was it four or five? I lost count somewhere along the way."

Anna shook her head slowly. "I wasn't counting, just enjoying. Who cares anyway, we had a good time."

He nodded with a tiny smile. "The best. We'll need to go a long way to beat last night."

Anna sipped coffee as she replayed parts of last night in her mind. He had been a good lover, attentive and sensitive to her needs, and she felt closer to him than she'd ever felt to any other man. It was this feeling that turned her experience from a sexually gratifying one to something on a higher plane. She didn't quite know how this was happening but accepted it as a new and unique feeling that they both enjoyed when they were together. She lacked the words to describe or discuss the feelings she experienced, so she remained silent and thoughtful as she finished her breakfast. *Did I have to wait over fifty years and travel to another country just to experience these new* feelings? she asked herself inwardly with a sense of satisfaction that was quite new to her.

"Mmmm, that was good," she said as they pushed their plates away. Could have done with some herring perhaps, and some tasty bread, but who's complaining, she thought to herself. She glanced across at Duncan who was yawning behind his hand. "Do you think you can stay awake long enough to show me where Hanover Street is?"

He nodded apologetically. "Of course, we'll get our coats and take a walk along the road. A bit of fresh air will do us both some good. I could show you some of the city when we've been to Hanover Street."

It will certainly do us some good, thought Anna with an ironical smile. It was hot in the hotel and even she was feeling a trifle sleepy. "Give me five minutes, I'll only dab some perfume on."

. . .

They strolled down Princes Street at a leisurely pace. The morning sun was delightfully warm, promising a fine day as they passed the Castle that towered over the east side of the main road. The finer details of the architecture were in the shade as the sun was behind the building but Anna knew that in a couple of hours the castle would be revealed in all its former glory. She hoped that Duncan would take her inside to see what promised to be a splendid old centre of history.

Hanover Street was a turning on their left opposite the Princes Street Gardens and just past the castle. Within a dozen paces she'd spotted the closed door of the tiny office that she needed to visit on Monday. They walked onwards, turning right to end up at the Scottish National Portrait Gallery. It was open for visitors and they spent the best part of an hour inside.

Later on they strolled up the hill to find the Scotch Whisky Heritage Centre located behind the castle. Anna gazed up at the walls of the enormous castle. "I'd love a chance to go inside there and walk around," she murmured as she squeezed Duncan's arm.

His laugh was spontaneous as his face lit up. "Glad you said that. I have two tickets for us to do just that tomorrow morning. It's open to the public till about 6 pm so I thought we'd walk there after breakfast. Tomorrow's Sunday so there'll be a crowd inside from about two o'clock, but if we arrive at, say, ten thirty or eleven, we'll be on the way out as the crowd comes in."

She turned and planted a gentle kiss on his cheek. "You make me feel like a teenager again on a voyage of discovery in this beautiful city of yours." Her words were genuine; she was enjoying the feeling as they walked round, all the sights being so new to her.

Duncan smiled as he glowed with pleasure. He'd never before met a woman with such a zest for life, whose enjoyment came from such small things. In fact he felt it was she that made him feel like a teenager in his first flush of love. He sighed, "Okay, let's pop into the Heritage centre? D'you like whisky?"

"Oh yes, but I don't know a lot about it."

"Well, you soon will," he said with assurance. "You'll see how it is made, there's a model distillery, they'll even show you the different regions where the spirits are made, and we can get a nice lunch at the Amber Restaurant inside."

. . .

The weekend passed far too quickly for both of them. The Whisky Centre was interesting and Anna left it reluctantly, but with a boxed litre of Isle of Jura single malt that Duncan insisted on buying for her. Their tour round the castle next day enthralled her and they took their time, making sure they saw everything on show. The restaurant he took her to that evening was obviously one of the best in Edinburgh, providing a meal that was beyond reproach.

Monday morning dawned bright and sunny, but there was the threat of rain coming later on in the afternoon according to the local weather forecast.

"This has been the best weekend I have had for years," murmured Anna as she relaxed in Duncan's arms. They were half sitting in the bed with the curtains drawn as they contemplated going down to breakfast soon. "You have to come to Stockholm in the near future and I'll show you around in return." She kissed him and grinned. "I can't promise any decent whisky, but we can enjoy a good selection of Vodka or beer if you like that?"

Duncan nodded slowly. "Don't know much about vodka, I'm afraid. I've had it, of course, but I'm sure there are plenty of varieties available that I would like to try." He wasn't about to tell her that he thought vodka was rough and uninteresting to his palate. "Anyway I think I could take a long weekend sometime next month. I'll suggest some dates and we can organise it later, okay?"

Anna nodded in turn. That suited her well as she didn't want to enter this relationship too swiftly and find disappointment, although she certainly didn't feel that this was going to happen. They seemed to get on so well, just like brother and sister in many ways. Her answer was a kiss that lingered as their mutual passion rose once again.

. . .

Later at breakfast Duncan expressed his concern at leaving Anna alone in the big city. "Just call me if you get into trouble, or get lost or have any difficulties, okay?"

Anna smiled at him over her coffee. She knew he was concerned but she was used to coping on her own and her English was sufficient to keep her out of difficulties. "I'll be fine, don't worry. If I do have problems I have your mobile number." She reached across and squeezed his hand gently. "I'll telephone you anyway, and you'll only be a couple of hours away, so I'll feel safe and secure."

Half an hour later Duncan drove away, leaving Anna standing outside watching as he disappeared off down the street. She sighed as she began to feel a sense of loss for almost the first time in her life. In the past she'd been all too pleased to see the back of the men she'd slept with, but this time she felt that she couldn't wait to be with Duncan again, she was missing his company as much as anything.

There were tears in her eyes as she turned and walked slowly back into the hotel.

. . .

An hour later Anna set off to visit the offices in Hanover Street.

True to the earlier forecast, the clouds could be seen to be building up over the horizon, and the temperature had dropped by a few degrees already so Anna carried a coat over one arm and her briefcase in her other hand. The offices were open when she got there and she walked into a small reception area where a bespectacled lady was seated behind a desk.

Anna smiled cheerily at the lady as she set down her coat and briefcase.

The lady flicked her dark hair back and frowned at her over the top of her glasses. "Sorry, we're not interested in buying anything you might have for sale," she said in a decisive manner.

I guess I must look like a sales representative, thought Anna as she sat down on the chair before the desk.

"I'm not selling, I'm actually a customer," she continued cheerfully.

The reaction was immediate, the woman breaking into a smile and apologising for her error in judgement. "We get so many sales reps here, and they always carry a briefcase, expecting us to purchase stationery, equipment, filing systems, you name it," she said with a grin, "and only last week we had some young woman here selling what she called 'marital aids'! I never asked her what she meant by that, but I have a good idea."

She looked at Anna and winked. "Batteries not included, of course." She took off her glasses. "Now what can we do for you?"

Anna launched into her explanation about her father, how he was stationed in Edinburgh in 1942, and how she'd like to see where he lived and maybe speak to the person who rented his accommodation if that was possible.

The receptionist's face clouded momentarily. "That was over fifty years ago, my dear. I doubt that the landlord will still be alive today, but we can find the address for you all right."

She smiled apologetically as an afterthought struck her. "You do realise there is a fee for the service, I'm afraid." She named a price and Anna put her purse on the desk, produced the money and pushed it across to the lady.

"If you write down the details for me, his name, rank and service number, if you have it. I'll also need proof of your relationship, I'm afraid. We get quite a few people looking up names for odd purposes and we do insist on blood relations only before we give out any details."

Anna nodded, she was expecting this. "That's good to know. I would feel uneasy if you gave out details about my pappa to just anybody." She opened her briefcase and rummaged round for a moment. "I have his Military Commissioning Certificate here. That gives the details you need," she said as she produced the old document along with her birth certificate, marriage certificate and Swedish driving license. "These should act as proof of my family connection."

Ten minutes later she was led into a small office with a desk and a chair. An ancient ledger was laying on the desk, open at the appropriate page.

"If you need any help just call out," said the receptionist, whose name Anna now knew was Gwen. "I'll leave you alone in here," she said, "most of our clients prefer to do this bit on their own where nobody can see if they get emotional. Just yell if you need anything. I can bring you a coffee or tea if you like."

Anna nodded her thanks and sat down. The first thing she noted with surprise was that the ledger was handwritten in fading blue-black ink. The handwriting was very clear, the old fashioned copperplate style, and it took only a few seconds to discover her father's name printed boldly at the start of a row that showed his number, rank and accommodation address in the city.

DOCHEWSKI, LADYSLAV: 1st Lieutenant: Billeted at 106 King Charles Mews, Edinburgh. Landlady—Miss M.S. Macmillan.

Anna smiled when she read the entry and the coincidence in names, but she knew that Macmillan was as common as Smith in England, or Svensson in Sweden. She called Gwen and asked if she could have a photocopy of this entry.

Gwen took the ledger and returned with a sheet of A4 paper with the entry copied legibly on it. Anna noted that she'd covered the other entries and only hers was shown.

"Here you are," said Gwen as she handed the copy to Anna. "I'm afraid that King Charles Mews and most of the other tenements in that area have probably been demolished since the war. I think some of them have been kept as a sort of mirror of the older style housing between the wars, and this might possibly still be there. You'll need to see."

Anna asked where they were.

"Why, just around the corner. Just walk down the road about a hundred yards, turn left and what is left of them will be on your right.

The street is now called Rathgovan Street, but there is a sign up on the old mews that still bears the original name and numbers."

Anna thanked her and left with a ripple of excitement building up inside her.

Chapter Fourteen

Rathgovan Street turned out to be exactly where Gwen had said. Ann pulled her coat over her shoulders as she walked, clouds having built up sufficiently to occlude the sun and the temperature had dropped a couple more degrees. She gazed for some moments at the rows of flats lining the street, and noted that one old tenement block had been left standing at the end of each side of the street.

Approaching the tenements on her right she found a plaque that indicated this had once been numbers 2-6 King Charles Mews. Crossing the street she discovered that block had originally been numbers 1-5 King Charles Mews. That put number 106 towards the end of the right hand side of the road.

She walked briskly along the terrace and approached the final block on the right, noting that this too was one of the old ones. All the newer flats had been constructed between the old ones, and those having probably had a face-lift at the same time. Turning right at the end she located the plaque that said this had been numbers 104-108. The flat was still standing!

She turned into the front of the building and approached the first door she could find. All the doors had been renumbered and she had no idea which might have been number 106. She rang the bell and waited for somebody who might be able to help her. The door opened a crack and a muffled voice from within asked who she was and what did she want. She could see a chain inside that stopped the door from opening any further.

"My name is Anna Petersson, and I'm trying to locate the flat that was originally number 106 King Charles Mews. Can you help me please?"

"Just a minute." The door closed with a thump and she heard the rattle of a chain, then it was pushed open again to reveal a woman in her sixties, her head covered by a yellow duster and wearing a cardigan with the sleeves rolled up to her scrawny elbows. She saw Anna looking at her with surprise. "T'day is Monday, we do our washing, cleaning and dusting on a Monday here," she said with a scowl.

"Oh," said Anna. "I didn't realise, sorry to interrupt you. Where I come from we traditionally do this on a Friday."

"Ah," the lady said with a triumphant grin. "Ye're foreign! Thought ye must be. Ah'm foreign tae, I come doon fra' Aberdeen ye'ken."

"Number 106?" asked Anna, not wishing to explore the psychology of doing housework on a Monday.

The lady directed her up the stairs that she could now see at the end of the building. "Second door on the left," she said dismissively. "It's Mrs McCormack ye'll be after then?"

Anna nodded as if this was the answer to her life's problems and thanked her. In fact it was as near to the magic answer as she felt she would ever get today.

The stairs were of bare concrete and sorely in need of the attention of a bucket of warm water and a hard broom. At least, she mused as she climbed the steps, the place didn't actually smell of dogs urine and other forms of excreta. Number 106, now renumbered to 88, had a freshly painted white front door. She thumbed the bell push and waited.

"Yes?" A voice sounded from the inside. The occupant hadn't even deemed to open up yet.

"Mrs McCormack? Could you spare me a few minutes?" Anna called at the front door. She wondered whether she ought to yell through the letter box.

"What d'ye want? I'm bust and I'm nae buyin' ye ken!"

"I just need to talk, I'm not selling anything. I'm after some information about the previous occupant."

Moments later the door opened and dark eyes surveyed her for some seconds. Then the door was pulled wide open and the small lady who stood there had dark hair and rosy cheeks. On closer inspection Anna found that Mrs McCormack was made up like a ageing Hollywood star, make-up layered onto her face, dark eye shadow, vivid red lipstick and spots of rouge on her cheeks. The word 'hideous' popped into Anna's mind momentarily.

"Well? Ah haven'y all day ye ken."

"I'm asking about a Mrs Macmillan who lived here in 1942. Is she still alive? I would love to speak with her if so."

The Hollywood Queen burst into laughter, cackling in a most unladylike manner behind her hand like an ageing rooster. "It'll be a séance ye'll be needing, my dear. Old Sadie's been dead these past fifteen years, bless her."

"Did you know her?"

"Didn't everyone? She ran the Crawford Lounge down on Princes Street in those days. Place is long gone now, been turned into some fancy bar full of foreign muck on sale for the young bucks." She eyed Anna up and down for a moment. "Come on inside and have a cup of tea, or even something a mite stronger perhaps."

Anna thanked her, stepped into the hall and the front door banged shut behind her. The atmosphere of the flat was a far cry from what she'd expected, it seemed as if time had stood still.

The living room, on the right from the entrance hall, was bright and spotless much to Anna's surprise. An old two-seater settee and a single armchair in what had once been top quality upholstery were fronted by an equally retro glass-topped mahogany coffee table. Other furnishings in the room were of similar quality and carefully polished, making Anna slightly apprehensive about sitting down. She looked at the ornaments that abounded on the shelves and on the walls and the array of healthy plants that adorned the window sills. This was one lady who tried to take great care of herself and her home.

"I'll go and make some tea," the lady suggested with a welcoming smile. "Just make yourself comfortable." She disappeared into an adjoining room that Anna presumed was the kitchen.

Anna was reluctant to flop down on the settee so she walked over to the sideboard on which stood several framed photographs of people unknown to her. These must obviously be the lady's family, she mused as she inspected the orderly squad of portraits. One particular picture, slightly larger than the rest that held pride of place in the middle, was of a handsome man with wisps of grey hair, a tiny smile on his face paid token to a loving and caring personality.

"Ah, that's Angus, he passed on four years ago now," said Mrs McCormack's voice from behind her.

Anna turned. "Oh, I'm so sorry Mrs McCormack. That must have been very sad for you. He looks such a nice man."

"Yes, he was probably the best husband in the world, and I do miss him so." She paused for a moment to take a deep breath. "Please, call me Jessie, everybody else does. Do you take milk with it?" When Anna nodded she turned back to the kitchen and disappeared again.

Anna went back to the settee and sat carefully down as Jessie returned bearing a tray with cups and saucers, teapot, milk and sugar which she set down gently on the table. The crockery was fine bone china and Anna saw that she'd placed a small bottle of Famous Grouse on the tray as well.

"Would you like a wee dram in your tea?" asked Jessie as she poured. "It'll warm you up a mite."

"Well, just a touch, perhaps," agreed Anna, "as long as you're having some as well." She'd never drunk tea laced with scotch before and was interested to discover what it tasted like.

Jessie poured a measured half teaspoon into each cup. "There, that's about all ye'll need, any more would ruin it." She passed a cup to Anna. "Now, you were asking me about Sadie Macmillan? What exactly do you want to know? I'm not sure I can tell you much though."

Anna sipped at her tea, surprised that it tasted so good. What exactly do I want to know? How much information do I really want to have? She began to wonder if this had been such a good idea after all.

"I'm not sure what to ask now. My father lived in this apartment from 1942, she is listed as his landlady and I guess I'm just interested in where he was and who he knew. This was some time before he met my mother after the end of the war, so he was only a young officer when he was here."

Jessie nodded thoughtfully and sat quietly in thought for a few moments. "I was born at about the same time as Sadie's daughter, Veronica, she was just a couple of months younger than me, I think. My parents lived in number 95, and Veronica and I were friends. I was often in this house. Auntie Sadie, I called her. We all did. She was a lovely lady as I recall, everybody liked her."

She sipped her tea with a tiny smile on her rosebud lips. "She never married so far as I know. I don't recall anybody staying with her, but the invasion of Europe was under way and no doubt your father had long gone by that time." She glanced across at the photographs on the sideboard for a moment, as if for inspiration. "My mother, bless her, once told me that Sadie had a guest for a year or so, a foreign soldier billeted out from the local Army Camp."

With a smile that widened for a moment she suddenly told Anna the most important piece of information. "Mother also hinted to me that there was a romance of some sort, and that Veronica was the result. I never ever saw Sadie out with, or friends with, any man that I can recall."

Jessie raised her eyebrows to Anna as she put down her cup. "Is that of any help to you?"

Help isn't quite the right word, thought Anna. "It gives me a lot to think about, and at the moment I'm not sure where to start. Is Sadie buried here?"

"Oh, aye. She's in the Rosebank Cemetery. That's a way out of town on the Leith road. You'll need to take a bus if you want to visit."

Anna jotted down the details and resolved to visit sometime later today if it didn't pour down with rain. "What about her daughter, Veronica? Is she still alive and somewhere around here?"

Jessie shook her head slowly. "I don't know, my dear. We lost touch some years ago when she moved away. She had quite a bad time of it."

Anna raised her eyebrows in mute question.

"She was such a quiet little girl when we were friends, even tempered and so pleasant to everybody." Jessie smiled with her memories. "Too nice really, for her own good. Her biggest problem was that she always fell for the wrong men, wasters, yobs and good-for-nothings most of them. Eventually she ran off with some Sassenach, Eddy Hobbs was his name if I recall. He was up from London, a real shady customer. Rumour has it that he was related to the Kray twins, cousin or something like that, and fell out with them. That's why he was up here, to hide from them."

She leaned back with a sigh. "They must have caught up with him in the end though, his body was found up near the Forth Bridge." She smiled again. "Though not before he'd knocked up poor young Veronica."

This all sounded a bit sordid to Anna. "The Kray twins? Who or what were they?"

"Ah well, ye may ask. They were twin brothers y'see, from the East End of London, criminals of some sort I gather. Ye'll need to speak to somebody who knows about that sort of thing. I know the name and recall they were in the news sometimes in the 50's or 60's." She sat up again and leaned forwards. "Anyway, Veronica ran off with Hobbs, returned home a couple of times with bruises I remember, black eyes, that sort of thing." She grinned. "Sadie was mad as hell. It wouldn't surprise me if she didn't get some of her customers to deal with him, who knows?"

"So, what happened to Veronica then?"

"Well, shortly afterwards Sadie sold her interest in the Crawford Lounge, and rumour has it that some of her money went into buying a cottage for Veronica somewhere far away from here. By that time she had the bairns, twin boys, and a few months later she disappeared. We never heard from her again."

Anna finished her tea, which by this time was all but cold. So her father possibly had an affair with this Sadie, producing a daughter, Veronica, who might or might not be her half sister. Veronica had twin sons and disappeared somewhere away from the city. They would then be her nephews if Veronica was really her half-sister.

"I guess that means I may have a half-sister, and a couple of nephews somewhere out there?" Anna set down her cup and saucer with a grin. "That serves me right for asking all these silly questions, doesn't it?"

"Sometimes," said Jessie slowly, "it pays not to ask too many questions. Now see how the answers have complicated your life?" She smiled across at Anna.

"Have another cup of tea?"

. . .

Anna left the flat just before lunch time, making her way back to Princes Street where she found a cosy café that advertised baked potatoes with various fillings. The rain still hadn't started to fall when she came out half an hour later so she hailed a taxi and asked to be taken to the Rosebank Cemetery.

The journey was less than a couple of miles but she didn't fancy walking back so she asked the driver to wait for half an hour. Once she was inside the cemetery she realised that this was indeed a special place, beautifully maintained and providing space to many important headstones dedicated to local merchants and ship owners who lived or were born in Leith.

After searching for ten minutes she discovered the grave she was looking for. A modest headstone, at least in comparison to most of the others, situated in a quiet corner announced the resting place of one, Magdalena Sadie Macmillan, born in Leith, who passed away on 19th October 1990. The inscription underneath indicated that Sadie was missed and much loved by her daughter, Veronica. Simple and to the point.

Anna took a picture of the headstone and inscription in case she needed it, then walked slowly back to where the taxi waited. She wondered what she was going to do next, if anything, to further her research.

. . .

Next day the British Midlands Airbus touched down at Heathrow exactly on time. Anna walked into the departure lounge and immediately spotted Justine seated at a quiet table near to a coffee bar. Justine rose and waved cheerily.

"Hi Anna, good to see you again, I've missed your company. How did the weekend go?" She put her arms round Anna and gave her a hug and a kiss on the cheek.

"The weekend was like a dream come true. Duncan had to go back to work on Monday morning so I had a day to do some research."

"Is coffee okay?" asked Justine as they sat down. Anna nodded and her friend waved at a waiter in the bar. "I got him briefed so coffee is on its way. How was your flight?"

"Perfect," said Anna as she extracted the package from her bag and handed it across to Justine. "This is for you from Superintendent Vickstrom."

She took the package and nodded as she stuffed it into her bag. "I know what's in that, the records from the jeweller in Russia for sales to Macmillans over the last few years."

Anna's heart missed a beat, she knew she must warn Justine before she looked at the documents. "There'll be discrepancies. Duncan explained to me that his brother, Robert, had taken several of the crucifixes without paying." She gazed at Justine with concern. "I know he's worried about it and hs's been trying to protect his brother."

Her friend assumed a serious expression for a moment. "Okay, so what do you know about his brother?"

"Not much. He works away for most of the time. I don't know what he does, but I get the feeling that it might not be strictly legal." She reached across and touched Justine's hand. "For God's sake don't let on that I told you this. Duncan and I are now very close and I know he'd feel betrayed if he found out that I'd spoken to you about him and his brother."

"His name is Robert, isn't it? I'll do a search under his name and see what comes up. We can do some work on that and probably uncover most of the information you've told us. Don't worry, I'll not say anything out of line and your name will never come up."

Anna relaxed as the coffee arrived.

"And how did your research go? Have you traced where your father lived?"

Anna took a deep breath and started on the story as Jessie had done. When she got to the bit about Veronica and the twins she stopped and asked a question. "Who were the Kray twins? Eddie Hobbs was apparently connected to their family."

Justine raised her eyebrows in surprise. She put down her coffee cup and thought for a moment.

"They were bad news in anybody's book, especially during the early 1960's. Ronnie and Reggie Kray, they came from Hoxton in the East End of London. I understand they did some boxing in their early years, turned professional for a time too. By 59 or 60 they were well into armed robbery, arson and extortion. They got hold of several properties and started night clubs there. They were very successful and soon became known as a part of the 'swinging London' scene."

She sipped her coffee thoughtfully.

"It was about 1967 that their careers came to a head and they were accused of two murders, somebody called McVitie, like the biscuits, and someone else whose name escapes me right now." She looked up with a grin. "Now, funnily enough, it was from Scotland that the police got their best evidence against them. They sent somebody to Glasgow to buy explosives to make a car bomb and things went wrong and he told all to the police. Anyway they were arrested and both got life sentences. Ronnie was certified insane, surprise, surprise, and died in prison. Reggie was let out in 2000 and died soon after from cancer."

She put down her empty cup. "Now you know. So this guy Hobbs was on the run from them? They'll have got him in the end, their hold on the underworld was very powerful." She laughed quietly. "You know they even made a film about them, Britain's answer to Al Capone. You could probably hire it when you get home if you like violent movies."

Anna shook her head. "I think I'll pass on that one."

An announcement came at that moment over the speakers that her flight was being called, and Anna got to her feet.

"Sorry, I guess I'd better go off to the gate now. Thanks for the coffee."

They hugged again and promised to meet soon, then Anna walked thoughtfully away towards the moving walkway that would take her to her boarding gate.

Chapter Fifteen

Stockholm

Arina Kovalenko sat stiffly in the lounge of the Viking Ferry, her back against the rear wall as her eyes searched the other passengers for a familiar face. Ari was frightened, and she was running for home. The ferry was due to leave in twenty minutes time and she mentally tried to will time to speed up as she knew she would feel safer once on the high seas, but for now her stomach churned and nausea threatened to overtake her as she watched fearfully for any sign of Bob Scott.

As if spurred by some vindictive spirit, time now seemed to run slower than normal, the twenty minutes feeling more like a full hour as she fidgeted in her corner seat. After an eternity the ferry began to move and Ari started to breathe more easily. She closed her eyes for a few moments and thought back to those special days three months ago when she'd first met Bob. Then he had seemed so sophisticated and adult, a safe and caring lover who wooed her like a story-book hero.

Ari hadn't been a virgin, she'd been with a couple of boys of her own age in the past, but to her this had been a whole new and wonderful experience. She had lost count of how many times she had fallen asleep with her body still tingling from the aftermath of their love-making. Experience had followed experience and about a month later Bob had suggested a new way to enhance their nights together.

The white powder had looked so innocent at first, but when inhaled it changed her whole nervous system. Every stroke, thrust and orgasm took on earth-shattering proportions, she had never experienced anything like it before. A few weeks later he introduced a new experience, sex with three in a bed, Bob and one other man both working to ensure her satisfaction. It was too good to be true, and of course, it wasn't. The icing was rapidly melting from the cake of her desire.

Ari gazed from the porthole to see the harbour slipping away as they moved slowly towards the open sea. She felt she was safe now, just so long as Bob hadn't boarded and was hiding on deck waiting for her. That was a possibility she preferred not to consider as the evening was warm and the sea calm as the ferry rumbled on towards Helsinki and thence to Tallin where she intended to catch a train to her parents' house in Riga.

With a sigh she recalled how lucky she'd been when she'd had the idea of hiding her passport from Bob. It had only been a joke initially as he'd asked for her passport several times once she started to entertain 'clients' for him as a member of his 'escort service', be nice the them, in other words he wanted her to behave like a prostitute. The first couple of times had been fun, the clients were young and respectable, and their demands were normal. Later the clients began to be anything but normal, older and more physically revolting with desires for things she couldn't understand and which seemed to have little to do with sexual satisfaction. When she complained to Bob he smacked her, swore at her and demanded her passport again.

"I don't know where it is, I think I must have lost it," she had cried, tears streaming down her face as she was determined not to give in to his demands.

Promptly he hit her again, harder this time, making her reel back and collapse on the floor. He began to tear her room apart in a vain hope of recovering her passport. Of course he didn't find it. She'd had the sense to hide it in the tiny deep freeze compartment, inside a pack of individual pizzas that she'd opened but not liked very much.

The next morning she started to plan her escape, and a few days later, when Bob went out at midday she took her bag, passport and some cash she'd saved up in the freezer with the pizzas, and jumped onto a train to Stockholm Central station. She travelled light, taking with her merely a change of underwear and the cross he'd given her at the beginning. That cross, she knew, was worth quite a lot of money and hoped she could pawn it if she needed more cash. Now she fingered the crucifix and whispered a short prayer, then she stood up and walked slowly towards the doors that led onto the foredeck.

At this late hour most of the passengers would be at the bar or restaurant and the deck was all but deserted. She walked slowly round the ship looking for any sign of Bob, but there was none. She reached the bows, well away from any other passengers, and leaned on the rail as she watched the sea birds swooping and diving along with the ship in the hope of an easy meal.

I very nearly made a real mess of my life, she mused with regret. My place at University is long gone, I'm being pursued by some sort of madman and all I want now is to get home and start all over again. If only . . .

"Well, well, the fleeing maiden is here after all," the voice whispered in her ear. "You almost made it, didn't you!"

Ari whirled round to confront her Nemesis, gazing past him to see if there could be any help at hand. Nobody was in sight as she opened her mouth to let out a loud scream. Bob's hand came up and grasped her throat round the windpipe, stifling the scream before it left her.

"Don't try that or I'll break your fucking neck here and now," he warned with a growl. "Are you going to return with me on the next ferry back?"

Silently Ari shook her head. Enough was enough and she had no intention of subjugating herself to this man any further, whatever the consequences. She knew she'd rather die than exist like he wanted her to.

"Okay, if that's what you want, then . . ." he brought up his other hand clutching a wicked looking knife.

Ari didn't even think, acting out of pure instinct. There were several things about her that Bob never knew, and one was that she'd taken extensive lessons in self defence before journeying to Sweden. Her right knee jabbed swiftly upwards between his legs while her right hand index fingers aimed for the spot at the base of his throat where a nerve cluster lies. Her fingers connected with a satisfying feeling.

Bob staggered backwards as if given an electric shock and Ari tried to run past him. Unfortunately he was quicker than she'd anticipated and he managed to grab her sleeve, insert his other hand under and between the legs of her jeans as he lifted her off the deck and swiftly over the side. All the time he was watching to see if there were any witnesses, but the deck was deserted.

She never even screamed as she plunged off the ferry. What Bob was unaware of, apart from her self defence lessons, was that she had recently been the first reserve for the Latvian Olympic Swimming Team. As she fell she twisted her body so that she entered the water smoothly and disappeared beneath the surface. Angling her dive carefully she tried to put as much distance between herself and the ship as possible. The propellers were her most immediate worry as they would chop her to pieces if she made contact with them.

Up on deck Bob stood at the rail, taking deep breaths to ease the pain between his legs and watching for the dark hump of a body to appear somewhere on the surface. He was aware that the next minute was crucial, and if she was spotted by passengers or crew he could be in big trouble.

After half a minute there was still no sign of anything and he started to breathe more easily. Perhaps she'd come up under the keel and been knocked unconscious, or maybe the propellers had done their work for him. He stepped slowly to the other side but there was still no sign. One further careful scan and he felt he was now safe from immediate danger.

Taking a cigarette from the pack in his pocket he lit up and eased his body against the rail, the pain subsiding slowly as he drew the smoke into his lungs. A beautiful evening for a trip to Helsinki, he mused with a tiny smile. Perhaps an overnight stay and return at leisure tomorrow. No doubt about it, Bob, you're the best, he thought with a wider grin.

. . .

The water was surprisingly cold for the height of summer, but Ari was used to that. She surfaced about two hundred yards behind the ferry, bobbing around as the wake washed over her. She watched the ship ploughing away from her and subdued a moment of panic as she turned to see the coastline as a dark smudge on the horizon. She estimated the distance as about four or five miles, well within her capabilities as she was used to swimming at least that distance most mornings in the bay when she'd been training before.

Her will to survive took over from the bitterness and anger and she forgot about the pain in her arm and throat where Bob had clutched her as she began to swim carefully back the way the ferry had come. After some minutes she found herself wondering what Bob was going to do with her bag that had fallen to the deck as they struggled. I expect it'll be floating in the sea somewhere behind me, she thought, and then recalled that her passport was in the back pocket of her jeans. It may well be ruined, she thought, but at least it will be proof that I'm not trying to enter the country illegally.

After another quarter of an hour she began to notice the weight of the gold crucifix hanging round her neck. It was comforting to know that she still had that as it could provide her with some money should she need it. Her immediate concern was whether or not to go straight to the police. After weighing up the pros and cons of that action she realised that if she didn't then some poor soul might suffer similar treatment in the future, or even worse.

Turning onto her back she floated for a few minutes then she began to use her back stroke for half an hour. When she eventually turned over again she could see that the land was clearer on the horizon now, and even better, there was a boat of some description headed towards the harbour not very far from her. She changed direction to a course that should intercept the boat in the hope that they might spot her. As the boat drew nearer she lifted an arm and waved.

After the third time she noticed it start to turn slowly towards her.

. . .

The boat was a fishing vessel with two men on board, one old man in his sixties and a younger version, she thought, in his early thirties. The older man cut the motor whilst the younger one threw her a line and helped her on board, his eyes admiring as she rolled over the side with her soaking wet tee shirt clinging to her body. Ari was neither interested in nor complimented by his gaze.

"What are you doing swimming out here?" asked the old man in coarse Swedish that spoke of a local upbringing.

"I was on the ferry and was attacked. He threw me overboard," she replied in her halting Swedish. "Lucky for me I'm a good swimmer. Can you help me to speak to the police when we get to the mainland?"

The younger man introduced himself as Gunnar Svensson, and told her that the older man was Rolf, his father. He quickly produced a cup of thick hot black coffee from a battered flask, then he went off into the cabin and returned with a warm blanket and a kindly smile. "I will go and radio ahead to the police. They will be waiting on the dock for you when we get there."

Ari summoned up a thin smile. "Thank you for your kindness," she said as she sipped at the coffee.

. . .

True to his word, Gunnar spent a few minutes on the radio in the cabin and returned with a broad smile. "They are on their way and will be bringing an ambulance in case you are hurt."

Some minutes later she was helped onto the jetty and straight to the ambulance where the attendants checker her over carefully. She had been lucky and, apart from bruising on her neck and arm, there were no lasting injuries that might need treatment. She was handed back to the police and the ambulance left.

She was helped into the Volvo by a gentle policewoman and they were driven off to police headquarters. Once there she was interviewed by a Sergeant who took her name and address and her passport to try to dry it out. A younger Inspector replaced him and she went through her story slowly and in detail. By the end he seemed to be more interested in the crucifix that still hung around her neck. When she explained that it had been a gift from the man who attacked her he nodded, saying that this was possibly significant and he must speak to his superior.

A hot meal followed and then she was given a change of clothing and the chance to shower away the remains of the sea water. Once showered and changed she was shown to a sumptuous office where the occupant introduced himself as Superintendent Vickström.

"I think you may well have had a very lucky escape, young lady," he said once she had sat down on the chair he pulled across for her. He offered her a cigarette and lit it for her. "That crucifix you're wearing round your neck shows me just how lucky you have been. I'll explain it all later, but for now I want you to tell me all that has happened to you since you arrived in this country."

Ari sat back and began her tale of how she met Bob Scott, their sham romance (on his part anyway) and what followed subsequently. She didn't know any of the names of his clients, nor of any of his friends, but she tried not to leave anything out. When she was done he sat and gazed frankly at her.

"You are indeed lucky; even if you probably don't feel it. Now please tell me all you can about this man." He pushed a photograph across his desk.

She gazed at it with a chill. The photograph in front of her was of Bob Scott, a similar snap to the one that he had given her early on in their romance. She noticed with horror that this one had been splashed with blood.

Chapter Sixteen

Anna put the final slice of chicken into her mouth and speared the last piece of fried potato when the telephone rang. After a few chews she swallowed and picked up the receiver with a grin. "Hello Duncan, you're early," she said in English. "I've only this minute finished dinner. How's my darling tonight?" She took a sip of the red wine she'd opened for the evening.

There was a curious silence for a moment or two. "Is that Anna Petersson?" asked an unfamiliar voice on the other end.

Anna felt a little embarrassed as she realised this wasn't Duncan after all. "Er, yes. Who is this?" She hoped it might be a wrong number, or somebody who didn't know her.

"*Jaha!* Superintendent Vickström here." His voice was suddenly recognisable. "Are you very busy?"

Apart from waiting for Duncan's call and feeding the cat, she had the evening to herself. "Well, no, not really. I've just finished eating. Is there a problem?"

"I mustn't say too much over the telephone, but it is quite urgent. Can you come in to the office?"

Anna's heart sank. Of all the times for him to pick it would be when she had her feet up and was waiting for Duncan to ring. "I am expecting a telephone call any minute. In fact I thought this was him. Is this something that cannot wait until tomorrow morning?"

"A serious new development, interesting and important. You've been involved from the beginning and your help would be very useful." He paused for a second. "I can send a car if you like?"

Anna considered this. It would give her time to call Duncan and ensure he knew she had been called out. She'd also had a couple of drinks so she couldn't drive, and the trains were not as frequent during the evening. "Yes, that would be a good idea. I can't drive at the moment."

"Okay. Be ready in twenty minutes."

The phone went dead.

"*Fy fan!*" she exclaimed, using the Swedish equivalent of 'damn'. The last thing she wanted was to go out right now. Since her recent visit to Edinburg the weeks had become quite hectic for her, and so different compared with the times before her first visit to London just over a month ago. She had since found herself turning down invitations to parties and dances, a life she'd previously enjoyed, preferring nowadays to stay in her flat and enjoy the peaceful surroundings of her home.

There were many times when she found she was looking forward to these quiet hours at home after a busy day at the University or in Police headquarters in Stockholm. There were also times when she sat at home and tried to recall her youth, reliving in her mind her bonds with her parents and relatives. The more she dwelt upon her childhood, the more a picture of her father's sad eyes became important to her. Was there something or someone she wasn't aware of hiding behind them?

At one stage she'd found a picture of her father in the company of two young women. It had been taken during the war at some unknown place or time, but there was nobody who could give her any information about this photograph. She knew she was seeking answers without even knowing the proper questions to ask.

She shook her head slowly with a long sigh. She dialled Duncan's number at home and he answered almost immediately.

"Ah! I was just about to ring you," he said.

She could tell by his voice that he was smiling, which made her feel happier. "I'm sorry, but I've just had a call and have to go out for an hour or two. I hate when work interrupts my evening. Can we speak tomorrow at the same time?"

"Right, not a problem. I miss you a lot. We can talk about my visit then. The booking can wait for another day, the plane won't go away."

They said their goodbyes and she replaced the receiver before checking the contents of her briefcase. Going into her bedroom where Mendelssohn was sleeping curled up on the duvet she changed into a skirt suit and white blouse. As an afterthought she put the Russian Orthodox crucifix round her neck to complete the outfit.

The doorbell rang just as she was scooping the remains of dinner into Mendelssohn's dish. She placed it on the floor and picked up her coat.

. . .

After being chauffeured to the centre of Stockholm and dropped by the front doors of the police building Anna was ushered into Vickström's office. He stood up as she entered and walked round his desk.

"Thank you for agreeing to come out at this late hour. I wouldn't have called you if it could have waited." He pulled a pair of armchairs across to the low coffee table under his window. "Coffee will be coming shortly," he said as he pulled a third armchair up to the table.

Anna gazed at the third chair and raised her eyebrows in puzzlement.

"Somebody will be joining us in a few minutes. We've had another incident relating to the Bovok case."

Anna's heart missed a beat. "Oh no! Not another murder?"

Vickström shook his head. "No, not this time. The young lady was extremely lucky, and she's here at the moment. She'll be with us soon." He went on to explain what had taken place on the ferry to Helsinki earlier this evening. "So you see she should have been just a further body on the slab, but luck was on her side. She's identified the man in our photograph as Bob Scott. We have his address and officers are there at the moment searching the place for any clues as to the people responsible for these atrocities."

"So he's still on the ferry?"

"As far as we can establish, yes. He could have jumped overboard, of course."

"So are we to presume that he'll grab the next ferry back here tomorrow? Couldn't you just arrest him when he gets in?"

He nodded slowly. "I expect we will. We can hold him for extradition if we turn up sufficient evidence to prove he was the man wanted in England, or we can just charge him with murder if we find sufficient evidence. What we really want is some evidence as to who might be behind the organisation, who's putting up the money to pay people like him and rake in the profits."

Anna was shocked at the turn this was all taking. "What you're saying is that you're willing to risk losing track of this murderer for the sake of trying to arrest some 'bigger fish' somewhere? They're the ones you really want?" She was not amused at the thought of using this man as a way of getting to his bosses. "Seems to me that this man probably has murdered at least two young ladies, he's got many more probably hooked on drugs and using them for prostitution. The man's a menace to our society, especially to young girls in this city."

She got up and paced about for a few moments. "I'd sooner see him caught and convicted than risk losing him to get a couple of fat businessmen or politicians who are very little danger in themselves." Her cheeks were flushed as she sat down again.

He nodded. "Okay, point taken. I understand what you say, but! My superiors are working from a different agenda, one I must take cognisance of. They see the 'fat cats' behind these set-ups as being of prime importance. The likes of Scott are merely petty criminals in the scheme of things." He leaned forwards holding her eyes with his. "As far as I think, he deserves to be removed from society just as much as the so called 'fat cats' above him. We'll do our best not to lose him if we don't get the evidence we want. Don't forget that he is a visitor to our country and will be deported to England whatever happens now."

Anna nodded slowly, she could see Vickström's position, but that didn't relieve the frustration she felt that somebody like Scott might get away with murder if something went wrong. With a sigh she said, "Sorry, I didn't mean to go on at you. Perhaps I'm getting too close to all this." She smiled apologetically. "That was really unprofessional of me."

He shrugged and offered her another cigarette. As she leaned forwards to take one he caught sight of the crucifix round her neck. "Ah, you have one of the crosses. It looks good on you."

Anna reached down, pulling it from under her blouse and looked at it. "Yes, I bought one in Glasgow, from Macmillan's a couple of weeks ago."

At that point the door opened to admit an officer pushing a trolley with coffee cups and jugs on it. Just behind him walked a tired looking young lady who went to the chair that Vickström indicated and sat down wearily. She glanced across at Anna and extended her hand as the Inspector began to introduce them.

Suddenly the girl's face drained of its colour and she shrank back, her hands rising to her face as a scream bubbled up inside her.

. . .

Ari followed the officer into the room, watching as he set out coffee for the Inspector and his guest. The woman was attractive and middle aged, at least to Ari, and there was something about her face that held her gaze. The officer put out a further cup for Ari herself before retiring from the room and closing the door softly. She looked closer at the woman and saw something about her face that struck a chord within her. What was it, she wondered as she tried to analyse what made the face seem so familiar to her. Her eyes perhaps? She got the distinct feeling of déjà vu. She shook her head slightly and looked away.

Vickström introduced the woman as Anna Petersson as she lowered herself into the seat. Anna leaned forwards and extended her hand across the table towards Ari with a smile. A gold chain and crucifix suddenly swung forwards out of the woman's blouse and Ari's heart missed a beat as her breath caught in her throat and she tried to cut off the cry that was erupting inside her.

This was her cross, the cross that Bob had presented to her. Her mind was suddenly thrown into turmoil. What did this mean? Was this Anna woman in league with Bob Scott? Then, by association, was the Inspector also in Scott's pocket?

She was badly frightened at the idea that Scott's influence could possibly extend this far.

"What's the matter?" asked Anna with a look of concern. She glanced downwards and saw the crucifix dangling from her neck. "Is it this?"

Ari nodded dumbly, tears running out of control down her cheeks. She could see the expression in Anna's eyes, an emotion she didn't expect from anybody associated with Bob Scott. Could her first assumption have been wrong?

"Don't worry, this has nothing to do with Scott," said Anna softly, "I bought it in Britain when I was there recently." She placed her hand behind the crucifix and lifted it to admire the workmanship. "It is lovely, isn't it? I like it very much."

Vickström leaned forwards and pushed a plastic envelope holding a similar crucifix across the table. "And this is yours. It must be worth some money so you'd better have it back."

Ari picked up the packet and shoved it into the pocket of her jeans. She wasn't sure that she'd ever be comfortable wearing it again.

"As I was saying, Anna has been working for us. She is one of the country's best criminal psychologists, and you can trust her implicitly," continued Vickström with a kind smile. "What we would like from you is your story from the beginning. Take your time and tell us all about yourself."

Ari's breathing and heart rate had slowly returned to normal. Now she sat back, picked up her coffee as she gathered her thoughts, and began to speak.

. . .

Anna could have written Ari's story without any direction from the girl herself, she'd interviewed so many students in the past from the universities. Their lives and problems had, in the main, been so similar and the approaches during their times of hardship were predictable. Men like Bob Scott were very good at their jobs, showing concern and a willingness to help save the girls from their desperation at the beginning. Then the slow entry into a sexual relationship that soon extended past what is conventionally termed 'normal' during the first month. This was followed by a casual introduction of 'soft' drugs to enhance the sensations, leading to an addiction in many cases as they were eased into their new life of prostitution.

Ari had not appreciated the attentions of the older men, their predilections of role-play, sado-masochism, bondage and other sad perversions. She still hadn't entered into the world of hard drugs and hence retained a reasonably clear head. She was obviously one of Bob's less than spectacular successes.

When she finished speaking she sat back sipping at her coffee and willing Anna to criticise or censure her. There was a certain challenge in her eyes that warned Anna of how she was thinking.

Instead of censure, Anna smiled across the table and touched her hand. "You did well not to let yourself fall into his trap. A weaker woman would now be a corpse drifting somewhere in the Baltic Sea." She quickly changed the subject. "How many swimming competitions did you win when you were in training?" she asked.

"I was first reserve for the Olympic Team at one stage and I won quite a few local championships and was placed very well in the Nationals," answered Ari with a shy smile.

Vickström rose and walked to his desk, picking up some papers that were in the centre. "We have Scott's address here in Stockholm, my officers are there now. We have the ports and other points of entry covered for his return. Once he comes back we'll have him and will be able to get on with our jobs." He gazed sternly at her for a moment. "I take it that you'll be willing to give evidence against him if needed?"

Ari nodded vigorously. "Of course I will. One problem though, will you be prepared to pay my fares back here from Riga if you want me?"

Vickström gave a tight smile that never reached his eyes. "I suppose so, but hopefully that will not be necessary. We'll take a full statement from you before you're accompanied back to your country." He handed her a small card. "This has my telephone number on it. If there is anything about the case that springs to mind later on, please don't hesitate to call me here."

"That's all very well, but you've got to get Scott first," said Anna quietly.

"That's a foregone conclusion," asserted Vickström as he held out a pack of cigarettes. Ana took one and Ari refused with a shake of her head. "He'll never escape us now that we know who he is." He lit Anna's cigarette and placed a copper ash tray between them.

Anna wondered just how much of what he'd said was really based on hard fact. She got the distinct feeling that things were no quite so clear-cut as Vickström had indicated.

Chapter Seventeen

The old ferry pulled slowly out from the terminal at Helsinki while Bob Scott watched from the upper passenger deck. Leaning casually on the rail he could see the lights of the Finnish capital dwindling slowly behind them. For some reason he had never much liked Helsinki and was glad they had not stopped there for very long. Flicking his cigarette butt over the side he stood up and wandered back towards the warmth of the passenger lounge, hands stuffed deep into his pockets.

The trip had been smooth once they'd reached the relatively calm waters of the Finnish coast, and now the short journey across to Tallin in Estonia should be equally as pleasant. He liked Tallin, it was quite a modern resort on the Baltic, and he looked forward to strolling its streets and perhaps doing some shopping before returning to Stockholm.

Closing the passenger lounge doors behind him he wandered to the bar, ordered a scotch and soda and retired to a quiet seat at the far end of the room well away from the other passengers who were becoming increasingly raucous. Groups of people enjoying themselves with too much to drink tended to irritate him at the moment, so he would avoid them rather than endure the discomfort brought on by the proximity of their company.

The television set was showing a chat show of some kind in Finnish or Russian, he wasn't sure which, and he watched idly as his thoughts dwelt on the incident earlier this evening. The girl, Ari, had not made it easy to find her unlike the other girls who had tried to escape from their organisation. Her planning had been very good, almost perfect in fact, and he'd felt himself lucky that she'd booked her passage over the internet rather than through a travel agent. Using his computer had been a stupid thing for her to do, and possibly her unfamiliarity with computers had been her downfall.

Bob had liked Ari, she had been the only girl with whom he'd felt a pang of remorse once he'd put her to work with the clients. Slowly he began to drift off to sleep only to be awakened suddenly by a roar of laughter from the other side of the lounge. Checking his watch he discovered that he had been asleep for almost an hour.

He gazed at the television set to see the news commencing. The world news headlines, although he couldn't understand the language, were predictable. Scenes from Baghdad and the Middle East crisis, world cup football, and then some local news. His eyes were beginning to close when suddenly he spotted a familiar face on the screen. It was Ari being helped by police, wrapped in a blanket, outside the police headquarters in Stockholm. The commentary was unintelligible but the message obvious, she was still alive. That meant that he might be targeted within the next couple of hours, if not already. He was certain that Ari would now tell the police everything she knew.

He looked around the ship's lounge but there was no way he could get off, he was caught on this ferry with nowhere to hide. Panic began to surface within him and he walked swiftly out onto the deck to get some fresh air and think. As he made the railings he stopped in surprise, there were lights ahead. The ferry was approaching Tallin already! With a wave of relief he knew this might be his best chance, a quick exit and then lose himself in the crowd.

At this moment he was glad that he'd not brought any bags or cases with him. Disappearing would be just that much easier for him.

. . .

Once through the terminal without any problems Bob began to think about his next move. Steal a car? Probably not such a good idea as it might direct attention towards him. Take a bus? Again not a good idea as the local buses were exactly that, local. A train perhaps? If the police had been asked to stop him they might be on the lookout at the stations, scrap that idea. So what to do? He pulled out his wallet and notebook, checked that he had sufficient local currency, and then headed for the nearest telephone kiosk.

The number in Riga rang three times before a voice answered. "Yes?"

"Scott," he said simply, then "I have a problem."

There was silence on the other end of the line for some seconds before another male voice answered.

"Tell me."

Quickly Bob outlined what had happened on the ferry. There was a pause as the person he was speaking to thought for a moment. "Where exactly are you?"

Bob explained that he was just outside the Tallin ferry terminal.

"There is a late night café just around the corner called 'Olga's', it stays open until two am. Go and take a coffee and wait there for somebody to pick you up."

The telephone went dead.

Bob smiled to himself, Marek Sołtysiak was always in control; he would be safe now. He left the kiosk and started walking slowly round the corner, eyes skinned for anybody who appeared to be observing or following him. The cafe was about a hundred yards away and there was an illuminated sign outside. He hurried to the door and closed it behind him with a feeling of relief.

. . .

The car, an old black Mercedes that had seen better days, stopped outside Olga's. Bob watched as the driver got out, recognising her as Christina, Sołtysiak's live-in girl friend. As he pushed his half empty cup away and stood up he wondered how she'd managed to get there so quickly. Riga was over an hour from Tallin so he'd expected to be met by a more local contact in the organisation.

Christina was blond, pale and stacked, a trophy that Marek took with him wherever he went, except if it was dangerous. She undulated into the front door of the café and nodded to him as their eyes met. "You in trouble?" she asked as they walked to the car and he slid into the passenger seat.

"Yeah, the little bitch Ari did a runner. I caught up with her on the ferry and dumped her overboard. I gather she was rescued fairly quickly and I saw her face on the television news about half an hour ago. She'll be spilling the beans to the Stockholm police by now and it's just a matter of fucking time before they come searching for me over here."

She smiled to herself, amused that the smooth Bob Scott had messed up at last. They'd never got on with one another since he'd made a clumsy pass at her, and now she was sure that Marek would be less than pleased with him. She was well aware that Marek never suffered fools lightly and she felt that Bob would be lucky to get away with his life.

As she slid into the driver's seat Bob asked how she managed to get here so quickly. "Were you already in Tallinn?"

She pulled away from the kerb before answering him, driving towards the main road leading out of town southwards towards the border with Latvia. "I was here delivering a package to Ernest when you called. He asked me to pick you up as it only meant a short diversion. So now I have your company all the way back to Riga."

She glanced towards him, her eyes hard. "Remember that I put up with your company only as a favour to Marek. If I had my way you'd walk to Riga."

Bob fought an urge to grab her by the throat and strangle her. He knew that Marek would probably kill him if he did anything to hurt his busty trophy. Instead he forced a laugh and settled back in the seat, closing his eyes.

They drove along in silence.

. . .

Crossing the border into Latvia proved not to be a problem, the barrier had been left raised and unmanned, the small guard hut dark and quiet. Bob breathed a sigh of relief as he realised that the police or border guards hadn't yet been alerted to his presence. Christina motored through the border unconcerned, then turned to him and said:

"It was open like this when I drove up earlier." She accelerated away on the Latvian side. "I think there's a football match of some sort happening tonight." She threw him a glance. "You're lucky; usually they stop everyone and check their papers and passports."

Bob grunted and closed his eyes. He wasn't about to show her just how concerned he had been. He wasn't sleeping, he was carefully going through an inventory of what he owned in his current identity. It was just the flat in Stockholm, which he rented, and his possessions inside that didn't amount to much. He couldn't think of anything that pointed to his intended new identity, his flat in Riga or even his proposed final destination in UK. He was aware that he needed to ditch the Bob Scott identity no sooner than he reached Riga and assume his alter-ego, Daniel Burns. He'd had a new passport and identity card prepared for just this purpose, and the flat in Riga was already registered in that name. But what should he do after that? How was he to return home to Glasgow?

He was in no hurry to return to his brother; Duncan could be such a prissy old sod at times. He'd often wondered if they really were twins, maybe they had been separated at birth and Duncan was the wrong baby substituted for his real brother at that time, an unknowing impostor. He smiled inwardly, it often seemed that way to him.

As he mused silently the lights of Riga began to appear on the horizon and he realised that he must have been daydreaming for some hours. They were almost there already. He glanced at his watch to find that it was nearly three thirty in the morning. He sat up and felt in his pocket to establish that he had the key to his flat ready, then he relaxed into the seat and dozed off for the last quarter of an hour of the journey.

. . .

"Marek will see you later this afternoon, if you manage to wake up that is," said Christina with a glare as she cranked the old car into gear and rattled away into the night.

Bob consulted his watch, the time was just after four in the morning and the sky was beginning to brighten on the eastern horizon. He felt tired but knew he'd probably not be able to sleep as his mind was buzzing with random thoughts, the least of which were about Marek and what sort of reception he was likely to receive. Marek was an enigma, there were times when he could be charming and others when he was totally unpredictable, not a man to be crossed. He was aware that their forthcoming meeting could be a veritable lottery and he should be ready for anything.

Slowly he climbed the stairs to his flat on the first floor of the drab building, opening his front door silently. Inside the flat was cold, dark and inhospitable. He felt for the torch that he kept on a small table by the front door and used it to light his way to the fuse box where he threw the switch to turn on the power.

The hallway was suddenly flooded with light and there was the sound of the freezer and refrigerator starting up after months of disuse.

He walked round the flat turning on all the lights and checking quickly that everything was still in place as he'd left it. He considered the double bed in the bedroom, still rumpled on one side from the last time he'd risen before leaving for Sweden many months ago. Shaking his head slowly he turned and went to the kitchen alcove where there were some pans left unwashed in the dry sink. They emitted an unpleasant smell that he knew would soon permeate the whole atmosphere now that the heating had been activated.

First things first, he thought, turning back to the living area and walking over to his desk. He opened the drop-down flap and rummaged in the drawers pulling out a small folder. He tipped the contents onto the desk surface, a pair of passports and identity cards, one set was for Robert Macmillan and the other was for Daniel Burns. He picked them up and looked at his photograph on all four documents before pushing those for Robert Macmillan back inside the folder and stuffing it in the drawer. These could wait until he really needed them.

Pulling his passport and identity card from his inside pocket he strolled back into the kitchen and took his cigarette lighter from his pocket. He touched the flame to the passport that identified him as Bob Scott. He watched as the document began to blacken and turn to ashes, then he added the identity card to the pyre before he put the remains into the sink to flush away the ashes.

"Goodbye Bob Scott," he murmured quietly. "You did well for a few years."

Chapter Eighteen

Anna sat in the office talking with Ari whilst Vickström made appropriate arrangements for Scott to be apprehended at airports and seaports throughout the country, now that he was wanted for questioning for one murder in Stockholm and one attempted murder earlier this evening. The police were also aware that he might be wanted in connection with the murder in England on Wimbledon Common. When told all this Ari was devastated, tears erupting within a few seconds.

"Come with me," murmured Anna sympathetically, "we'll find a quiet spot where we can get some coffee and talk about all this."

Vickstrom reminded her that the canteen would be closed and he gave Anna a key to the main door. There was a coffee machine inside that was switched on, so they sat quietly in a warm alcove over paper cups of hot coffee-flavoured water while Ari opened up to Anna. She knew that Ari needed to talk and this interval could be very important to her.

"He was so nice," she started as she stirred the coffee. "I know he was quite a bit older than me, but that didn't seem to matter. He bought me presents, this was one of the first," she said tearfully as she fingered the crucifix that she'd replaced round her neck. She sniffed and then blew her nose. "It was only later that I discovered that several of the other girls had also been given crosses like mine."

She attempted a wan smile.

"Funny how that seemed, at first, to pull us all together, like members of a club, but later on we realised that it was a symbol of so much more. Then he tried to give me drugs, but I said 'no', so he tried lacing my drinks and I realised what he was doing after the first time. He tried lacing my food and even tried to make me swallow the pills forcibly. I kept them in my mouth and spat them out as soon as he turned his back."

She dabbed at her eyes with a tissue. "Most of the girls were hooked within the first couple of weeks. I seemed to be the only one who wasn't so I watched and tried to imitate them, their behaviour, things they said and how they acted in front of him. I even got him to give me small supplies of pills, then some white powder. I flushed it all down the toilet as soon as I could."

"Did you ever find out where he came from originally?"

She shook her head. "No, I don't think so. I know he isn't Swedish, he speaks the language so badly, but he seems fluent in English, but even that isn't quite right at times. I studied English at school and some of the words he uses are not in any dictionary I know. He has a flat here, I gave the address to the policeman, and he goes away to Latvia from time to time to do some sort of business, he says."

"Do you know exactly where in Latvia he goes?"

She thought for a few seconds. "I think it is Riga, where I live. He has mentioned the town a few times and places he's mentioned are near my hometown." She leaned back and studied the ceiling for some moments, then changed the subject. "The clients got worse each week; it was as if we were taking a course. At first they were young and good looking, and I was not unhappy about having sex with them, it was almost a pleasure. But later they started to get older and they wanted me to do things that were nasty, I didn't like it."

"Like?"

Ari looked embarrassed. "For example, one night the client, an elderly politician, I think, wanted to handcuff me to the bed before having sex. I kept saying 'no' and eventually he walked out. Next day Bob was very angry with me and wouldn't give me any of the powder I asked him for. He said that he would beat me if I ever did anything like that again." She sighed slowly. "That was the time I realised I had to get away at any cost."

Anna nodded thoughtfully; the picture was getting clear and was one that she was familiar with. Bob was doing a job and playing a part. Break her in gently, get her hooked on drugs of some sort then use her to satisfy various desires of his client group. Only Ari had been too clever for Bob. She hadn't allowed herself to become dependent on the drugs so she would not be forced to endure the depravities of frustrated old men who wanted young girls for their nefarious purposes. Faced with the options of doing what Scott wanted or running off, Ari made the only sensible choice she could live with. She knew that the girl was very brave indeed.

At that moment a police officer came into the canteen to ask them to return to the Chief's office. Anna locked the door behind her and looked at her watch as they walked back. She discovered to her surprise that the time was already after three in the morning. They entered Vickström's office and Anna pulled out chairs for her and Ari. The Inspector was seated behind his desk with a satisfied look on his face.

"So far so good," he started with a smug expression. "We've got all the major ports covered and pictures of Scott have been circulated. Arrangements have also been made to keep a lookout at the major airports. If he tries to enter the country we'll have him. That's about all we can do for the moment."

Ari looked up and raised her eyebrows in question. "Surely he will know by now that you're after him?" She spoke quietly but firmly. "There was a television camera crew outside the police station when I was brought here. I recall that quite distinctly, and they were filming my walk from the ambulance to the front door."

Vickström's brows knitted for a few moments, and then he thumbed his intercom. "Can you come in, please," he asked the duty secretary. Moments later a lady in her early forties entered with a notebook and pencil in her hand.

"You won't need that," said Vickström. "I believe that Miss Arina Kovalenko here was filmed by a television crew on her arrival. Can you get straight onto the news main desk and check whether or not anything about her has gone out over the air? If not, ask them not to broadcast it before speaking to me."

The lady nodded and retreated quietly.

Vickström looked vaguely troubled. "If a broadcast has gone out it could well have alerted Scott. That'll probably mean he will disappear and not return. I'll get on to the British police and bring them up to date on what's happened so far, he might try to go straight there." He looked across at Ari with a tiny smile. "Thank you for your help. Now we need to find somewhere for you to stay until we know what is happening."

He looked at Anna. "I don't suppose you could . . . ?"

Anna had actually been on the point of volunteering her services anyway, so she agreed to have the girl stay with her for a week. She hoped Duncan hadn't arranged to visit too soon or she'd have to put him off.

. . .

"Here," said Anna as they walked into her study. She indicated the settee that lined the wall behind the door. "That opens out into a bed. You can sleep on that in relative comfort."

Ari gazed round the room taking in Anna's desk, computer and fax machine with a certain awe. "But surely you need to work in here?"

Anna grinned and patted her on the arm. "Yes, sometimes, but I'll make sure I finish well before you go to bed. I promise I won't disturb you. In any case I have a laptop in the bedroom. Just shut the door or Mendelssohn will only come and jump up on you when you're sleeping."

Ari had already been introduced to Anna's cat, who she loved on first sight. She smiled. "I wouldn't mind that at all." Her eyes twinkled suddenly with humour. "It would make a pleasant change from some of those loathsome client's of Bob's."

Anna suddenly had a thought. "I have something to show you, it's an old photograph I have. I would be interested to see if you are reminded of somebody you might know." She opened her desk drawer and pulled out the old album that lay on top. Opening it at the portrait of her father she laid it on the desk. She switched on the small desk lamp as she did this. "What do you think?"

The girl gazed down at Anna's father for some time without speaking, then she turned to Anna and asked, "Where did you get this picture? Was it in Bob Scott's flat by any chance?"

Anna almost jumped at the thought. She hadn't really expected Ari to pick up on the likeness so quickly. She shook her head. "No. This is a portrait of my father. It was taken in Poland about forty years ago, just after he was discharged from the British army." She saw Ari's nervous expression. "Do you see somebody else?"

Ari nodded. "Yes, it looks a lot like Bob Scott. It made my blood run cold for a moment." She summoned a tight smile. "Uncanny, don't you think?"

"It worries me too," replied Anna, recalling her first reaction when she'd compared the photographs a couple of months ago. "That is one reason why I've been so involved in this case. I spotted the resemblance immediately and wanted to find out more about this chap Scott. So far I know very little about him."

Ari nodded quietly. "Most people don't know much about him. I think that's how he likes it."

"He does seem to be a creature of habit, like giving these crucifixes to his favourite girls. I know he has a violent temper and wouldn't hesitate in resorting to murder if it suits him." She touched Ari's arm again, a gentle, comforting gesture. "You are a very lucky young woman."

Ari smiled and nodded her agreement. Then she yawned.

"Come on, I'll make up the bed for you. We can sleep late tomorrow morning." Anna went to her hall cupboard to fetch sheets, pillows and a blanket.

Chapter Nineteen

Daniel Burns, AKA Bob Scott, awoke after about four hours of sleep. Picking up his wristwatch he saw that the time was a shade after eleven and he had a few hours to make his preparations before he went to Marek's house. He intended to use this time carefully. Whilst Marek was his boss, in charge of running things efficiently, he had few illusions as to his personal safety should Marek decide his use had come to an end. On a good day he'd seen Marek laugh and tell one of his staff to do better next time. Conversely he'd seen a similar situation when the man in question had been taken away for execution, his body dumped in the woods.

First he wanted a weapon, one that could easily be concealed, and then he needed an escape plan that was immediately available and fast. These things were his first priority after eating something. Pulling on his clothes after a quick shower he went to his small safe and took out a couple of bundles of Lats, the local currency, before stepping out of the front door and locking it firmly behind him. As a final precaution he pulled a hair from his head, licked it and stuck it across the door jamb at the bottom so he would know if anybody had entered during his absence.

Food was first, something to keep him going even if the last thing on earth he wanted to do was eat. The sky was grey as he stepped onto the pavement and walked round the corner of Blaumana, a side street off the K. Barona, to where there was a small but reasonably clean café that he used from time to time. He lived fairly centrally and not very far from the Latvian University, a position that suited his needs. As he walked he gazed at the buildings around him, many newly renovated and painted brightly in contrast with the drab exteriors of others that included his own apartment block.

He shouldered his way into the small café, sat down and ordered *Pîrâgi*, local bacon buns, some crepes with *Jânis* cheese and coffee. As he waited for his food he decided that his plan needed to be such that it could take him back to Britain fairly quickly. His best route would be to cross over into Poland and fly from Gdansk as there was a new cheap airline operating between Gdansk and Glasgow.

He expected there was a good chance that the local police would be close on his tail soon, so he must move quickly. His movement to Poland should be sometime tomorrow if possible he thought, and for this he needed a car, preferably not one that was stolen. He had to find an old banger that would get him where he wanted with some semblance of reliability. He would abandon it at Gdansk airport if necessary. His funds would cover the expenses, as well as the flight, so he relaxed for the time being, his mind made up.

Breakfast completed, he walked out into bright sunshine, the clouds having disappeared as if by magic. He turned towards the University, passing it on his right and onwards to *Kronvalda* Park. Once through the park he found himself in the *Veoriga* district where he knew a dealer who would sell him a car that would get him to Gdansk, also one he could use to get to Marek's house in the *Babite* woods from where he operated. His reception there would determine his next move.

The garage he was looking for was a run-down back street operation that always gave the impression it was terminally closed unless you knew the code signal. Three raps on the door, followed five seconds later by two more, succeeded in gaining him entry. Once inside, the grubby exterior was a thing of the past, the rooms were spotless. The owner, Goran, sat at his desk, his face twisting into a smile as Danny walked in.

"Ah, Danny Burns, or is it still Bob Scott today? A long time, eh?" He stood up and they shook hands. "What will it be?"

"Yeah, Bob Scott is dead now. I need wheels to get me to Poland, like now, or at the very latest this evening." Danny had known Goran for many years, since the time he'd tuned up motors for use in illegal operations and eventually graduated to a garage of his own, still doing roughly the same thing.

"How much can you pay?"

Danny grinned. "As little as possible. I don't have unlimited funds."

"Will I be able to get it back?"

"Yeah, in a couple of days."

Goran nodded, this was nothing new to him and he trusted his customers or they never returned. "I have an old BMW outside. It's fast, if you need speed, and it is good for long journeys. Treat it carefully, no overland driving or pushing it too hard, okay?"

"When?"

"You can have it right now." He named a price that seemed fair to Danny. "That takes into account that you'll leave it in a certain spot when you finish with it, keys up the exhaust as usual."

Danny nodded, exactly what he'd hoped for. "One other thing. I need a shooter, small and efficient. A Walther PPK would do just fine."

Goran looked dubious. "Not easy, but I have a P5 Compact, almost the same if not better. Magazine holds eight rounds of 9mm and you get a spare with it. Ammunition?"

"One box should be plenty; I'm not expecting to massacre the whole Polish Police force! In the glove box, eh?"

Goran named a price that almost doubled his original figure. "Walther is popular this year," he murmured.

Notes were exchanged and they shook hands. The deal was done bar the paperwork for the car.

. . .

Before he drove out to see Marek, Danny went to his bank in town and transferred the bulk of the balance to his account in Scotland; a precaution he felt was probably wise in view of what might happen in the next few days. This was an involved transfer, going via another of his accounts in a Swiss bank so it would be difficult if not impossible to trace. After that he drew out a good amount of Zloty and some Euros for his use during the journey.

His next stop was a local RIMI supermarket where he bought sufficient provisions to take with him on a long journey, or to use at home, depending on his decision later. He packed the foods into the trunk of the car, smoked a cigarette thoughtfully, then climbed back into the driver's seat and switched on the engine.

He now felt that he'd done sufficient to cater for whatever he was about to undertake and he drove sedately out of town on *K. Valdemara,* crossing the river by the tilting bridge and onwards up towards *Babite*. Soon the woods began to close around him and he could feel a tension building up inside himself, his adrenalin flow increasing. What was essentially a very picturesque drive was rapidly becoming a minor ordeal. With a sigh he pulled into a parking space about one kilometre from Marek's cottage and cut the engine. Taking the Walther from the glove box he first checked it was loaded, then he pulled back the slide to lever the first round into the chamber.

As the sun cast mottled shadows across the roadway he sat in the BMW and thought of the time when he and Marek first met. It had been in a bar in Warsaw, more a seedy dive than a regular bar as he recalled, inhabited by various forms of riff-raff and minor criminals from the poorer parts of the city. A fight had started and he'd quickly been caught up in it for no reason other than he'd been there at the time. Two shady characters had picked on him immediately because he was foreign and they obviously thought he would be an easy target.

As if from nowhere Marek had appeared by his side and taken out one of the men with a swift head butt and a hefty kick in the crutch. Danny had dealt with the other one with ease and they'd scrambled for the door and run off laughing. That had been the start of a friendship that had lasted for the past ten years.

Now Marek was the organiser of the group in Riga and Danny was one of his trusted associates for Scandinavia, but the money had changed Marek and he was no longer the same man that Danny had met in that bar. He'd become unpredictable and tense since he had taken Christina under his wing. Danny felt that she might be poisoning Marek's mind against anybody she disliked, and he was well up on her list in that category.

He looked at the Walther again, now snug in its holster, wondering if he should take it with him. He knew that going to see Marek with the weapon strapped to his ankle was not a good idea under any circumstances, so he slid the gun into the deep car door pocket and stuffed some papers over it. It was readily available if he needed it once he was back at the car. With a smile he gunned the motor back into life and drove the last kilometre towards Marek's bungalow.

He hadn't visited this retreat for almost a year so the overly ornate wrought iron gates came as a surprise. He stopped the car and gazed at the open gates, black and shining with some sort of crest on the tops of each that looked a bit like a lion's head. Sadly he shook his head as he coasted onto the long driveway that had been surfaced since last year. Looking over to the left he noted that the trees had been cut down and a new stable block with paddocks had been built. Three horses grazed in one paddock, while the other had been laid out with low jumps for schooling them. He suddenly recalled that Marek's teenage daughter, Tanya, was deeply involved in show-jumping, hence the latest additions.

As he approached the house he saw that it had been extended outwards and probably back as well, new brickwork showing up cleaner that the original. A new front door had been added, solid oak and brightly polished, as well as a pair of pillars to make the entrance look almost regal. He parked the car in a space marked out between a new yellow Porsche Boxer and a enormous black shiny Mercedes. Marek used to drive an elderly Mercedes as he recalled, rather like the one that Christina had been driving last night. In all probability, he guessed, it had been the same car.

As he closed the car door Christina emerged from the depths of the house wearing jodhpurs and a riding hat. Suddenly he remembered that she'd originally been engaged as Tanya's riding coach some years ago. She had been extremely attractive in the past, but now with her dyed blond hair to cover the grey, too much make-up plastered onto her face, and a glittering array of ostentatious gold rings on every finger, she reminded him of an old English saying, 'mutton dressed as lamb'.

Christina stopped and looked at him with a sour expression on her already sour face. "He's expecting you," she said in an unwelcoming tone. "Just go through to the study, if you can find it." Leaving the door open she strode off towards the stables, her jutting breasts bobbing with her movements.

Danny realised that she must have had implant surgery sometime recently, she's never been that endowed in the past. He smiled as he saw that Marek had never outgrown the immature breast fixation of his younger years. Stepping into the hallway he noticed it was at least twice the size it had originally been, and immediately his senses were overloaded with the trappings of the neo-rich. Hideous but expensive velvet drapes lined the hall and a very large marble statue dominated the centre. The statue looked as if it was of some Greek mythological figure, perhaps a god, but he wasn't sure who or what and he doubted that Marek would be able to correctly identify it either. Marek's basic education had been gleaned from the back streets of Warsaw.

The door to the study was ajar so he pushed it open as he rapped on the polished wood panel.

"Yes?" Marek's voice boomed out from within.

As the door opened further Danny saw him seated behind a brand new curved mahogany desk littered with electronic gadgetry. Marek was a large man with a drooping moustache that needed clipping, dark eyes and several teeth missing in front. "Ah, Bob, or is it Danny now? You have slept?"

Danny gave a tight smile and nodded as he stepped into the room. Bookcases lined one wall, filled to bursting point with books of all descriptions that he guessed Marek had never even opened let alone read.

Marek rose to his feet, emerged from behind the desk and embraced Danny in his typical East European fashion. "Come my friend, you must see my house, we've had so much done here since you last came." He led Danny back out of the study and across the hall to the statue.

"This is my inspiration, Achilles, the Greek God of War. We make our own tiny war against the bourgeoisie in our fashion. What you think?"

Danny thought that the statue looked more like Zeus than Achilles, and neither was the god of war, Greek or otherwise. "Fantastic," he enthused. "I didn't know you were so familiar with Greek mythology. I congratulate you on your choice."

Marek grinned from ear to ear with pride. "There is much more. Follow me." He led the way to the main lounge that was festooned with expensive kitsch, marble telephone, giant plasma television screen on the wall and old fashioned heavy reproduction furniture with dark red upholstery that looked decidedly uncomfortable. In the front of the picture window, in contrast to the red furnishings was a pale green chaise longue that had definitely seen better days. Marek pointed this out as being very old and a real antique.

Danny thought it was better not to say anything. He looked back at the room and noted the paintings on the walls, mainly reproductions of the masters, Renoir, Van Gough, Constable and Picasso, all intermingled like a multi-national buffet. "Wow," was all he said as he moved to the window. Outside he could see a large swimming pool glittering azure in the sunlight.

Marek joined him at the window, an arm round his shoulder. "You like the latest addition? Christina spends much time in it."

Danny felt that was hardly surprising with the choice between the overblown and glitzy lounge or the warm pool. "Spoiled for choice," he said as he clapped Marek on the shoulder. "You've come a long way since that bar in Warsaw."

Marek poured drinks for them both from a heavily decorated crystal decanter. "Here's to you, my friend." They touched glasses and sipped at the treble whiskeys he had dispensed.

At least the scotch is not so bad, thought Danny as he knocked his back with relish. It was the real thing and probably almost impossible to get in Riga. He grinned at Marek, relaxing as he drank.

"So, tell me now. What happened yesterday?" said Marek with a smile.

. . .

Marek shook his head slowly when Danny stopped speaking. "You didn't do your homework very well, did you? Have you not got a computer?"

Danny nodded his head. "You know I have. I keep my accounts on it, mail money to you and other details. Why do you say that?"

"Come round my desk and sit beside me. I'll show you."

Danny took a seat just behind Marek's right shoulder from where he could see the screen clearly. He watched as the computer logged onto the internet.

"How do you spell her name?"

Marek typed in each letter laboriously but carefully and after a few moments a list of hits scrolled down the screen. There were several pages.

"You say she was from here, Riga?" He added RIGA to the search string and sat back as another, shorter, list appeared. He opened the first site but it evidently had nothing to do with Ari. The next, however, came up instantly with her picture, it was the Swedish newspaper site, Aftonbladet, and by the smaller pictures, the story of her rescue was recounted, albeit in Swedish.

"Can you read Swedish?"

Danny shook his head. "Not well enough to decipher all this."

"Okay." With a nod Marek went back to the list of hits and selected a further site that proved to be the Riga news bulletin. "Here you are, it says she survived because she was an Olympic swimmer! Now you know what happened." He turned to Danny. "Did you not know this?"

A shake of the head. "No, she never mentioned it."

"That is what I mean when I said you didn't do your homework properly. Looking at this report, I would suggest that you lay low for a while until it quietens down." He turned and smiled at Danny. "We have been friends for many years, and I will ignore this error because of that, but if you screw up again things could be different."

Marek turned further round and gazed searchingly at his friend. "You know that you have an enemy in Christina? She had given me some grief over our friendship. Have you ever done anything to upset her?"

A thousand thoughts ran through Danny's head as he sighed. What to tell Marek? How would he react to the truth? Would a small lie suffice or would Christina suddenly come out with the truth later? That seemed likely at some point. He realised that it would be better to come clean now while his friend was in a good mood than allow it to surface later when he might not be.

"When she first came here I made a stupid pass at her. I didn't realise that you were serious about her or that would never have happened, and I apologise to you. I have regretted it to this day, my friend, as I would hate a woman to come between us." Danny had chosen his words carefully as he knew roughly how Marek's mind worked; even so he was relieved when his friend's face split into a wide grin.

"I like honesty," he exclaimed as he logged off the internet. He turned back to Danny. "You remind me of my countrymen in so many ways." He held Danny's eyes for a long moment. "Are you sure that you have no Polish blood in your family?"

Danny shook his head.

"Och, no. We're Scottish through and through."

. . .

Breathing a long sigh of relief, Danny walked to his car and pulled out carefully before coasting down the driveway to the gates. He could see Christina on a black horse in the jumping paddock. With a tiny smile he watched her as she schooled the horse over the hurdles. She was good, there was little doubt of that, but now he knew he had the advantage over her, an advantage he must keep to himself.

He pulled out from the gates and turned back towards the town, the sun low in front of him as he drove sedately through the trees. Things had gone far better than he had hoped; Marek had seemed genuinely pleased to see him again and had not criticised him too severely for his oversight in not fully checking Ari's details.

From what he'd gleaned from the news reports the police were concentrating mainly on the ports of entry into Sweden, which meant that he could make his way back to the United Kingdom at his leisure. He could take some time out to enjoy the sites of Gdansk and other Polish places of interest before flying from there to Glasgow.

He was in no mood to go back to his home at the moment, especially when Duncan was involved with his latest girl-friend. He knew that wouldn't last, they never did.

He relaxed in the driver's seat. Life was beginning to look up once again for Danny Burns alias Robert Macmillan.

Chapter Twenty

Anna stepped out of the front door to where the stretched white Cadillac awaited. The chauffeur, handsome in his pristine black uniform, smiled warmly at her as he opened the door and ushered her into the sumptuous interior.

"Is it Glasgow this time?" he asked as she slid onto the soft seat and took the glass of champagne he offered her.

As she nodded and opened her mouth to affirm their destination, her eyes opened. She was still in her bed. Was this only a dream? It seemed too real and immediate to be merely a figment of her subconscious. She could still smell the leather, the newness and freshness of the car's interior.

Rolling from her bed she crossed to the window to check if there really was a white limousine parked outside the front door of her block. She felt let down when there was not a sign of a car, black, white or any other colour for that matter. The street was bare of traffic as the streetlamp reflected orange on the damp pavement below.

She turned slowly and studied her bedside clock, the time was a quarter past two in the morning and she knew she had obviously been caught up in a vivid dream, a very strange dream indeed. It had been so unlike her usual night-time horrors where she was swimming in deep water and never finding the shore, or suspended high on top of a tall building and needing to climb down backwards on an exposed ladder. It was strange because she had been happy in the dream, it gave her both hope and excitement.

Glasgow? Edinburgh? Scotland? Her head was crammed with thoughts, fleeting ideas and possibilities these last few hours since

Ari had immediately noticed the likeness between Bob Scott and her long-dead father. Up until now she'd felt it was only her mind playing tricks on her, but Ari's reaction only confirmed her speculations and had now added a new dimension to the fears that crept silently through the corridors of her mind.

Was it really possible? Could her father have led a double life over there in Edinburgh? No, a double life hinted that he was being unfaithful to both women, and Edinburgh had been some years before he had married her mother. But her initial research had shown that he had lived with Sadie Macmillan, possibly had an affair with the woman, so why had he not returned to her after the war? Why father a child and then never return? That was unlike the good man she knew her father was. Perhaps there was another reason, unknown to her, that stopped him from going back? The answer to these questions had long since died with her father and Sadie. There would be no definite answer now, just more questions.

Did he ever return? She didn't think so, but she had no idea what he might have done before she was born. She knew that her father had returned to Poland during 1947, having stopped on in Germany with the occupation forces for a couple of years before taking his discharge. Had he been uncomfortable with the idea of returning to his home with no family to speak of, just his elderly mother?

She had never been told exactly how her parents had met. She had asked her mother on more than one occasion but the question had always been ignored or otherwise left unanswered. Childhood had not been an easy time, food was scarce even though they lived in the country, and there were little in the way of home comforts. Her parents, as she recalled, were often touching and embracing, spontaneous demonstrations of their love she presumed, but there were also times gathering in frequency when she would find her father sitting outside on a warm day, his mind far away as if in another world. Now she wondered if that other world could be anywhere like Scotland, or perhaps, she thought, she was being too harsh and he had only been concerned with the many problems of that time in 'old' Poland.

With a shake of her head she rose and walked to the bedroom door. Mendelssohn opened one eye and raised his head as she moved, stretching and following her towards the kitchen. The sound of deep breathing could be heard as they passed the study door where Ari was asleep. Had she been wise to so quickly offer the girl a place in her flat, or was this some kind of penance because Ari's potential killer had looked so much like her father? 'Analyst, analyse yourself'; she thought with a grim smile.

By now she was wide awake, all the threads of her dream having dissolved away as she contemplated her father. Her mind was suddenly in a turmoil and for the first time in her life she wasn't exactly sure what she ought to do, or who she could talk to. She had no close friends, apart from Duncan, and certainly none with whom she could confide her innermost thoughts. Neither did she have any close relatives here, or in Poland, apart from her children and an elderly aunt in the south, nor did she have any wish to confide her innermost fears with any of the family. The only person who sprang to mind suddenly, and to her surprise, was Inspector Vickström. They had worked together for many years and she always found she could talk with him, even about things that were unconnected with the job in hand. Also, she had an obligation to him and knew she could trust him.

Switching on the coffee-maker she put in a measure of Gevalier and the room was soon filled with the rich aroma of fresh coffee. She squeezed a spoonful of Whiskas from the plastic pack into the cat dish and put it down. Mendelssohn wandered over, sniffed at the food, then walked away towards the bedroom with tail twitching in disgust. Obviously he had wanted a warm lap rather than feeding, she thought as he disappeared into the darkness. She poured coffee and sat down at the table, alone with her thoughts.

She attempted to analyse the situation impartially and not let her emotions sway the balance. Take as a starting point the premise that Scott was related to her father, could he be his grandson? If so, that would make her his aunt! Surely not, how could that be? The idea was preposterous to her, but she realised she must not discard any possibility, stupid or not.

Thinking back carefully she could remember her father speaking about being in Scotland, but not very often, and he never ever mentioned any friends he might have had during that time. His landlady, Sadie, was the only person Anna was aware of who knew him. Was there any chance that Sadie's daughter might recall him? Or even her mother speaking about him? She would need to locate Veronica and establish whether or not Bob Scott was related to her. Veronica could even be his mother for all she knew.

She took a piece of paper and pencil and tried to do the math, and decided that it was at least possible that Veronica might be his mother. She'd been born sometime in late 1944. If she had fallen pregnant when she was around twenty years old, that would make Bob in his late thirties or early forties. That seemed to make some sense, maybe! She threw down the pencil in disgust. Speculation based on a very shaky premise indeed. She shook her head.

Dawn was beginning to lighten the sky as she placed her cup in the sink. Turning off the light she made her way back to the bedroom, deciding that she must visit Scotland again very soon. First, though, she needed to speak to Vickström, and to Duncan. Her memory jogged her at that thought, Duncan was supposed to be visiting her sometime in the next fortnight, but so far he hadn't booked his flight.

Perhaps she ought to call him and ask him to wait for the time being, she thought as she climbed back into bed. He could always come later when she had resolved this situation once and for all.

Mendelssohn sniffed at her for a moment then settled down beside her.

. . .

"Sorry, but I can't see it," said Vickström after studying both photographs for several minutes. Slowly he pushed them back across his desk to Anna. "Perhaps I'm not looking properly but I can see virtually no likeness between them. Colour of eyes and shape of the mouths perhaps, but I can also show you hundreds of men with such similar features."

Anna shrugged away her disappointment. She knew from previous experience with the Inspector, that he would not be swayed by persuasion or argument. He would just become even more obstinate. She knew she must give up the fight in the most courteous manner.

"I'm relieved," she murmured slowly. "Maybe my worst fears have been unfounded, in your eyes at least. It just shook me when Ari spotted a likeness immediately. She was so positive."

Vickström nodded wisely. "I don't find that at all surprising. Remember that she's been terrorised by Scott and anybody who looks even vaguely similar to him will cause her some trauma. I would expect it will take some time before she stops reacting like that."

Anna gazed at him with half a smile. Here she was, a criminal psychologist listening to the Superintendent coming out with a sensible psychological explanation that she ought to have thought of herself. Am I becoming redundant, she wondered? She was well aware that she would get no further with him on this matter so she chose a different tack.

"How is the case going, have there been any sightings of Scott yet?"

He shook his head glumly. "Several, actually, but none were genuine. We're keeping a look out for the next few days but we simply can't spare the men for very much longer. Two days we've drawn a blank, so it looks as if he's gone to ground somewhere between Finland and Latvia, we think he's probably over there laying low." He offered her a cigarette and lit both before he continued. "The police in all those countries are helping us, and the Latvian officers have discovered a flat that they think might have belonged to him. It's empty now, except for some decaying foodstuffs, and they're about to wire some fingerprints to us for comparison with some we have got from the apartment here."

He grinned across his desk at her. "If we get a match I'll let you know."

"Do you have any plans for Ari? I think she wants to go home as soon as possible."

He hesitated for a few seconds, then said, "Er . . . yes, probably by the end of this week, I think."

Anna nodded with satisfaction. "Good idea. I presume that my presence will not be needed after she's on her way?"

"Not for the moment," he agreed. "Why d'you ask?"

"I need to go back to Scotland next week for a few days. I have some family business I want to finish."

"That's all right, just give me a telephone number where we can contact you if anything important crops up in your sphere."

Anna nodded, that was rather as she'd expected. He always liked to appear to be in control. "I'll telephone you once I know where I'm staying," she agreed with a smile as she rose from the chair.

That had gone better than she'd expected.

. . .

Anna met up with Ari in a coffee shop opposite the police headquarters. The girl was all smiles as she bounced in through the double doors.

"Wow! They're letting me go home in two day's time!" Her face bore token to the fact that she was delighted. She looked as if she'd won the national lottery.

Anna signalled the waiter to bring two cups of coffee.

"That is good news," she said, then paused as a thought crossed her mind. "Sorry, I didn't mean that I'm pleased to be getting rid of you. It's just that I know you can't wait to get away from here so I'm glad for you that they're letting you return home so quickly."

"Yes, I'm so excited to be going at last. I think I've had enough of 'University life' for the time being. I want to go home, see my mamma and pappa, I have so much to do. I don't want to lose the possibility of going back into training, back to swimming." She smiled wistfully as she sipped her coffee. "I still have my dreams." She looked Anna straight in the eye. "I want to get into the Olympic Team again."

Anna reached out and squeezed the girl's hand.

"Thank you for looking after me so well, I really appreciate it," said Ari quietly. "I do hope that you will come to my home one day. I'm sure my mother would love to meet you."

Anna wasn't quite so sure about the idea of travelling to Latvia. The old Russian bloc countries tended to make her feel uneasy. She knew deep down that her fears were probably groundless, it was the way she'd been brought up, but the feelings were deeply ingrained and she was sure that she'd never be able to relax if she was in any of those countries.

She gave a smile and nodded. "I'll try to come over one day. Keep in touch anyway. I may see you soon."

. . .

The telephone rang later that evening just as Anna was clearing away the supper dishes. Ari had gone into her bedroom to use Anna's computer and Anna was carrying a pile of crockery across the kitchen when the strident tones of the phone almost caused her to drop the load. She placed the dishes on the worktop and walked into the lounge where the telephone was striving to be heard. It was Duncan.

"Hello Duncan, I was going to ring you later . . ." she started, only to be cut off by his voice.

"I have a problem." His voice cracked a bit and she could tell he was very tense. Obviously there was something wrong. "I can't make it next week as we'd planned."

"Ah," said Anna with some relief. "That's all right, something has come up anyway over here and . . ."

"It's the police. They've been here again," cut in Duncan sharply. He was very agitated. "They've been grilling me for hours."

"Oh my God, why? What's the matter? What's happened?"

"It's that blasted discrepancy in the invoices for those bloody crosses. They were trying to find out if someone was stealing them and I was covering up for them. I said as little as possible, but they kept on about my brother Robert. They seem to think he might be mixed up in something illegal."

Anna recalled him telling her that his twin brother was always into some shady deal or another and toyed with the idea of just saying that the police might not be too far from the truth. After a second she decided not to stir the waters, just say nothing and wait for the possibility to occur to Duncan himself. Just now he was obviously not in a very receptive mood.

"Is he really?" She said with a grim smile.

"I don't know."

She got the impression that he really meant to say 'I don't want to know'.

"I just hope he has the sense not to do anything stupid," he continued. "I know almost for certain that he's taken some of those crosses, it couldn't be anybody else, but I'm not about to sell him to the police."

"So it's some sort of stalemate now?"

"Now they've confiscated my passport and told me I can't leave the country." He snorted with annoyance. "As if I'd run away and leave my business to cope without me." He sighed heavily. "I'm sorry to lay this on you but that's why I'm not able to be with you next week. It's bloody ridiculous."

Anna couldn't help smiling to herself at his words. He was so naïve at times and he seemed genuinely upset that he couldn't come to Stockholm and stay with her as they'd planned.

"That's not important now. Anyway, as I started to say before, I was about to ring you and tell you not to book up anything yet. I need to come over to Glasgow and continue with my family research, so I'll come to you next week. How does that sound?"

"Fantastic!" The change in his tone was instantaneous; he was suddenly filled with enthusiasm. "When do you plan to arrive? I'll pick you up. You can stay here with me at the cottage." He paused for a moment. "How long will you be staying?"

"Probably for three or four days," then she added, "but if you want I could extend it to a week." She could almost hear the crinkle in Duncan's cheeks as he broke into a wide smile.

"A week would be great. How about a month or two? Or even for the rest of your life?"

She started for a brief moment. What did he really mean? Was that some sort of proposal? No, not in his present mood, he wasn't capable of thinking rationally.

"That sounds nice, but I have too much . . ." She bit her words back. "Anyway I'm coming over and we'll talk about it then, okay?"

"Just let me know what flights you've booked and I'll be there to meet you."

Chapter Twenty One

Anna decided to go with Ari to Arlanda airport. She'd advised Vickström not to send the girl home by ferry and he had reluctantly agreed to arrange a flight for her, which left Anna wondering how he could be so insensitive. Surely he couldn't expect her to make another trip on the ferry when she'd so recently been almost murdered on the thing, it seemed ludicrous to her that she needed to explain to him how a young girl might feel to have to make that sea journey again so soon.

She stayed with Ari until her flight was called, and then walked with her to the departure gate. When the gate opened and the passengers began to move into the Departure Lounge Ari suddenly embraced her, kissing her cheek as if this was her last living moment.

"Thank you so much for all your kindness," she whispered to Anna as the tears began to glisten in her eyes. "I'll never forget you. I really hope that you can find the time to visit me soon." She disengaged reluctantly and picked up her bag. "I have your telephone number and I'll call you once I get home."

Anna smiled and nodded, suddenly tongue-tied. She didn't try to speak for fear of bursting into tears as well. She realised she was going to miss this girl more than she expected.

She watched as Ari disappeared into the lounge that would lead her to the Boeing standing outside on the tarmac, and then slowly she turned and started to walk back towards the terminal and the shuttle to Stockholm main station. She was sorry to see Ari leave; she had enjoyed having her stay. It had been like having her daughter back home again. She'd enjoyed cooking for two, eating together and the conversations they had long into the evenings, and she now realised just what she had been missing for the past few years.

She smiled gently as she walked down towards the shuttle, the Arlanda Express, maybe all was not lost. I should call my daughter, she thought . . .

. . .

Danny drove slowly back to his flat, his mind going over his intended journey back to Scotland. He knew he couldn't take the pistol with him as there was a chance the airport staff might discover it in his baggage at some stage so he decided he must hide it before setting off.

He opened the front door and entered his flat, carefully locking the door behind him. In the kitchen he had installed a small safe in the back of the food cupboard and he decided this was the best hiding place for the weapon. Pulling out a pile of tinned foodstuffs he opened the safe and placed the Walther inside after wrapping it carefully in a pair of tea towels.

With a sigh he locked the safe, sorry not to have the gun weighing down his pocket. It made him feel safe, almost invincible, while he had it on his person. He smiled as he recalled that he had a similar weapon, a Smith & Wesson 669 Semi-automatic Pistol that used 9mm rounds like the Walther he'd just locked away, in his bedroom in Glasgow. He'd hidden it carefully in case Duncan found it when he was cleaning the room. At least he would not be without protection for too long, he thought.

He packed his case carefully, making sure that nothing incriminating was inside, checked his UK passport and money, and went back downstairs. He was now Robert Macmillan once again.

. . .

When she arrived home Anna telephoned Justine but she was not in her office. She left a message on her answering service to call when she had the time, then busied herself by feeding Mendelssohn, packing Ari's bed linen into the washing machine and generally tidying up in the study her new friend had now vacated. She was suddenly surprised to discover that she didn't mind the mess that Ari's stay had created, it hadn't been bad but still needed tidying up, a job she drew some comfort from.

Her telephone sprang to life just over an hour later and Anna picked it up immediately.

"Hi, girl, how's it going?" Justine sounded very pleased with herself.

"Oh, I'm okay," murmured Anna, not wishing to mar her friend's enthusiasm. "How are you? You sound in good form from your voice."

"Me? I'm on top of the world at the moment. Things are actually going right for me just now. I've just been told that I'm up for promotion at the end of this month. To make matters even better, I'm off out on a date tomorrow evening. What more could a girl wish for?"

Anna grinned at her friend's excitement, pleased that she was happy. "I'm due to fly over on Wednesday and will be changing planes as usual at Heathrow. If there's anything I can bring you from here I'd be happy to do so."

"How about one of your famous Swedish blondes, slim with long sexy legs? Can you slip one into your case for me?"

"Ha, ha, very funny. I wonder what your British Customs officers would say?" Anna couldn't help giggling at the thought. "Seriously though, is there anything you want?"

"Not right now, but give me your flight number and I'll meet you for a coffee or a bite to eat. We can have a natter for half an hour or so."

Anna arranged to meet Justine at the same place they'd met last time.

"One thing I need to ask you," said Anna changing the subject. "Duncan Macmillan in Glasgow, they're giving him a hard time. He was planning on coming over here to meet me but they've taken away his passport. Is there a real problem, because I'll be seeing him when I'm up there and I wouldn't wish to embarrass the investigation by popping up unexpectedly?"

Anna had no intention of telling her friend that she planned to be staying with Duncan. That was strictly between the two of them.

After a short pause Justine said, "Not really any problem, it's just that we feel that his brother, Robert, may well be involved in this case. He seems to be the only person we can find who has had access to those crucifixes, and he travels around in East Europe quite a lot. His tax and bank records are extremely vague, yet I understand that he drives a new BMW or Mercedes or similar? It all smells a bit fishy."

"Fishy?"

"Sorry, an English slang expression that means it is a bit suspicious. We want to interview the chap but Duncan can't, or won't, give us any clue as to where he might be." Justine paused, then continued, "Basically we're trying to put Duncan under some pressure to see what might happen. We don't actually suspect him of anything underhand, the man's certainly not a criminal, but he's not being entirely honest with us, he's trying to hold something back."

Anna nodded to herself. "That's hardly surprising, is it? After all they are twin brothers. Duncan knows that his brother is basically a bad lot, but I think he still feels loyalty towards him. What would you do under the same circumstances?"

"Point taken," agreed Justine. "Anyhow, we'll meet at the airport and I'll fill you in on any further developments."

. . .

On Monday evening Anna picked up the telephone to discover a very worried Duncan on the other end.

"Are you all right?" she asked as the sound of his strained voice alerted her to his mood. "You sound a little uneasy." That was a gross understatement as he actually sounded almost suicidal.

"All right? No, not really. Those bastards served a search-warrant on me first thing this morning, at five o'clock. They spent hours pulling and prying into every bloody thing, taking fingerprints from each room as well. They even had the audacity to fingerprint me, 'just to check', whatever they mean by that. So, no, I'm not all right. I'm angry, humiliated and sodding well pissed off."

Anna could understand how he felt, but she could also see that the police were more or less justified in giving him the treatment. She wondered how she could sympathise and try to edge him in the right direction, then realised she shouldn't interfere.

"I'm sorry you're having a bad day. I would try to help make it better if I was there with you, but right now I have to be here for another day. I'll be with you very soon so try to cope with things, try to find something we can do together when I arrive, please. Don't forget that I love you."

That is about the best I can do for the moment, she thought as Duncan calmed down a bit and began to speak more or less normally again.

. . .

When Anna eventually replaced the receiver she put Preisner's 'Requiem for my Friend' on the player and poured herself a glass of Absolut Vanilia. Sitting down in her comfortable arm chair she sipped the vodka, her mind crowded with conflicting feelings as the first track, 'Officium', began to wash over her. She felt torn between her loyalty to Vickström and the case she was obliquely involved with, her research into her father's early life before he returned to Poland which made her feel slightly uneasy, and her feelings for Duncan.

So, what is really my main concern, she asked herself? That was a very difficult question as each of these options seemed to be of equal importance, not least of which was her emotional involvement with Duncan, a relatively new experience for her and more than a bit scary after all the years she'd spent alone. Her training had taught her that matters of an emotional nature usually assumed a priority greater than they really deserved, but in this case her instincts were saying something different.

If I could put aside the issue of my relationship with Duncan, she told herself, what am I left with apart from the emptiness? The case itself and my dealings with the police are, in reality, just a side-line and of lesser importance than my job with the University, she mused. That leaves my research into my family, or at least my father's life during the war. She knew this was an important part of her life, who she really was, where she came from and possible relatives she might never have known about previously.

How did all that stack up against her liaison with the Stockholm police? With them, her prime motivation up until now had been money. They paid, not very well, but an amount that couldn't be ignored in her monthly finances.

"Oh, *fie fan!*" she said aloud. "This is too much. It's crazy, ridiculous!"

Her instinct was drawing her towards something she was hard put to understand. These three issues appeared for her to suddenly have some kind of connection.

She shook her head, well aware that sometimes in the past her instincts would push her towards an unseen target, but was it possible that there really was some connection between these three matters? Goose bumps suddenly erupted throughout her body as she considered the possibility. She took a long sip of her drink.

"I need some rest," she said with a sigh. As usual Priesner's 'Dies irae' helped calm her as she tried to relax in her chair with the glass in her hand.

She never remembered falling asleep, the glass slipping from her hand and rolling away on the carpet.

Chapter Twenty Two

At half past nine on Wednesday morning Justine tapped gently on the Brigadier's door.

"Come in Justine." His invitation to enter made her smile. He invariable seemed to know exactly who was rapping on his door by some sort of internal telepathy, and he was seldom wrong. She'd tried to fool him in the past by varying the speed and loudness of her knock but she'd never caught him out.

Stepping into his tiny room she found Danny Kelso sitting cross-legged on his carpet in a Yoga pose, eyes closed.

"Shut the door behind you," he murmured as he slowly opened his eyes. "What can I do for you?" He rose to his feet in one smooth movement and smiled down at her. "Sorry about that, but if you will come around so early you have to take me as you find me." He sat down in an arm chair beside his desk, indicating that she take the other comfortable chair opposite him.

"No great problem, it's just nice to see that you're still a member of the human race despite your elevated status. I'm going to meet Mrs Petersson at Heathrow soon, she's changing planes on her way to Glasgow and we've arranged to have coffee during her wait between flights. Is there anything I need to ask her, or tell her?"

Kelso nodded slowly. "Will she be seeing Duncan Macmillan while she's there, d'you know?"

Justine grinned again. "That's quite likely, I suspect. Why? What's the state of play with him at the moment?"

The Brigadier reached across to a pile of papers on his desk, picking up the top bundle. "I've just got some news from Stockholm that concerns him this morning." He scanned the top sheet for a few moments, then looked up at her. "You recall that we had his place searched and fingerprinted recently? Well there were two other sets of prints beside his own and one of these we're pretty sure will have belonged to his brother. Stockholm has now confirmed that one of those sets of prints matches those found in the apartment used by somebody by the name of Bob Scott."

He met her eyes with his gaze. "That particular man is currently under suspicion of attempted murder of a young Latvian girl on the ferry between Stockholm and Tallin. I understand she was running away from him, trying to get back home. He apparently sets up girls as prostitutes, gets them hooked on drugs and uses them to please his clientele."

Justine's face darkened at his words, her mind working furiously. "Are we to presume that this man Scott is actually Duncan Macmillan's twin brother?"

Kelso shrugged expansively. "That would seem to be the case." He shuffled the papers for a moment. "And that's not all, I'm afraid. According to the Stockholm police, Scott has not returned to Sweden. They think he's trying to evade capture by travelling through Estonia and into Latvia, somewhere in Riga has been suggested. The Latvian authorities have pinpointed a flat in Riga rented under the name of Daniel Burns, and the fingerprints there are said to be a match for this Bob Scott."

"So Robert Macmillan, Bob Scott and Daniel Burns are probably all the same person?"

Kelso nodded. "That might well be so. I guess it's not really surprising that Duncan Macmillan seems to know so little about his brother if that is the case. The man is pretty deeply into this organisation and the Latvian police seem to think that he's closely connected to some character called," he glanced at his papers again, "Marek Sołtysiak. He's some sort of Polish gangster involved in everything illegal that he can get his hands on including drugs, gambling and prostitution to name but a few. They've been after the man for some years now and they feel that this might just be the lead they've been waiting for."

Justine sighed slowly. "Oh shit! Anna doesn't know what she's getting into, does she?"

Kelso nodded. "These are very dangerous men, they'll stop at nothing to get their way. People's lives mean little or nothing to them when compared to their own safety." He shook his head with a grimace. "Anyway, I gather they've taken this chap Sołtysiak in for 'questioning'— what that word may mean in Latvia one can only guess at." He sank back in his chair and tossed the papers onto his desk. "I'd say that both Anna Petersson and Duncan Macmillan are probably vulnerable, and possibly Macmillan's brother as well if he's running for cover."

"So, how much of this can I tell her?"

"Is she romantically involved with Macmillan?" he countered.

Justine considered his question for a moment. "Probably, I'd say. I know they've been out together but I don't know how far that has gone. She told me she's going to Glasgow to do some research into her father's past; he was stationed in Scotland during the war I believe. Whether or not she's seeing Macmillan, I can't say for certain, but I'll bet a week's wages that they'll meet up during the next few days."

"Best not to say too much then." He rose and paced about for a minute or two, picked up a pack of cigarettes and offered her one.

"We're not supposed to smoke in this building," she said with surprise.

"My predecessor never let that stop him, and I've just carried on from where he left off. You'll notice there's not a smoke alarm in this office. Now, do you want one or not?"

She nodded and took one, the Brigadier lighting them up before sitting back down.

He looked across at her with the ghost of a smile. "I would suggest that you pack and take a flight to Glasgow yourself. Don't use the same flight as Anna Petersson, best she doesn't know. They just might need some help in the near future." He blew smoke upwards in a blue cloud.

. . .

Justine was waiting in the business lounge at Heathrow's Terminal 1, pleased that she could use her contacts to give her the possibility of avoiding the crowded arrival gates. Anna's plane was ten minutes late, but her progress through baggage handling and customs seemed quicker than usual. She greeted her friend with a wave as Anna walked out towards her.

"How was your flight? Have a seat, coffee will be on its way in a moment. Would you like something to eat?"

Anna dropped her holdall by a chair and smoothed her skirt. "The flight was uncomfortable and I was beginning to feel a bit sick by the time we landed." She smiled at Justine as she sank into a comfortable arm chair with a sigh. "Oh, I do fancy that coffee now I'm here. It seems to have been a lifetime since I last saw you. How are things here in London now?"

Justine ignored Anna's question. "So you're off for a long weekend with Duncan, then?" She had decided that the direct approach would work best with her friend.

"Well, maybe I'll see him over the weekend," Anna hedged. She still didn't want Justine to know just how close they'd become. She was aware that the police already knew Duncan's telephone number so she reached into her purse and pulled out a card, pushing it across the table to her friend. "Here, this is my new mobile number. You can easily reach me on that at any time of the day."

"Not booked into a hotel yet?" Justine raised an eyebrow in question.

Anna shook her head. "Last time I was there I noticed a lot of places that offered a room and breakfast. I'll book into one of those when I get there."

Justine cast her a look of concern. "Are you sure you know what you're doing?" The expression on Anna's face indicated that her friend was not telling her the whole truth. "You might be better off by staying with Duncan than in one of Glasgow's grotty bed and breakfast dumps." She tried to disguise the smile that accompanied her words.

Remaining unmoved, it was obvious to Anna that Justine was seeking information for some unknown reason. She nodded her head slowly and grinned back. "I'm a big girl now. It might be amusing if one of the rich Scottish lairds decided to kidnap me, lock me in his castle and use me as a sex slave," she said with a laugh. "But I'll certainly tell Duncan it was your suggestion if I have to stay with him."

Justine was feeling bad about trying to pry information from her friend and changed the subject to a more serious note. "Have you heard anything from your Inspector of Police in Stockholm recently?"

A shake of the head. "No, not since I last saw him about a week ago. He told me they were going to compare fingerprints with some from Duncan's house, but he hasn't told me any more since then."

"Well, it's all a bit hazy at the moment. I understand as well that Duncan's brother Robert might possibly be involved in some way." She met Anna's eyes. "If you happen to run into the chap, just be careful. He could be dangerous if our suspicions are correct. I understand there's a warrant out for his detention but he's on the run."

Anna nodded. There was no smile this time, it was as if her inner fears were suddenly becoming reality and the jig-saw pieces were fitting into place, but she didn't like the picture. She felt that she really needed to trust Justine at this moment. Digging into her handbag she extracted a copy of the photograph of Bob Scott. As she did this the old photograph of her father fell from her purse onto the table. She grabbed it and returned it to her purse. Justine raised her eyebrows and Anna quickly explained that this was a picture of her father who died some years ago.

Gazing at the photograph of Scott, Anna said, "You know, this doesn't look anything like Duncan. How can that be if they are twins?"

"I don't know the details, but sometimes twins can look completely different from one another for some reason. All I know is that this guy could turn up out of the blue, and I don't want you in danger if he does."

Anna's sudden smile was genuine. "I appreciate your concern; it's good to know that you care even if you've been trying to pump me for information a few moments ago. I'm sure you have your reasons and I don't think I want to hear them."

At that moment the departure board flickered and the next flight to Glasgow was announced. They finished their coffee and Anna got to her feet. She hugged Justine and kissed her cheek, noting that her friend's embrace was slightly more than would be normal for the occasion. With a smile she started off towards the gate, leaving Justine standing beside the table, deep in thought.

Turning away from their table she walked along to a nearby bar, Justine bought herself a gin and tonic. She felt in need of a drink to calm her feelings. Sitting at a vacant table she sipped her drink and wondered why she felt so bad. It wasn't as if she'd let Anna go to Glasgow unprepared, as had been expected of her. She'd told her just sufficient to make her wonder about Duncan's brother, and with any luck she hoped that Robert Macmillan, alias Bob Scott, would not appear.

So why do I still feel uncomfortable, Justine asked herself? Is it because she's closer to me than I'd like to admit? I do value her friendship and she's one of the few women I would like to be close to. Should I have told her about the fingerprints, and the fact that he's already on the run from Latvia? And how come that Bob Scott looks so much like her father? Those eyes! Is there something more she's not telling me about? Could they really be related in some way? Surely that's not possible.

She shook her head, sighed and finished her drink. It was time for her to check in for the next flight to Glasgow.

Chapter Twenty Three

Anna cuddled into Duncan's shoulder as the evening sun warmed her through the partly drawn curtains. She was feeling loved, needed and satisfied even after the flights earlier in the day. Finding Duncan waiting for her at the airport, anxious to meet her again, provided her with renewed energy for the rest of the day. Her eyes wandered round the room in which they had so recently made love, surprised at the many pieces of decor that he had collected. It was as if somebody had placed the ornaments carefully to remind her of moments from her past, and she was certain that it couldn't have been Duncan who had furnished it. With a contented smile she snuggled deeper into his shoulder.

"I'd half-expected your brother to be here for some reason," she murmured as she stretched her legs towards the bottom of the bed.

Duncan raised his eyebrows. "Why d'you ask that? He's hardly ever here and this moment would certainly not be the best time for him, seeing all the interest the police have paid to the place recently."

She shrugged casually. "No particular reason, it just popped into my head."

He lifted himself onto an elbow. "Robert is the last person I'd like to share your company with. If he had been here I'd have booked a hotel rather than bring you home." He smiled into her eyes for a moment. "He's not really a nice person, even if he is my twin brother."

Anna nodded slowly with a feeling of unease, hoping that Bob Scott and his brother were not possibly one and the same. She had sensed this possibility no sooner than Ari had noticed the similarity between Scott and her father, but she had put it out of her mind when Vickström had not agreed about the likeness.

"Let's talk about something else," suggested Duncan with a gentle hug. "I want to take you to the Aberdeen Angus House for a special meal this evening, and then—maybe—back here to bed?"

"That sounds like fun, and I'm really hungry now. I could eat a horse if they sold such things over here."

"Great, I could introduce you to our speciality, Haggis, but you'll have to put up with the best Scottish fillet steak, I'm afraid, because personally I hate Haggis" he laughed. "Now, tomorrow, have you any plans? I have to go to the cemetery and leave some flowers on our mother's grave sometime during the morning, but I can take you wherever you wish before and after that."

She pulled him down and kissed him softly. "You're a good man, Duncan Macmillan, I love you for that."

. . .

The battered green surveillance van was standing in a lay-by about a quarter of a mile from Duncan's home. Justine pulled the rental Audi in near to the van, locked the car and walked past the side that bore the inscription 'McCormak Landscaping Services' on the worn metal in fading letters, and rapped on the rear doors. The doors opened and she flashed her identity pass before climbing inside. The occupant was a small, thin man with receding hair, a sallow complexion and breath that smelled heavily of stale whisky. She reckoned he must be somewhere about her own age, but looked ten years older.

"Busy?" she asked as he sat back down in front of the tape recorder and other electronic gadgetry. Hooking over a stool with her foot she perched beside him with a grimace.

The man shrugged and pulled a face. "They're still inside. Nothing has happened. She asked him a question about his brother but got nowhere." He glanced appreciatively at her for a moment. "They've been banging each other in there for about an hour and they're going out to dinner at the Aberdeen Angus House later on. Tomorrow he must go and leave flowers on his mother's grave."

"That's it?"

"Aye," he nodded with a sour grin showing blackened teeth. "Too busy doing what comes naturally to talk much at the moment." He turned towards Justine with an obvious show of interest. "I'm Gordon, by the way. Would you like a wee dram?" His head indicated a half empty bottle of Bells Whisky standing on a small shelf attached to the wall of the van.

She edged her stool away from him as she shook her head. "No thanks, not while I'm on duty." She frowned. "And neither should you."

Gordon glared back at her as he returned his attention to his electronics. "Get's boring in here after a few hours; a wee drink helps to pass the time."

Justine shook her head and got up. "I'm going to take a look around outside. I won't be very long." She slipped out from the back door of the van and closed it behind her with a feeling of relief, glad to be back in the fresh air and away from the smell of male body sweat and stale alcohol. She shuddered at the thought of even being touched by that man.

Walking leisurely she soon came in sight of the cottage. The place looked idyllic, set in a surround of pine trees with a small stream gurgling down one side to empty into another stream that ran along beside the roadway. She could see well-tended rose bushes across the front of the cottage ablaze with colour, and a spacious parking bay cut out on the left that housed a late-model red Vauxhall Astra, Duncan's she presumed.

She stood quietly, allowing all the details of the property to sink in, memorising both the building and its surroundings with a professional eye. Instinct prompted her to visualise both approach and exit routes and special places where one could hide from observation during the twilight. Gazing up at the windows she could see no signs of movement inside. She noted that the bedroom curtains were partly pulled and guessed that they must be in there at the moment. The thought of Anna with Duncan, offering him her body and doing things to him that she could only just recall, made her feel uncomfortable. With a frown she turned abruptly and strode back towards the van.

She was aware that they'd planted the bugs only a couple of days ago, and she knew it might be several more days before they gleaned any useful information, but the idea of inhabiting that stinking van in the company of Gordon the Groper was sufficient to make her want to leap onto the next plane back to London.

With a sigh she walked past the van and unlocked the doors to the Audi. At least her own company was preferable to the alternative.

. . .

Robert Macmillan eased back in his seat as the plane began its descent to Heathrow Airport. His journey to Gdansk had been uneventful and he'd stayed in a hotel near the airport for a day before taking the afternoon flight to England. Now he intended to stay in London for a day or two before taking the train up to Glasgow. He had left his car in the long-term park at Glasgow Airport so he was in no hurry to appear at their house and have to explain himself to Duncan who would no doubt ask questions as to the reasons for his early return.

There was a lady in Camden Town who he was hoping to visit for a couple of days and renew their acquaintance in the intimate way that they had parted last time he was here. The fact that she had actually thrown him out didn't seem to bother him unduly.

The plane came to rest at the terminal and the passengers began their frantic scramble to exit the aircraft. He sat back in amusement and waited until they were almost all gone before he rose and pulled his small case from the overhead locker. Saying 'goodbye' to the attractive stewardess he strolled along corridors to the main passport control and thence down to the baggage claim area where he found his small suitcase alone but for a couple of other large cases on the travellator. He grabbed it and strolled through the customs 'Nothing to Declare' exit where one officer was watching the passing passengers. He thought about smiling at the man then decided that this might be too much and could possibly cause him to become suspicious, so he walked on ignoring the official.

Once outside he breathed a sigh of relief and headed for the underground terminal that would take him to the Piccadilly Line and thence to Camden Town.

Chapter Twenty Four

The shrilling of the telephone from the living room woke them early next morning. Anna stirred and opened one eye as Duncan jumped from the bed and strode towards the door making signs for her to stay where she was. A couple of minutes of murmured conversation later he returned to the door with an apologetic smile.

"I'm sorry, but we'll need to change our plans for this morning," he said as he sat down on the edge of the bed beside her, gently running his hand down from her face to her shoulders and caressing her lovingly. "I have to go to the shop and speak with my accountant. It's important, tax matters, and it'll take a few hours I expect."

Anna nodded slowly, fully awake by now. "Do you want me to come with you or to stay here?" she asked.

"No need. I'll take a taxi and you can have the car. I'll get to the cemetery, St Augustine's on the Fife Road, and meet you when I've finished." He smiled down at her. "I'll go and put some coffee on and make some porridge, then you can wash and dress at leisure when I've gone. The car keys are on the hall table and there's a road map in the front car door pocket. I'll get myself to St Augustine's by about three and I'll take you out to dinner later on. Somewhere different from the steakhouse last night."

She sat up and swung a leg out of the bed as he rose. "No, you go and get washed and dressed while I make the coffee," she volunteered. "I think I can cope with porridge, we even eat it in Sweden you know." She kissed him lightly on the lips smiling inwardly as his stubble grazed her face, then pulled away before they got too close. "Time for that later on, you have work to do this morning," she laughed as she pulled on her dressing gown and headed for the kitchen.

. . .

Anna stepped out from the front door and locked it behind her before walking to the car and unlocking it. She adjusted the seat and pulled the road map from the pocket, studying it for a few moments. She pulled away gently and turned out onto the road heading towards the town. The way was well signposted and she concentrated on driving slowly and carefully as she hadn't driven in Britain for some years. The act of driving on the left hand side of the road was made more difficult by the position of some of the drivers' controls on the opposite side of the car to those she was used to. She discovered she needed to divide her concentration between the morning traffic flow and the unfamiliarity of the driving position. She soon realised that she would need more practice before she got comfortable driving in this fashion.

She pulled into the first large car park she came to, relieved to lock the car and proceed on foot into the main street. After strolling through malls and department stores where she found a new pair of shoes and a Gucchi handbag far cheaper than they would have cost in Stockholm, she spotted a small café in a side street. The smell of familiar food from her childhood made her curious to go in. Approaching the entrance door she was surprised to see the Polish flag on the wall inside. With a smile she pushed open the door and stepped into the small but clean eating area, noting that she seemed to be the first customer of the day.

"Dzień dobry," she greeted the tall, middle aged man who had the air of being in charge.

"Good morning, madam," he replied in a broad Scottish accent. "You are Polish?"

Anna nodded. "I presumed by the flag near the door that you would be as well."

His face broke into a warm smile. "Yes, and no." He indicated a table with two chairs. "My father was stationed here during the war. He met a local lady and when he was eventually discharged he came straight back here and never returned to Poland." He perched on the edge of the chair opposite her. "Do you mind if I sit with you for a moment?"

"Of course not. My father was stationed in Edinburgh at the same time. He was from Poland too and I was born in *Sopot* in North Poland."

The man, who introduced himself as William Kowal, nodded slowly. "Ah, I see. Well my father was originally from *Kościerzyna*," he pronounced it 'Costina', "but I understand the town was almost totally destroyed by the end of the war and his family were all lost, so he never went back there to live, nor wished to return later on." He looked slightly abashed. "I regret that my Polish is not all it ought to be and I can never properly pronounce *Kościerzyna* correctly. Please forgive me."

Anna laughed. "Your pronunciation is good for someone who doesn't speak Polish. But today *Kościerzyna* is a delightful place in the country. You ought to visit it one day," she suggested.

"What brings you here to Glasgow? It rains too much at this time of the year and isn't the best attraction for tourists."

"You're quite right," she nodded, "but the rain doesn't matter. Actually I'm here on other business. As I said, my father was here during the war and I think he might have some family who I never met before. If I'm right I could find my half-sister, or at least her grave, somewhere in these surroundings."

Kowal nodded, his eyes lighting up. "I might be able to help you. There is a Polish Cemetery not too far outside the town near Cambuslaing. It's part of the main cemetery of St Augustine on the Fife Road. Try that one first as there are many Polish graves there. Quite a lot of people who were 'associated' with members of that force have requested to be buried there."

He rose to his feet with a wide smile. "Now, what would you like to eat? For you, it's on the house."

Anna settled for *barszcz* with *smietana*, a beetroot soup with sour cream, followed by schnitzel with *mizeria*, a cucumber salad, and boiled potatoes.

. . .

The drive to the cemetery took her much longer than expected, mainly because she lost her way twice as she was having problems concentrating on the road names. Kowal's words were still echoing in her mind and she found herself often searching for the gear stick on the wrong side, knocking her hand painfully on the door opener as she tried to reach for it. Once she was on the Fife road, however, the cemetery was obvious as she neared it. She pulled the car into a lay-by opposite and walked across the road towards the tall gates that stood ajar. She stopped at a small mobile kiosk next to the gates and bought an appropriate bunch of flowers.

Once inside she turned to her right and started to walk round the perimeter, arriving at the entrance to the Polish section after about a hundred yards. The entrance had a tall wrought iron gate separating the area off from the main graveyard. It opened to her touch and allowed her to step through and arrive in front of a high stone monument topped by the Polish Eagle. On the stone was carved a dedication in both Polish and English; 'Poległym żołnierzom . . .' to the memory of Polish soldiers who died during the latter stages of World War II.

Most of the graves in this sector were heavily ornate affairs, the headstones having been worked by skilled craftsmen. She soon discovered that the majority were of Polish soldiers who had returned to this country, or been killed in action and had no home town or family in Poland. Some were obviously their wives and children as well. She walked slowly down each row reading the inscriptions where they were legible, in the hope of finding a name she might recognise. There were many from almost every town she knew from her childhood, but none were familiar.

The sun came out suddenly, warming her as she walked through the well-kept graveyard and some time later she checked her watch, surprised to find the time was almost a quarter past three. She turned and searched the area for any sign of Duncan, but apart from three other people also walking peacefully in the surroundings he was not yet in sight.

She continued to the end of the row and turned to make her way back to the entrance when she caught sight of a fairly new headstone. The inscription read 'Jacek Kowal—1922 to 1993'. A small vase stood beside the headstone holding a small bunch of white lilies which were beginning to wilt. She crossed herself instinctively and smiled at the thought of Bill Kowal's father returning to Scotland and the woman he loved. She sighed with memories of her father and wondered what had kept him from returning. She remembered him as a loving and caring father and she couldn't see him just abandoning the woman she presumed he'd loved. So what had actually stopped him from returning to Edinburgh and Sadie? She shook her head slowly in the knowledge that she'd never ever know the answer to that question.

Turning away sadly from the grave she walked across to the main monument and laid her flowers there before returning slowly to the entrance. She caught sight of Duncan as she stepped through the gates, he was kneeling in front of a grave some twenty yards to her right as he arranged a bunch of yellow roses in the holder provided. She strolled over to where he was and stood back as he tended his mother's grave.

Duncan turned and stood up, smiling warmly at her. "I saw you down there," he indicated the adjacent cemetery. "Thought I'd pay my respects first then come and meet you." He took her by the arm and drew her forwards to the graveside. "This is where our mother lies, God bless her."

Anna looked at the nicely finished marble headstone and well tended plot as she squeezed Duncan's hand, then she began to read the inscription. Her grip tightened as she froze, the words in front of her echoing through her brain as she almost jumped backwards with shock.

. . .

Justine had followed Anna for most of the morning and was now watching from a grassy hillside opposite the graveyard as her friend walked slowly round the cemetery. She was feeling self-conscious and like a traitor to their friendship as she followed Anna's progress along the rows of Polish graves through her binoculars. She didn't want to spy on her, the idea was unthinkable, but she felt uneasy about Anna's safety, reconciling her feelings with the knowledge that she was here more for her friend's protection than for any other reason.

In her mind was the fear that Robert Macmillan could turn up at any time, and if he did it was entirely possible that both Anna and Duncan could be seriously at risk if he was indeed the Bob Scott they were searching for.

She relaxed as she brought the binoculars up to her eyes again as Anna laid some flowers gently on the steps of the huge monument. As she lowered the glasses a movement to her left caught her eye and she trained the binoculars on a taller figure standing in the main cemetery watching her friend. She breathed a sigh of relief as moments later she recognised Duncan, relaxing once again.

Watching again as Duncan squatted down by a grave and carefully laid flowers by the headstone she never saw Anna approach until her friend suddenly appeared in her view behind his kneeling figure. Her focus was on Anna's face as Duncan stood and eased her friend towards the grave, apparently showing her the inscription. She saw Anna's expression change to one of shock and horror and take a step backwards.

Quickly she lowered the glasses and checked out the rest of the graveyard for the presence of any threat, but nothing was out of the ordinary. Returning to them she could see her friend and Duncan standing and discussing something heatedly, Anna gesticulating towards the gravestone he'd just laid flowers beside. There was something in Anna's face that she couldn't read, even in close-up through her powerful binoculars. She could tell that her friend was both shocked and upset, but what was the other emotion? She was looking suddenly very sad, drained, and not the Anna she was used to seeing.

At that moment she wished she was beside her friend, there to hold her close and comfort her in her moment of need.

Lowering the binoculars she sat back feeling very empty and alone.

Chapter Twenty Five

"Sorry," stammered Duncan as he stirred his coffee noisily. "Just stop there for a moment. Let me see if I've heard you right!"

Anna sat stiffly on the edge of her seat. She watched his hands trembling, making the teaspoon clatter on the side of his cup. Nervous as she was, she was somewhere relieved that they could sit alone in the tiny coffee shop on the corner of the street about a mile away from the cemetery. For the first time in her life she was unsure of her feelings, thousands of thoughts racing through her mind and of course she didn't know how he would react.

Duncan drew breath, his face pale as he began to speak. "So your father, when he was a young man, was stationed in Edinburgh where you say he met a woman who you think was my grandmother? You are telling me that they never married but he left her pregnant with Veronica, my mother; that's ridiculous!"

Anna felt goose pimples rising on her arms as he raised his eyes to meet hers for a few seconds. She felt she must justify her words to ease the blow. "I know this all sounds far-fetched, but I'm not stupid. You knew I came here to research into my father's background, I told you that when we first met, didn't I?"

He let out a sarcastic chuckle devoid of any humour. "So I now have an Aunty Annie, with whom I'm sharing my bed! I've never heard anything more daft in my life. Steven Spielberg couldn't make a better film!" His face changed as a look of sadness appeared in his eyes. "I was intending to propose to you before you left for Sweden, and now you're telling me that this may not be legal? You've got to be kidding. It sounds like my life's biggest joke."

Anna let out a sigh and shook her head. "No, it's not a joke. Right now I'm deadly serious." She opened her handbag and pulled out an envelope from which she took a photograph. "Look, this is a picture of my father when he was young. See for yourself." She pushed the photograph of a young man in uniform across the table towards him.

Duncan picked it up and studied the black and white print in a heavy silence for a couple of minutes. Slowly he looked up and their eyes met. "I would agree that he does look a lot like my brother Robert, but that's not proof of any relationship."

Anna took another piece of paper from the envelope, unfolded it and pushed that across to him. "This was given to me by the office in Hanover Street that I visited last time I was here." She reached across and pointed to the address in the text. "See, this is where he stayed during his time in Edinburgh. The landlady, Ms Sadie Macmillan was also the owner of the Crawford Lodge not far away."

His eyes widened as he studied the document, digesting the details on the extract. "Oh, shite! This really is my Grandmother!"

When their eyes met she could see fear and disappointment on his face, a deep frown creasing his forehead. He looked defeated. "Veronica took her mother's name but she must have been your half sister," he mumbled as he pushed his half finished cup away.

'Do you know the name of your father?'

Duncan frowned for a moment. 'I was told it was somebody called Eddie, I think. I didn't give it much thought as my mother told me he had died. Why d'you ask?'

Anna dug out her notebook from her handbag and flipped over a few pages to find the note she wanted. 'Eddie Hobbs?' she asked.

He nodded slowly. 'That sounds like him but I can't be certain, it was a long time ago.'

'Well, if it was Eddie Hobbs, he was a blood relative of the Kray twins, and as you and Robert are twins it seems likely that this Hobbs was your father.' She gazed at him with concern, knowing this was sensitive information. 'The Kray twins were bad news, gangsters from London who murdered several people.'

There was a flash of anger in his eyes suddenly as he banged down his cup. "Did you know any of this when we first met?"

"No, not at all. I had no idea," said Anna shaking her head. "But I do have another confession to make, something I really shouldn't be telling you. The reason why I was here in the first place." With a sense of foreboding she explained about the girl in the water in Stockholm that started this investigation, and all about her involvement with the Swedish police as a part-time adviser.

He sat back with half-closed eyes as if sorting all the facts into separate files. When she finished he sat up and asked, "So you were trying to track down the source of those Russian crosses? You weren't a tourist at all?"

Anna summoned a twisted smile. "Well, yes and no. I wanted the chance to go to Scotland to see where my father stayed during the war, and see if there was anybody there who might have known him. It was just by chance that this case presented me with the opportunity to have an expenses-paid trip to Britain, and even more of a coincidence that I spotted the likeness between your brother and my father. Once in London I soon discovered that you were the only importer of the crosses in the United Kingdom." With a sigh she summoned another tiny smile. "I think we were meant to meet."

After a moment of contemplation Duncan moved his seat back and took her hand gently. "I guess we were." He smiled for the first time since leaving the cemetery. "At least I now have a brand new aunt, one I love dearly, and I can't be angry with you." He squeezed her fingers. "I can't help feeling miserable now all my hopes and dreams have come to nothing. But I still have you, and I hope that we'll be together in one way or another from now on."

Anna squeezed his hand back with a sigh of relief. "I feel the same way about you too, that won't change. I guess I'll just have to get used to having a new nephew or two."

At this oblique mention of his brother, Duncan's face darkened. "But he'll never accept the fact that you are his aunt. Robert is nowhere near as open-minded as me and he doesn't change his opinions easily, even if we show him conclusive evidence."

Anna felt an icy stab of foreboding at his words. Her eventual meeting with Robert Macmillan was not a moment she anticipated with pleasure, but she realised that it must happen sooner or later.

. . .

Justine sat in her Audi with a half-smoked Marlborough in her hand as she watched the café from a safe distance. She'd followed them for a couple of miles along the Fife Road and saw them turn off into a small car park on the right. Beside the car park was a tiny tea shop with a sign outside advertising afternoon teas, cakes and various other local dishes, called the 'Fife and Drum teahouse'. There was a small red and white awning that extended down over a picture window as a sun shade. It looked very cosy.

She wished she could have joined them inside but she knew that Duncan would most likely recognise her from their earlier encounter at his house, and she thought he would become suspicious as to her motive for being there. The whole exercise in following Anna and Duncan was two-fold, firstly to catch up with Robert Macmillan and arrest him and secondly to act as protection for Anna who was vulnerable at this moment. There was no telling what Robert Macmillan might do if he realised they were under surveillance.

More important to Justine was that she felt personally involved with her friend. Anna had become much more than just a friend in her eyes, although she knew that Anna had no interest in any sexual involvement with her. Be that as it may she could do little about her personal feelings so she contented herself with fantasising about an intimate relationship with Anna and thoughts of a grand seduction and the possible delights that could follow.

Finding herself starting to become aroused, she changed position in her seat and pulled out the thermos of coffee, opening it and filling the plastic cup that acted as the lid. The coffee was still very hot, scalding her tongue as she sipped at it. Suddenly her eyes caught a movement beside the café and she saw Duncan leading Anna across towards the car.

Quickly she took another sip, intending to throw the remains of the coffee out of the open window, but at that moment her mobile began to ring. She gave an involuntary start of surprise and hot coffee spilled down her chin and onto her blouse.

"Shit!"

She dropped the coffee cup onto the car floor, pulled out a tissue and started to wipe her face and hands as the mobile continued to ring. She glanced down to see what mess the plastic beaker had made on the car seat as it bounced off it. Quickly she wiped the front of the driver's seat, picked up the empty cup and twisted it back onto the thermos before looking up again.

The Astra that Duncan had so neatly parked neat the car park entrance had now disappeared. The mobile was still shrilling in her ears.

"Oh, bollocks," she mouthed as she fumbled with the car keys. Jamming her foot down on the accelerator she turned the key and operated the ignition. The car wouldn't start. Two more tries proved fruitless, the motor turning over without catching.

"Fuck this bloody, pissing heap of junk!" she shouted. The mobile was still ringing, insistent as ever.

She lay back and picked up the mobile, snapping it open. She jammed it to her ear. "Yes! What the hell is it?" she snapped.

"You don't sound very happy," murmured a voice on the other end. She recognised the voice as Brigadier Kelso himself from his office in London. "Has something happened?"

"Sorry, yes, I've just dropped hot coffee over myself, Macmillan and Anna have just driven off, and this bloody heap of junk won't start. I think I might have flooded the engine."

Kelso chuckled. "I'm pleased that you're having an interesting day! I have some news so just relax and listen, I expect you'll catch up with them sooner or later, you're pretty resourceful."

She sighed and leaned back in her seat. "Go on then, make my day."

"We've just received information that Bob Scott has been spotted in Glasgow, so he's not so very far from you. You'd better be prepared for him to show up at any time."

Justine nodded. "Okay, I'll bear that in mind." Her mouth twisted into a grim smile. "How old is this information?"

"He was spotted at Glasgow Airport yesterday evening. We only got this tit bit about an hour ago, so don't blame us. I gather the Glasgow police were sitting on it for a while before notifying us."

Justine sat up and banged her fist on the steering wheel. "That bloody shit-for-brains Gorman, I expect," she spat. She had met Inspector Gorman some time ago and he'd made a clumsy pass at her during her stay in Glasgow. She recalled clearly just how pissed off he was when she'd told him to sod off and find somebody who wasn't so fussy. "That man's about as useful as a wet dream in a monastery."

Kelso chuckled again at her words. "I wouldn't know about wet dreams, or monasteries for that matter, and I don't know who held up the information. Just be aware that Scott, or Macmillan, or whatever he calls himself now, could be just around the corner. And another thing, be very careful, he's probably armed."

"Thanks, I'll be in touch if anything happens," she finished. Moments later the connection was broken. She closed her mobile and dropped it onto the passenger seat, turned the ignition key and this time the Audi sprung to life as if the recent problems had never happened. She frowned, wondering if the car stalling was an act of fate?

She pulled away slowly and began to make her way back in the direction of Duncan's house.

. . .

"I've booked a table at The Highlander Restaurant for eight this evening," said Duncan a few minutes after they arrived at the cottage. "I hope all this won't put you off your food because the Highlander is quite special."

They were sitting in his lounge in separate armchairs almost like strangers, both avoiding the settee in unspoken agreement. Anna was feeling uneasy, almost as if she was in a dream world, and the thought of dressing up and going out for a meal was just about the last thing she wished to do this evening. She shook her head slowly, deliberately not looking at Duncan.

"No, I'm not ready for that I'm afraid. Could we just have a snack here later? We need to talk more about this."

Duncan's face fell. "But this was supposed to be a special surprise and I've gone to a lot of trouble to get exactly the right table and a special menu. You can't let me down at the last moment."

He jumped to his feet and began to pace around the room.

Anna watched him for some moments, surprised at his reaction. Surely he must understand how awful she felt, she thought. He must realise that she would not wish to be in public after her discovery earlier?

"Can't you find something easy to put on, and just a touch of make-up?" he asked, stopping in front of the doorway.

Anna looked away, suddenly feeling annoyed that he hadn't appeared to understand the feelings that were implied by her words. "No, I couldn't face it," she mumbled, almost to herself. "Surely you cannot expect me to go out and act as if nothing had changed between us?"

"Why ever not? I could, even under these circumstances. Okay, so I won't be proposing to you, and the flowers can become a table decoration, but we can't let them down."

She sat up, even angrier now, and grabbed an ash tray from the table beside her. *"Jävla Skit!"* she exploded in Swedish as her temper rose suddenly inside her. "I didn't realise what a selfish pig you could be! Why can't you think of anybody but yourself? You're just like all other men, bloody self centred!" She drew back her arm and the ash tray flew across the room.

The missile missed Duncan's head by a couple of inches to crash into the doorframe behind him. It was made of thin copper and it buckled as it hit, finally finishing in a twisted lump on the carpet. He stared at her for a couple of seconds, his breath taken away by her outburst.

Anna collapsed in tears back onto the chair as Duncan watched from the other side of the room. He took two quick steps across to where she sat and pulled her to her feet, holding her tightly against him as her sobs racked her body.

"I'm sorry," he whispered, "I didn't realise this had affected you so much. Of course we don't have to go out; I'll get a takeaway or find something in the freezer for tonight." He held her close and kissed her on the cheek. "Please don't cry, it tears me apart."

A few seconds later Anna felt her anger dwindling away and she clung to him and let him kiss her. She really wanted him to kiss her on the lips, carry her up to bed and make love to her, but she could feel his control as the kisses continued to be more friendly than erotic.

Things had changed between them already.

. . .

Three hours later Anna pushed her plate away with a satisfied smile. "That was great, tasty and very different. What was it again?"

"Haggis is supposed to be the national dish of Scotland, but it isn't everybody's taste I'm afraid. I'm pleased that you enjoyed it." Duncan grinned across at her. 'I told you before that I don't like it but this brand isn't so bad.'

Anna nodded, she'd found the spicy taste of the haggis interesting when set against the blandness of mashed potatoes. It reminded her of homemade *Pölsa* she'd eaten in Sweden, but more spicy. The sliced vegetable served with it had been delicious but she couldn't identify it. Duncan had called it *'Neaps'*, but that meant nothing to her.

"I'll wash the dishes," said Anna as she planted a kiss on Duncan's forehead. "I'm sorry I lost my temper and threw that ash tray at you. Just relax and enjoy another drink. You've had a difficult day and you deserve it."

Duncan chuckled quietly for a moment. "Not a problem, I didn't like the ashtray much anyway." He took her arm gently and kissed her hand. "I'm proud to have my aunt staying in my home, and I'll need to make suitable arrangements for tonight. We both need to rethink everything between us."

Anna had been dreading this moment all evening. She hated the idea of sleeping alone, but under the circumstances she knew that she oughtn't to continue to be intimate with him. They were related after all.

"I think I ought to sleep down here on the couch," she said quietly. She hated herself for making this decision.

Duncan shook his head vehemently. "You'll do no such thing while you're in my house. There is another bedroom upstairs and the bed has been aired. Robert would usually sleep there but you can have it while you're here. If he returns I'll use the couch."

This was the first time he's been so positive about anything and Anna was impressed with his manner. "All right, you're the boss," she murmured with a wide grin.

She turned and made her way towards the kitchen.

. . .

She discovered that Robert's bedroom was smaller than Duncan's. It was furnished well but seemed bland and impersonal, no pictures on the walls and no ornaments. A single bed made up with a small table beside it on which stood a tiny reading lamp, a cheap chest of drawers and wardrobe with a mirror door made the room comfortable if nothing else. It felt just like a hotel room.

Anna moved her clothes into the wardrobe, pushing aside the few things that were Robert's, and then she changed into a nightdress.

Normally she would sleep without anything on but for some reason she decided that the nightdress might help keep her warm instead of just cuddling up against Duncan.

With a final look around her she cracked open the window a fraction to admit some fresh air, climbed into the bed which was more comfortable than it looked and turned off the bedside lamp. She soon found that sleep was to be a long time coming as her mind dwelled on the events of that afternoon, recalling how pleased she had been at first when she discovered she was related to Duncan, followed by the sudden realisation of what this actually meant to their situation. Now she found herself beginning to regret having been so thorough in her search for her father's movements during the early years of the last war.

So what would have possibly happened to her if this information had not surfaced when it did, she wondered. Would she have agreed to marry Duncan when he proposed as he said he intended? A part of her mind told her that she would have most likely accepted, embarking upon a new life with excitement, but where? She couldn't have expected him to move away from his successful business and live in Sweden, so would she have made the break and come here to Scotland?

Reluctantly she admitted to herself that she probably would have moved to be with him, a thought that opened up a vista of possible outcomes, the worst of which being that some time after their marriage their actual relationship would have come to light. She shuddered at the idea. How much worse would it have been then, she wondered.

With an effort she turned over, closed her eyes and tried to relax and summon sleep. After ten minutes her eyelids began to droop and she lapsed slowly into a sleep troubled with dreams about Scotland, cemeteries and driving a car with which she was not familiar.

. . .

Outside the cottage in the darkness of the hedgerow, Robert Macmillan stood quietly, watching. He'd been there for nearly an hour surveying the area carefully for any sign of police presence or any surveillance on the property. He was well aware that the Glasgow police rarely mounted such operations using their own people. They were short staffed and usually hired one of the local companies who specialised in this. Surveillance was always very costly in terms of manpower and time, two qualities they sadly lacked.

There was one ageing green van tucked in a lay-by some way down the road that he was a bit suspicious of. Painted in large letters on its side was 'McCormack Landscaping Services', the whole thing looking rather unprofessionally done in his estimation, which was one positive aspect in his eyes. Normally any surveillance van would be carefully prepared for each job and this one didn't look as if it had even been washed for a long time. A quick check on its doors ascertained that they were locked and there appeared to be no signs of life.

As he watched two shadows moved behind the curtains of the cottage, they appeared to be his brother and another person, possibly a woman by the shape of the silhouette. He waited patiently, he was in no hurry and he didn't want anybody to know he was in the area. It was obvious to him that he must leave the country as quickly as possible, and the cash he'd stashed away in his room would be sufficient to buy a new identity and a passage to Brazil. There would even be enough to set him up there where he had friends. He had planned for this eventuality for several years, and now the time had come.

The light in the living room was turned off and moments later Duncan's bedroom light came on. Robert smiled, so his brother had a woman staying over, good for him. Give her one and go to sleep, he thought.

A couple of minutes later he was annoyed to see the second bedroom light up. Fuck it, he thought, what's he doing in my room? Surely he's not trying to be a gentleman and give her the spare bed?

Twenty minutes later he saw both lights turn off, Duncan's first, then his room, which meant there was probably one of them in his bed. Give them half an hour to go to sleep, he thought, and I'll give somebody an unpleasant surprise. If it is a woman I might even give her one myself and keep her happy, that is if she's young and pretty enough. He leered to himself as he settled down for the next thirty minutes.

The night was quite warm and the moon was just rising over the trees as he approached the front door of the cottage. He had waited for almost an hour to make sure they were well asleep and now he pulled the key from his pocket and eased up to the door. First he used a tiny oil spray on the lock to ease the barrel, recalling how it would be stiff and sometimes squeak when it was dry. The key slid in easily and the door opened silently. He crept into the darkened hallway pulling the door shut behind him.

. . .

Something woke Anna suddenly, a waft of air perhaps or a noise, she wasn't sure. Lying quite still she listened for a sound, but there was nothing. Then there was a smell, sweet and cloying, very familiar to her.

Moments later she recognised the odour, a man's eau du cologne, Marionotte. She recalled it specifically because that was the cologne her ex husband used all the time, and she hated the sickly stink. There was somebody else in the room with her she realised, and it wasn't Duncan.

With a swift movement she reached for the bedside light and switched it on. Immediately she noticed that the door had been opened, but there was nobody there. She started to turn to see behind her bed head as she smelled the perfume again, stronger this time. Before she could cry out a large, coarse hand descended over her mouth and a sharp metal edge was pressed against her throat.

"If you move, fight or scream, that'll be the last thing you ever do, hen. Just lay still and keep quiet!"

Chapter Twenty Six

Justine had volunteered to man the surveillance van for the night as privately she was anxious to hear what they were talking about as their behaviour had looked suspiciously like a breakdown in their relationship, but why? If that was the case she didn't want the morons who were currently manning the post to hear what was going on. Settling into the van at six she wasn't due for any relief until six the following morning.

Another reason for volunteering for this night shift was a flash of intuition that tonight could well be the night that Bob Scott paid a visit to the cottage. There was nothing to substantiate why this feeling had arisen but she had learned over the years to trust it.

Listening to their conversation, Justine was stunned to discover that they appeared to be related and she could hardly understand how all this had come about. Recalling a conversation sometime ago with Anna about her enquiries into her father's movements in Edinburgh, it seemed somehow relevant, but how on earth could this be related to the Macmillan twins? Listening to them only made her more confused, so in the end she removed the headphones and left the recorder to do its job.

Opening the packed supper she'd brought, and a bottle of spring water, she started to eat slowly, but moments later the sound of footsteps outside the van alerted her to switch off the internal light and sit silently in darkness. This was probably some drunk on his way home, she mused, but there was always the chance this could be Scott, or Robert Macmillan checking out the van, and one chink of light might give the game away.

The footsteps slowed and hesitated beside the van, and then somebody tried the rear doors. She smiled to herself, pleased that she'd had the sense to lock herself inside or the whole operation could be compromised. A minute later the cab doors rattled as the intruder made his way to the front. The last thing she heard were footsteps retreating along the road in the direction of the cottage.

With a sigh of relief she continued with her supper, only turning on the lights after about a quarter of an hour of silence. Settling back in her chair she began to read a book, turning up the sound sufficiently to be able to hear if there was any change in the occupation of the cottage.

About half an hour later a discussion about sleeping arrangements reached her ears and shortly thereafter the sounds ceased. Realising that they'd gone upstairs she was suddenly aware that the listening points were limited to the ground floor rooms and hall as the local police had seen little point in bugging the bedrooms at the time, but now it appeared that this cost-cutting exercise might cause a problem. She turned up the volume even more.

After another hour Justine was beginning to become sleepy when the microphone in the hall picked up an unexpected noise that alerted her instantly. It sounded like a door opening and brushing across a mat. Automatically she increased the volume to the full capacity of the powerful speakers that were capable of magnifying even the tiniest of noises to a level which filled the van. That was at least one positive aspect of the operation. The sound of the door closing, magnified in the confines of the van, was unmistakable—there was an intruder inside the cottage! She thought for a moment, then wondered if this could be Duncan or Anna going outside for some purpose.

More sound began to fill the room, tiny creaks from floorboards or stairs as somebody moved around slowly. The sounds were too stealthy to be either Duncan or Anna, this was more likely to be Robert Macmillan, she guessed, or an intruder bent upon some nefarious purpose. She sat back and considered her options.

Do I rush in and arrest somebody? Do I call the police for back-up? Or do I stay here and wait, listen and do nothing? What if he slits their throats while they sleep? These thoughts ran through her head as she checked her handgun to make sure it was properly loaded and ready for action. For this particular assignment she'd been issued with a Walther, lighter and smaller than the usual Browning or Smith & Wesson normally used by the police, and up until this moment she'd never even taken it from its holster.

Carefully easing the clip out, she checked that it was full. Replacing it she levered a cartridge into the chamber, applied the safety catch and replaced the gun in its holster, pushing it round her waist until it nestled in the small of her back where it would be less obvious.

At that moment she heard a stifled sound from the speakers, distant but still clear enough to recognise a muffled gasp. Then there was a voice in the background. She couldn't make out the words but the tone of voice was sufficient to tell her that Robert Macmillan must be inside the house.

After less than a second of deliberation Justine pulled out her mobile telephone and activated the number that connected her to the Night Duty Officer at Glasgow Central Crime Squad. "Now is the time I'll need help," she murmured to herself.

. . .

Anna lay still and watched as Robert pulled up an edge of the carpet, pushed the chest of drawers along the wall and then exposed the floorboards beneath. From one of his pockets he produced a small screwdriver and quickly loosened two screws, finally releasing them with his fingers and removing a short length of floorboard. Reaching into the hole he slowly withdrew a blue plastic holdall before replacing the floorboard, carpet and chest of drawers.

He looked across at her with half a smile. "This is my ticket out of here," he said with a note of triumph. "I'll be on my way very soon, but first . . ." He approached the bed slowly as he took off his coat and began to loosen his belt.

Anna could easily guess what was to come next and frantically tried to think of a way to avoid his attentions. Screaming might well lead to a quick demise, as he had threatened, but perhaps another option was available to her. What startled her the most was the man's eyes, so much like her father's, but cold and his smile didn't hold the warmth that her father's used to do. She sat up and gave him a scornful look as he put out a hand toward her.

"*Pasjol!*" she said in a loud voice, 'get away from here' in Russian, then when he continued to approach she continued, "*odpierdol się*", which meant the equivalent of 'fuck off' in street Polish.

At this Robert stepped back a pace. It was obviously an expression he knew. His face changed to one of disgust and he tightened his belt again. "So you're one of those girls from Poland! And I suppose Duncan thinks you're a lady! I'll not touch you with anything, I might get infected!"

He pulled out a black metal object from his pocket and unfolded a wicked looking blade from within the handle. "You can have this instead," he said with a growl.

Suddenly there was a sound from behind Robert, and Duncan entered wearing a dressing gown over his pyjamas. "What the hell is going on?" he asked. "What are you doing here? You know the police are looking for you?"

"Get the fuck back to bed while I finish this bitch," said Robert wielding the knife towards Duncan. "I'm going in a moment and you can't stop me!"

His brother raised his hands in submission. "I'll not stop you, just get out of our lives and leave Anna alone, she's done you no harm."

Anna could see an artery throbbing in Duncan's neck and she knew he was far more nervous than he was letting on. She was amazed at his calmness in a situation in which most people would be having a major panic.

Robert glowered at his brother for a moment. "D'you know what she is? She's just a common whore from Poland!"

Duncan laughed at his words. "She's your aunt Anna, you fool. We only discovered that yesterday. Now get out of here before the police find you."

"Aunt Anna? There's no such person. We dinna have an auntie, and this bitch is never related to us!" He turned towards the bed. "I'll make sure you don't fool anybody ever again!"

At that precise moment the tension was suddenly broken by the sound of loud banging at the front door.

. . .

Duncan glanced towards Anna, who shrugged with a 'do as you think fit' expression. He turned to his brother. "I ought to answer that," he said quietly.

"If it's the police, get rid of them," growled Robert. "I'll be here with your 'lady friend', remember. Any trouble and she gets it." His pronunciation of the words 'lady friend' left little doubt as to her status in his eyes.

"What if it isn't the police?"

"Just get rid of them as quick as you can, okay?"

Duncan nodded and started down the stairs slowly, worrying about leaving Anna with Robert, not knowing what his brother had in mind. The hammering on the front door started again as he reached the hall. He opened the door carefully. The figure outside seemed familiar to him but he found it difficult to discern her features in the dim light.

"I'm so sorry to wake you up at this time," said Justine in her best 'young girl' voice, "but my car has broken down outside and I need to use a telephone."

The woman's voice seemed familiar as well and he stood there unsure of just how to react. Normally he would have invited her in immediately, but now . . . ?

"It'll only be a couple of minutes, then I'll go back outside to the car and let you get back to sleep, okay?"

"Er, well . . ." He wasn't sure what he ought to do under the circumstances. He felt he shouldn't leave a young lady standing out by the road.

"Let them in, for Christ's sake!" His brother had followed him down and Anna was beside him dressed in an old bathrobe.

Duncan opened the door wider and immediately recognised the young policewoman from London who had been with the local force about a month ago. Her eyes met his and she gave a small shake of her head. "Thank you all so very much. I really appreciate this," she enthused as she stepped into the hall and looked around for the telephone.

"It's in the lounge," said Anna, who'd recognised Justine immediately. "We'll come in with you if you don't mind." She was relieved that her friend was here, even though she was nonplussed at her presence when she thought Justine should still be in London.

Duncan escorted Justine into the small lounge and showed her the telephone. Robert pushed Anna across to the front window, staying close to her. Once Justine picked up the telephone he peered out of the window to see if there was any movement round the cottage.

"Oh damn, it's engaged," said Justine with a show of petulance. "Could we wait a few minutes and I'll try calling again?"

Her innocent face was perfect and Anna smiled inwardly at the thought of the real personality behind the air of naivety. "Why don't I make us all a cup of coffee?" she suggested lightly.

Robert was having none of this. He stepped up to Anna and gripped her arm so tightly that she suppressed a cry of pain. "What the hell is all this? The Vicar's tea party?" He gazed at Justine closely and said with gritted teeth, "Just make the call or clear off!"

Justine had noticed Anna wince when Robert grabbed her arm and realised that the man was holding them under threat. She smiled into Robert's face. "Okay," she murmured quietly, "I'm so sorry to cause you all this trouble." As she said this her right hand slid round behind her. She turned with the receiver in her left hand, swinging her arm forcefully so that the receiver caught Robert full in the face with as much force as she could use. At the same time she drew the Walther and brought it round hard to the side of the man's face. Blood gushed and splattered as the barrel caught him on the cheek and split the skin with the sight.

With a yell of pain Robert sprawled across the hearthrug. His knife bounced on the floor and slid under the sofa. Blood was flowing copiously from the gash on his face and pooling on the floorboards where he lay. He started to get to his feet but Justine was standing over him with her gun in her hand.

"Stay on the floor!" she yelled as she kicked his supporting arm away from his side. He fell back onto his face. "Put your hands behind your back, now!" She had a pair of cufflinks in her left hand.

"Bollocks!" he cried, rolling away from her to be stopped by the legs of the bureau. He started to get up again.

"Out of the way." Justine said to Duncan and Anna who were still standing in the middle of the room. They both stepped back out of her line of fire.

"Police," said Justine somewhat inaccurately, but he wasn't to know. "If you try anything I'll take great pleasure in shooting you. Now lie still."

Robert lay on his back glaring up at Justine as she pulled out her mobile. She thumbed the buttons and spoke briefly into it. "He's here. I have him under cover. Front door is open, come in quickly." She looked down at Robert. "Do you know how much I'd love to pull this trigger? Just give me the slightest reason and I'll start by blowing off your balls." She smiled sweetly at his bloody face as she lowered her aim in accordance with her threat. "Next will be your kneecaps."

Heavy footsteps from the hallway announced the entry of the local police.

. . .

Within a few minutes the handcuffed figure of Robert Macmillan was led away by two large policemen and Duncan was escorted to the kitchen to provide a short statement. Justine lowered herself onto the sofa beside Anna, who was looking pale and very shocked.

"Are you all right?" Justine put her arm around Anna's shoulder.

Anna nodded slowly. "Yes, I think so. It was all so quick in the end." She looked at her friend with the beginnings of a smile but suddenly broke into a flood of tears.

Several minutes later she was able to speak again. "Thanks, you were wonderful." She sniffed. "I've never in my life been so pleased to see somebody when you walked in. How did you know that he was here?"

Justine handed her a pack of tissues. Anna sniffed again then blew her nose, dabbing at her eyes afterwards. Her friend wanted to explain how she came to be here but she felt this was not the right moment to tell Anna that the room had been bugged; so she kissed her gently and carefully so as not to appear too enthusiastic.

Anna didn't respond to her kiss, just laying her head on her friend's shoulder allowing Justine to cuddle her for a moment, then she sat up again with a wider smile and moved further away.

"I'd love to be able to return your feelings," she murmured with a shy look, "but I'm just not made that way, you understand." Softly she took Justine's hand in hers. "Let's just try to be friends, real friends. I don't want any complications, especially right now."

Her friend nodded, this was no more than she'd expected. "One can always hope," she said quietly with some emotion in her voice.

"You were brilliant, and I do love you. But it's not quite the love I think you want, I'm afraid." She leaned across and gave Justine a peck on the cheek. "You probably don't know that Duncan and I are no longer romantically involved. Can you imagine we discovered only today that I'm actually his aunt?" She looked at her friend's expression of surprise. "It's a long story which I'll save for another time."

"So you have a couple more relatives now, one of whom will probably be spending a long time in jail by the look of things."

Anna nodded again with an expression of regret.

"But I'm going back home to Sweden with at least one wonderful new nephew, thanks to you and the local police." She rose to her feet and stretched. "Nobody can take that away from me."

Epilogue

"Would you like to come with me to a soiree at the University on Saturday? It is the Lucia celebration and some of my pupils will be performing," asked Anna. "I think you would enjoy it." She glanced up from the letter she'd opened to see Duncan grinning at her. The photographs he'd been leafing through were still in his hand, new from the processing laboratory.

"Look!" He held out a photo for her to see. "Do you remember taking this? It's my great Aunt Jula." His grin widened. "I never dreamed that I would suddenly have such a large family." His brow creased for a moment. "What was it you asked me just now?"

Anna got up and joined him at the coffee table, picking up the photograph and studying it intently. It was only a couple of days since they'd arrived back from Poland after their visit to both the north and the south of the country. Duncan had felt he wanted to meet his new-found relatives and he'd been anxious to see the country of his grandfather. December hadn't really been the best time to visit the country, extreme cold and stormy weather had given problems when they'd visited Warsaw and delayed their return to Sweden.

Somewhere inside himself Duncan had felt this visit was very important and it was no time to hesitate just because of inclement weather. Recent unpleasant experiences, added to the disappointment about his brother, had been keeping him awake during the nights, but after a time he learned that life goes on and Anna's company these couple of weeks was helping to calm his anxieties.

They had both discovered their new relationship was stimulating and were both full of respect for one another. Duncan knew as well that this was also a difficult time for her, and now he found himself trying to make decisions for the future. "So, what were you asking me?" he repeated.

Anna laughed as she saw his serious expression. "We are invited on Saturday for a Lucia soiree. I would like you to meet some of my friends, and even my children."

Duncan frowned. "What is Lucia all about? I've never heard of it. Is it a girl?"

With a sigh Anna got to her feet. "I'll get you a cup of coffee, and then I'll tell you the story of Lucia." She headed for the kitchen.

When she returned she set his coffee on the table and sat down beside him, explaining how this was a traditional Swedish ceremony on the longest night of the year. Lucia lighted the night with a crown of burning candles and a cortege of beautiful virgins sung traditional Swedish psalms. "There will be refreshments afterwards, of course, and maybe even a dance. What more could you wish for?"

Duncan's face saddened for a moment. "There are a lot of things I could wish for, but maybe it is already too late. We haven't really discussed our future; perhaps this might be the appropriate time?" His face reflected an inward pain that Anna understood without the need for explanations.

She took his hand gently. "You could move here to Sweden. Live here and we could be together. You will like my kids and the people here and there is so much we could do together to catch up on all the years we've lost. What do you think?" She squeezed his fingers before letting go.

For the first time since leaving Scotland she was feeling eager for something she wanted to do, and the thought of having him with her was giving her strength as each day passed.

"You see," she continued quietly, "before, my life was so empty. There were some men of course, but only for a night and I never enjoyed their company. I couldn't stand their selfish needs for sex and their lack of interest in the person I am. Being with you has taught me to understand myself. You appreciated my company without trying to push me into bed. That was a new experience for me, and I enjoyed it."

As Duncan opened his mouth to reply the telephone broke the silence between their words. Anna jumped to her feet and picked up the phone.

"Yes? This is Anna. Hello?"

She spoke in Swedish for about five minutes, gesticulating occasionally to some person on the other end of the line. Duncan could understand only a handful of her words, but her tone suggested that someone wanted her to do something for them that she was reluctant to undertake.

When the call ended she threw herself back onto her chair with an annoyed expression. "That was my boss, Superintendent Vickström from the Central Police Headquarters here in the city. Robert is going to stay in a British jail for many years to come and he's not permitted to communicate with anybody now in the beginning. Also I'm afraid that during the early part of next year it looks like I may have to go up north on a new assignment, but I don't know exactly when or where."

For Duncan this was a blessed release, he hadn't wanted to make any decision right now. He didn't feel comfortable with moving to Sweden but had no intention of letting Anna know this.

"Anna, that's great. I promised you I'd stay here over Christmas, but after that I must go home and take care of the business. My Russian supplier has broken off contact with me, you understand, and I need to make some administrative changes before the start of the next financial year." He sat forward on his seat and put a hand on Anna's knee. "I would love to live here, it all sounds so interesting, but I don't think that would be possible at the moment."

Anna smiled as a shiver went up her leg. "Your dreams are where your future begins, and of course Swedish law is much more open-minded about marriages." She shrugged inwardly with the thought that they would still be in contact whatever happened.

Duncan grinned at her words, the unsaid meaning penetrating immediately but it didn't settle his uneasiness. "Yes, I'll come with you on Saturday. Lucia sounds like fun and I would be pleased to meet the Queen of the darkness."

Slut (The End)